## PROLOGUE

"*Öffnen!*" a voice in German barks for the third time to open the door.

After glancing achingly at my children who're huddling by the stove, I lift my trembling hand to turn the key in the lock. Within a strike of a match, sets of black boots stomp on a hard floor.

"We're ordered to search this hut," a soldier in a steel helmet snarls while his rifle shoves me to the side, then four of them surge forward.

I clutch my hand to my throat, overwhelmed by the sensation of choking on the sickening acrid odor that they leave.

My mind races like a bullet from a fired pistol. They can't discover my secret, not now, when I've been able to hide it from them for so long and keep my children alive.

"No reason to fret," Johann says, making me aware of his sudden presence, his pale blue eyes fixed on my lips. He stands in the door frame looking wickedly handsome in his Nazi uniform. "You have nothing to hide, so it will end faster than it started," he adds and smiles. "Your family is safe."

This coward ordered his soldiers to search my home while

playing friendly since his arrival in our village last month. "Yes, of course," I say, forcing myself to return his fake smile. If he only knew the truth, we all would have been dead a long time now.

"Commander, I spotted a hidden entrance to an attic in one of the bedrooms." The soldier's out of breath voice reverberates along my nerves, stiffening my spine.

The reality that they're about to discover the very secret that will bring death upon my children, rips my heart out of my chest.

Johann nods and follows his soldier without another glance at me. It's like he has anticipated this moment.

Everything in me screams while I run after him...

# ONE
## ANETA

Five years earlier, Late August 1938—Władysławowo, a fishing port on the south coast of the Baltic Sea

I walk barefoot on the soft sand, tuned to the waves hitting the shore and the *mew* and *ha-ha-ha* sounds of seagulls. I've arrived at my aunt and uncle's summer cottage only hours ago leaving behind my crowded city.

But soon I pause transfixed by the way a fisherman at the shore seems to be in harmony with the sea. He suddenly looks up and our gazes meet. There's something magnetic about him that I can't stop staring into the intensity of his bluest eyes.

He sets his fishing pole beside a bucket before nearing me.

His bold gesture makes me feel shy, so I look away.

"I'm Johann," he says in German and holds his hand out, his smile friendly. He looks to be around my age of seventeen.

"Aneta." I don't return his smile but extend my hand. His touch electrifies my skin. It's a weird feeling, so foreign to me.

"Do you care if I join you on your walk?"

I pull my hand away. "Sure."

"What do you like the most about the beach?" he asks like we're old friends.

"The smell," I say and look up to meet his gaze. "The briny scent of the sea that can't be imitated by anything else."

"It's like you read my mind," he says and brushes the strands of milky-blond hair from his forehead. "Are you from here or just visiting?"

"I live in Gdańsk."

He blows out a long breath and smiles. "So do I."

"What do you do over there?"

"I study business but the plan is that one day I take over my grandpa's brewery in the Oliwa district."

"Is this something you want?"

"Yes, very much. But tell me about yourself."

"I'm fascinated with history, but I will not go to university, so it doesn't matter."

He draws his head back and says, "Why not?"

"My stepfather's decided to marry me to a rich man who's twenty years my senior," I say and sigh with resignation. "You see, our family owns a small boutique with dresses and that's our pride, so getting more connections in that world is important to my stepfather. Besides, he doesn't believe that women should go to university."

"What about you? Do you believe it?" His voice is still quiet and there is this sadness that emanates from it. It touches me, and I like him more and more.

"I do. Women are as smart as men. I'm sure you heard of Maria Sklodowska-Curie."

"Then don't let your stepfather tell you how to plan your life. Take it in your own hands."

"It's not that easy," I say, contemplating his words.

He frowns. "I can help by getting you a job at the brewery. This way you can be independent."

I like how he makes it sound so easy. "Be careful as I might take you up on your offer." I attempt a lighthearted tone as if forgetting the dreadfulness of my situation at home.

He stops walking and squeezes my hand, and for a moment longer we remain like this, looking at each other with curiosity and wonder.

"I like you," he says.

Warmth builds in my cheeks. "You don't even know me."

"Maybe we knew each other in the life before this one." His words reflect in the intensity of his now stormy blue eyes. He's wise beyond his young years, something so hard to find among the boys my age. At the same time, the pull I feel toward this practical stranger scares me. It must be my loneliness that makes me so desperate.

I resume the walk, determined to go back home and never see him again. German boys nowadays don't take interest in Polish girls like me. He's only teasing me, so later he can laugh with his Hitler-Jugend mates at my expense. I can't be so naïve or stupid.

But he takes my hand in his and urges me to follow him.

This gesture brings an unwanted mellowness in my gut though his touch feels so safe. I force myself to say, "I should go back because my aunt will worry."

Without a single word, he lifts me into his arms and runs into the water.

"No, please, stop," I say while laughter bubbles in my throat. "Let go of me."

He pauses when we are in the sea. "Are you sure that you want me to let go of you now?" His eyes move to my lips and I anticipate he wants to kiss me. When our gazes meet, his is so soft and yearning that suddenly I *want* to feel his mouth on mine. Everything in me melts and I feel this softness spreading through my veins.

"Go back to the shore and then put me down." My demand sounds weak even to my own ears.

His lips brush mine so gently as if wondering if I'll protest.

Tantalized by the blissful feeling that claims me with the speed of a thunderbolt, I succumb to it completely, wanting more and more. I never felt this way, like I would be flying into the magic of the star filled sky.

He caresses my cheek with his thumb. "Tell me to stop," he whispers, "because I want you so much." His eyes gain this darker shade of blue again.

I run my fingers through his damp hair and feel him shivering. "I want you too. I don't even understand it, I just feel that way." The rebellious need to cherish my first time with him instead of with the old man I'll be forced to marry is so strong that it takes my breath away.

When a few days later I'm back in Gdańsk, I look forward to our first date in the city. We are supposed to meet tonight, so all day I can't focus on my tasks in my stepfather's shop. I end up volunteering to make a delivery for a client in Oliwa. The thought that it's also Johann's district makes me smile.

Just when I near the tenement where our patron resides, there are weird noises, like someone is crying, but then a familiar voice shouts in German, "Dirty Jew, you thought you'd hide from us."

I stop behind a courtyard's gate to see what's happening but the moment I lay my eyes on the blond boy in Hitler-Jugend uniform, my heart stops. Johann is the one that shouts these awful things and presses a pocketknife into the neck of an elderly man.

What I witness next, breaks my heart into a million pieces...

# TWO
## ANETA

Five years later, July 1943—Aneta's village near Zamość, a historical city near Lublin in southeastern Poland

After a short snort from a horse, comes across a firm voice in German, "Excuse me, Fräulein, how far to the nearest village?"

I feel like I'm in one of my dreams, hearing again this haunting voice that belongs to only one man in this entire world. It can't be, it just can't be... It's surely not Johann. Not in these secluded fields and dense forests.

I lean forward and grab a small handful of hay, now warm from the sun, then I inhale the sweet and soothing scent before swirling around to meet his eyes. Those eyes... The eyes of the only man that I've ever loved. I have no more illusions that it's not him. My heart makes a painful skip as I pray that he doesn't recognize me. It's been five years and I'm no longer the city girl wearing fashionable dresses, now I'm a village woman. I want to run far away from this man.

His piercing blue eyes narrow as he takes me in, stunned disbelief painted on his arrogant face with a hint of color on his cheeks from fresh air and horse riding. His high cheekbones and proud chin make him look unapproachable. Typical pompous follower of Hitler's sickening propaganda.

I don't know how long we stare at each other while I'm so overwhelmed by his presence, so lost and confused even though all I want to feel is disgust. Kostek's throat clearing brings me back to reality.

I glare at Johann's gray-greenish uniform, so over adorned by the brainwashed believers of the maniac, and say in cold voice, "Only two more kilometers, officer." I turn away to tend to the hay raking. I'm fluent in German thanks to the fact that I grew up in Gdańsk, the city on the Baltic shore, with around eighty percent of the population being German before the war.

I expect him to shout or even shoot at me for not showing enough respect to one of such *rulers of life and death* as they all pretend to be, but he only says, "Thank you." His voice is so quiet that it gets quickly lost in the neighing of the horse, probably stolen from one of our people.

When the galloping grows more distant, I whisper to Kostek with urgency, "Take the shortcut on your bike and warn the Steins, so they stay in hiding, and tell my mother-in-law to keep Janek inside till I'm back."

He gapes at me, revealing his missing upper tooth, his confusion visible in his eyes. "Do you know this German?" His voice is as rough as when he recovers after a prolonged binge of drinking.

"He's no good, so we must be careful," I say. "Please, go now."

Without another word, he jumps toward the wild apple tree on the other side of the field where his bike rests in the shade.

My husband hired this good man, now in his late forties, many years ago as a farm helper and he's proved over and over his faithfulness. His only weakness is that he hits the bottle way too often, and because of it there are days when he's not in our sight at all.

After I watch him drift away, I turn to glare at the small unit of German soldiers led by Johann. I gather both rakes and set on a walk to the village, taking the alternate route through fields. Meanwhile, my mind is a chaos of rumbling thoughts that slowly emerge from the hidden surfaces. What are the chances that he'd come here, of all places? The thought that they're only passing our village on their way to Zamość brings the needed hopefulness.

My youthful infatuation with Johann was gone the moment I saw his cruelty toward the innocent Jewish man. That day I forbade myself from loving him.

And now he keeps his evil stand by wearing this despicable uniform. I spit to the ground while continuing my march. For as long as this bastard stays here, I must protect my son from him. Thankfully, the German squads never station in our village for more than a couple of days, always favoring other locations with an easier access to main roads and more *civilization*.

I hate the shakiness I feel after encountering him but the brisk walk and freshness of zephyr caressing my face helps me calm down. I pose to fix my chestnut-brown hair, now disheveled after hours of field labor. After re-gathering it into a tight knot at the nape, I cover it under a pearl-gray scarf and resume my strut.

I must protect my son at all costs. Johann doesn't know that Janek is his and I will do everything to keep this secret away from him.

Now our situation is going to be even more dangerous, with the Jewish couple hiding right under the noses of the Germans. What if Johann or his soldiers find out that I shelter the Steins in my barn? Shivers run up my spine when I realize what the outcome would be: our immediate deaths.

# THREE
## ANETA

July 1943—Aneta's village

It takes me a solid fifteen minutes before I enter my village. I've lived here since I was forced by my stepfather to abandon my childhood home in Gdańsk.

Our cottage of wooden walls and thatched roof sits at the end of the tiny village that consists of only seven households. We are hidden deep into woods, so *visitors* like the ones today are rare, but we get them occasionally.

The German soldiers in steel helmets already hustle in the yard of the neighboring house where the Ramniwski family used to live, before they were dragged out like criminals and shot in cold blood by the Germans for sheltering a Jewish family of three.

I suppress my tears at the memory of our dear neighbors, and without glancing the soldiers' way, I push the gate of wood planks to my courtyard, cursing fate under my breath for bringing them here. But before I pass through, I sense someone standing to my right.

Johann takes a drag from his cigarette and after exhaling

clouds of smoke, he says, "We were instructed to station on this abandoned farm. I hope you don't mind that we will be neighbors for a while."

If I didn't know any better, his gentle tone of voice would fool me into believing in his courtesy. But I feel now the same way I felt all those years back when I witnessed his cruelty.

His golden hair in the slicked back undercut style of the length on top and short on the sides, make him look so different from the easy-going and charming boy I'd met in Władysławowo.

I keep walking with my head up while feeling his gaze following me.

"It's rude not to answer," he remarks.

I will not let him provoke me. I must appear like I have nothing to hide, sure of myself.

"Mamusia." Janek runs into my embrace when I cross the threshold of the cottage. "There are soldiers there and Kostek said to stay inside."

It's in this very moment that I start to truly breathe again, when I'm sure that my little boy is unharmed. I stroke his milky blond hair and kiss his forehead. "Yes, darling, it's safer to stay here until they leave." Unfortunately, he looks just like his father, the same blue eyes, the same nose... "What have you been up to?"

"I was drawing with the pencil you bought me in town, and I'm almost done making a special surprise for you."

"I can't wait to see it," I say and kiss the tip of his nose before letting him go back to his activity in the guest room adjacent to the kitchen. Well, we call it a "guest room" but we use it ourselves all the time.

I pour some water from a bucket into a tin bowl right next to the white-tiled, wood-burning stove with hanging pots, wooden spoons, dried herbs and mushrooms. After washing my face and neck, I feel so much better and ready to begin putting my thoughts together, so I perch on the wooden bench right beside the stove.

"Where were you?" my mother-in-law, a thin and pale woman with pure white hair and sharp bony face, barks at me. She never liked me, but since her husband and son died, she's grown to despise me.

"We were raking the hay," I say quietly, not letting her sharpness affect me in any way.

"Well, now we have Germans snooping right under our noses." She listens for a moment, then switches into whispering, "You must think of Janek. Tell the Jewish doctor and his wife to leave. If the Germans find them in the barn, they will murder us all. You remember what happened to our neighbors."

I sigh. "I can't do that. We must be extremely careful, that's all." Since last year, we've been hiding Mr. and Mrs. Stein, the Jewish couple who fled from Zwierzyniec before they were forced to the ghetto. Prior to the war, he was a physician who saved my son's life during my labor when the baby appeared to be in the breeched position. So, when they arrived at our door asking for help, I hadn't the heart to turn them down despite my mother-in-law's protests. They've been living here since, only stepping out of the hideout in the barn at night when it's safe.

It's been a quite emotional and fearful journey for all of us. Germans conduct frequent searches throughout villages, and we dread that one day they'll bang on our door too. Now, with Johann and his squad here, the stakes are even higher. It may happen at any moment. Still, I can't imagine not helping our friends. They deserve to live just like anyone else and I will do everything to keep them safe.

She forms her mouth into a thin line and waves her bony finger at me, the sharpness of her features making her look like a lizard. "Then you should've taken the gold they wanted to give you."

"Mother, we must be decent human beings. Zygmunt

would agree with me, you know that well." My husband and his father died while fighting to protect our borders from the Germans in September 1939. She never accepted the loss and lives like they're going to arrive any moment, always blaming me and the entire world for everything. We still don't know the whereabouts of Zygmunt's younger brother, Władek.

"You don't care about your own child," she says and shuffles pots on the stove releasing clattering noises and savory flavors that make my stomach gargle.

Through the whole conversation, I've been sitting on the bench, thinking that I owe it to Zygmunt to show his mother love and patience. "Where is Kostek?" I ask, knowing well that it's best to ignore her complaining.

"He—" She's interrupted by a loud tap on the door, and her panic-stricken small eyes glue into mine.

"The Germans," she says weakly and brings her hand to her neck, "they're here to search the house. They will find the Jews in the barn and kill us all."

I jump forward and shake her arms. "Stop, Mother. Compose yourself and act normally. Please take Janek to the other room, fast."

When she obeys, still trembling, I walk to the door and after swallowing hard, I open it to reveal Johann with his proud chin and strong arms. The man who once took my heart with the force of a storm is here now as our assassinator.

His gaze is stern, "May I speak to your husband?"

"My husband is dead," I say without betraying any emotion, like I was discussing what was for dinner. But even after four years, the loss of the kind man still hurts like blisters on a scorching day.

His surprised gaze takes me in before he says with pity in his voice, "Please accept my condolences." He clears his throat. "I'm here to inform you that some of my soldiers will be sleeping in your barn. I wish we could avoid such inconvenience to you and your family but we've no choice."

Suddenly I feel as if someone just cut my oxygen, but I strain for a neutral voice. "I suppose I must comply," I say, avoiding his gaze, not wanting my eyes to betray the panic inside me. If they discover the Steins in that barn, we will all die. It's the punishment in Poland for hiding or aiding Jews. So, I must play this right...

"Actually, it's all in disarray in that barn right now, so I would need some time for organizing and cleaning," I add.

"No need. My soldiers will do it when they move in tonight." His voice is crisp but also assuring.

I hang onto that thread, his need to assure me, I guess, the remnants of his conscience. "Please, let me make sure it's hospitable there for them," I say like I would really care for the comfort of his damn soldiers. "You know how they say: A guest in the home is a God in the home." I miserably fail to remove the sarcasm from my voice.

He narrows his eyes as he scans my face. "How touching." The corners of his mouth twitch. "Well, you have till tomorrow."

The relief sinks like vinegar into a sponge. "Thank you. I promise to have it ready by tomorrow night."

"I trust your word is worth something now unlike five years ago," he says, unmistakable displeasure written on his face.

"I see nothing has changed when it comes to you though, officer," I bite back at him pressing on the last word, restraining myself from slapping him. Then, I swallow my anger because I know that while he can show his, I can't for the sake of my son and the good people I shelter. So, I swallow again, this time my pride and anger, and quickly add, "I apologize, officer. I had a rough day in the fields and now must tend to my cattle."

He nears his rigid face to mine. "You act like I hurt you, when in fact you stood me up and made a fool out of me." He smells of wood and tobacco, a far cry from the musky cologne he had on that day when we first met. Yet, his raw masculinity teases my nerves.

I get no chance to answer because a high-pitched and urgent voice rings out, "Commander, we've found something that you must see right away."

# FOUR

## ANETA

July 1943—Aneta's village

"What is it, soldier?" Johann says without turning his inflamed gaze from me. It's as if he takes pleasure from my distress.

I'm trying not to show it on my face, but I must be a bad actress judging by the way he looks at me right now. What could they have found in the Ramniwskis' cottage? Maybe the partisans decided to stay there over one of the nights and left something behind?

"We found some items in the basement that clearly belong to Jews."

Johann narrows his eyes. "I will be there in a minute," he says in a rough voice.

The soldier clicks his heels and salutes before marching away.

"I can explain this, officer," I say lightly, like I don't care.

"I'm listening," he says and folds his arms at his chest.

"There was a Jewish family sheltering there but everyone was killed, including the owners of the hut." *By your peers, you bloody puppet,* I think but keep it to myself. "It's why your soldiers found those items."

He gives a silent nod while not meeting my eyes.

I'm sure he doesn't know the taste of remorse, the damn slaughterer. "If you'll excuse me now, officer, but I must tend to my chores." I close the door behind me and edge away toward the farm courtyard.

"I'm not like them," comes his quiet and tense voice.

But I wander away from him, wiping the single tear from my face, the one for what could've been if he was a decent human being.

I bring a fresh batch of hay from the barn for our old mare and our black cow, then I use a chaff cutter to prepare some nettles for the pigs. I place a stack of plants in the hopper, and as I push it forward with one hand, I turn a crank handle with my other hand. A set of blades cut the nettles into small pieces.

When done, I mix it with boiled potatoes, grinded rye and hot water. I pour it into the pig trough and for a few seconds I watch how they enjoy their meal.

I fill the steel bucket with water from the well with the sweeping pole and bring it to all the animals. Then I milk our only cow.

We used to have plenty more cattle but since the start of the war, I've had to downsize. It's all I can handle right now and I only grow some rye and potatoes but still maintain meadows, letting other villagers to use the rest of the fields.

Since the spring of this year, the contingents that we are to deliver to the Germans became even harsher. I produce very little, so they can't expect much from me. The soil here is very fertile, so it's often possible to sneak in some extra harvest goods.

"Good girl," I say and stroke the cow's soft belly after I'm done with the task. I put a white cloth over a tall can and transfer the milk into it. Then I pick up the cloth, now with a yellow sediment and dirt particles on it, and wash it. When I'm done, I place the milk can inside a larger container filled with cold water set in the cellar.

Close to midnight, I listen to any noise from the neighboring property but there is only silence. It's possible that there might be soldiers on guard, so I must be extremely careful.

I sneak into the barn and whisper while lighting up a tiny candle I brought with me, "Dr. Stein, it's me. Are you alright?" I stay still, attuned to the eeriness of the barn spoiled only by high-pitched squeaks of mice skittering through the walls.

"We're fine," comes the doctor's whisper and there is movement in the part of the barn used for storing hay and straw. When the Steins first arrived, we dug out something like a cellar under the hayloft. The opening of it is camouflaged with straw. During the days they just stay in the barn and only go into hiding underground when someone visits us. At night they sometimes go outside for fresh air, but not tonight since there are Germans next door.

Because of what happened at the Ramniwskis' home, we decided this is the safest way to survive, but now it all has changed.

"I have to take you to our attic because starting tomorrow the German soldiers will be sleeping in the barn," I whisper.

Dr. Stein takes my hand between his. "This is too much danger for you and your family. We will go to the forests." The dim light of the candle sharpens his facial features into despair, as if he's ready to give up.

"No, Doctor, it will be too hard for your wife. Please stay with us. We will do everything to keep you safe. You're part of our family."

In the end, I succeed in convincing Dr. Stein to go with my plan, and we carefully edge into the cottage. It's hard for Mrs. Stein who has trouble walking due to her illness. She breathes heavily for long minutes when we finally climb into the attic.

The attics and cellars are the most searched places by the Germans, but it's not like we have much choice right now. With Mrs. Stein's fragile health condition, she would not survive long in the forests. They must stay here with us. I just pray that we won't have to pay the ultimate price.

# FIVE
## ANETA

July 1943—Aneta's village

The next morning, I perform the usual farm chores, unable to chase away my worries about Janek. While awake at night, I settled on bringing him to my friend Bronka who lives in another village about ten kilometers from us. He will be much safer there; I trust my friend like no one else.

The fact that Kostek still isn't back unnerves me even more. It's not the first time the rake has fled a sinking ship, leaving me alone with everything.

But watching Johann and his soldiers galloping away brings the anticipated relief and more courage to go ahead with my plan. I throw the leftover rye into the yard for the chickens and enter the cottage. As I walk through the hallway and open the white double doors to the kitchen, the inviting smell of grain coffee travels to my nostrils, awakening my senses.

Janek is playing with a wooden airplane toy on a woven runner in colorful stripes and my mother-in-law is crocheting while perched on the bench beside the tiled stove.

My son lifts his head and runs toward me, his smile reaches

his eyes. "Mamusia, why couldn't I help you this morning?" His angelic face and earnest look melt my heart.

"I'm sorry, darling, but we must be careful now when the German soldiers are next door. Though I was hoping that you could help me bring breakfast to Mr. and Mrs. Stein. Would you?"

He jumps up and claps his hands together. "Can we do it now?"

"Yes, they must be hungry." I fill two mugs with steaming coffee made of roasted rye grains and apply a thin layer of apple marmalade onto two chunks of black bread.

In my bedroom, I put the tray with food aside and take out a folded ladder from under the bed to place it against the wall. After climbing it, I tap the right spot on the ceiling five times. Originally there was a visible entrance to the attic in the hallway but before the war Zygmunt got rid of it and moved it here. For someone not aware, the panel is so well camouflaged that it would be difficult to find it at first glance as it almost doesn't stand out from the rest of the ceiling. Almost.

Soon the panel lifts and a bearded face appears. "Hello, Dr. Stein," I whisper and smile. "I brought over some breakfast and Janek would like to visit. Is that fine with you?"

He smiles back. "Of course, my dear, of course. It will be our honor."

Once we manage to get up there, my son runs into the embrace of Mrs. Stein who sits on the pallet propped against a red brick chimney. He has an affection for this elderly lady with her soft face and salt and pepper hair. Dr. Stein explained that she suffers from a condition called osteogenesis imperfecta, a genetic illness that causes bones to break easily. It also affects her muscles and ability to walk. Still, there is always a smile on her face.

"Mrs. Stein, would you tell me a legend today?" Janek asks while sitting on her lap.

She nods but I interfere, "Janek, please let our guests have their meal in peace."

"I'm going to tell you this," Mrs. Stein says in a gentle voice. "I will enjoy this feast you brought for me first and then I will tell you a special story. How does that sound?"

Janek jumps out of her embrace. "Good plan," he says and winks at her while we all laugh.

The attic is large but while before the war Zygmunt liked to store grain in here; now it's mainly used for keeping junk. The Steins put their pallets and a few belongings near the chimney area. At least they will be warm in the winter. I make a mental note to bring more blankets and other things to them tonight, so they are more comfortable, especially Mrs. Stein.

While they eat, we discuss the current situation. I always make sure to bring them any newspapers I get hold of and books for Dr. Stein. His wife enjoys crocheting like my mother-in-law, so I supply her with the materials.

"Hopefully the German soldiers stationing next door will leave soon," I say.

"We will be extremely careful," Dr. Stein says, giving me an assuring glance.

"It's so unfair that you must hide here like this."

The doctor gives me a long look. "Thanks to your gold heart we are still alive. Besides, I don't waste my time anymore contemplating the unfairness of this world. I pray that one day this madness ends."

I sigh. "And so do I."

After we leave, I can't help but worry about our future. It all seems so overwhelming and impossible that we won't get caught at some point. I shake my dreadful thoughts away knowing that only clarity in thinking and acting will secure our well-being. With the risky move of bringing the Steins to our attic, I must keep my son safe. But can I manage it?

# SIX

## ANETA

July 1943—Aneta's village

An hour later, I scan the property next door for any soldiers that might have stayed on post, but it seems there is no one there. It's the perfect time to get on the road, before Johann is back. I attach a harness to the horse and connect it to the wagon, then I lift Janek to the wood bench in the front of the carriage.

I take a seat behind him and place his straw hat on top of his head. "You always forget your hat," I say softer than usual. My heart breaks at the thought of our upcoming separation but I know it's the only way to make sure Johann doesn't spot him. My son would find ways to sneak outside even if I forbade him from it. Still, it's the first time he will be away from me, and that makes me so uncomfortable.

The dirt road swirls through forests populated with pine and oak, and occasionally some birch. But today the trees strangely stand still, their leaves dangling in the torrid July heat, despite the morning hours.

As we move forward, Janek chats about his dream last night in which he sailed the sea as captain of a pirate ship. As I listen, I inhale a crisp and pungent scent from the air that mingles with the sweetness of sunbaked flowers and herbs. This smell is like nectar to my suffering soul, a balm to my troubled heart. I feel as if I'm breathing in the pureness of freedom, one that can be experienced only within nature, far away from humans.

Bronka's village is situated down the picturesque valley in the Roztocze Hills. Soon we approach her cottage with a wood shake roof and walls of tarred planks. To my relief, my friend is home as she's talking to her neighbor Faustyna, a friendly brunette in her mid-thirties, through a wooden fence. Bronka holds baby Jordan in her arms while the neighbor's two little daughters, Sabina and Jasia, play in the dirt.

After I exchange pleasantries with the neighbor, Bronka invites me inside while Janek stays to play with the girls.

"Roman and his parents went to the mill, but they should be back in a couple of hours," Bronka says as we enter the threshold that smells of the dried rosemary that Bronka's mother-in-law carefully uses in her herbal cures.

"That's actually good because I need to talk to you," I say and take a seat at a round table in the center of the guest room decorated with loom-woven carpets.

She lifts her brows, her sandy-blonde hair shining in the sun rays that infiltrate the white curtains. Her blue eyes and fair skin are a far cry from my chestnut hair, green eyes and tan skin. She's the light and I'm the darkness. "What's with the gloomy look on your face? Is everything alright?" she asks.

I sigh and regard the replica of *The Last Supper* painting on the wall with a silent prayer that dances in my soul. "If you make that raspberry tea of yours, I will tell you all."

After she hands the baby to me, she heads for the kitchen then soon comes back with a tray of two glasses with a steamy liquid and pieces of rhubarb pie with crumble topping. Then she picks up her little Jordan and begins nursing him while sipping on the tea. "I'm all ears now, my friend. You've really got me worried with that resignation written all over your face."

"Johann is here," I say, having this sensation of dropping a bomb from my chest.

She tips her head to the side. "The Johann from Gdańsk?"

"Yes, the one." I fill her in on what happened yesterday. She knows my past, so she understands the seriousness of the situation.

"Did he see Janek?" She rises from her seat and moves the sleeping baby into the cradle.

"No, and I've been doing everything to make sure he never does."

She takes another sip of the tea. "I would say leave him here with us, but it might be too much for you not to have him close."

"You know me so well. I was going to ask you about that. It does kill me to separate from him, but I trust you and I know he will be much safer here than at home. I would do anything to keep him away from Johann."

She puts her hand over mine. "Of course, you know I will treat him like my own. He can stay with us as long as you need him to."

I blink away tears of gratitude and relief. "I don't know how I can thank you for this."

She winks and says, "Start with having some of that pie. It's not as good as my mother's but I hope it's edible."

Without another word, I dig my fork into a handsome piece on my plate. "I'd rather die than let Johann take Janek away from me; it's what he would do if he knew he had a son." I chew on the rhubarb appreciating the pleasant tart flavor mixed with the sweetness of the crumble. "This is heaven," I say and smile.

She chuckles back at me. "Only you can change from a dreadful topic to a sweet one within practically a sentence."

"You know how unbalanced I can be. Living under one roof with Zygmunt's mother does that to people."

Bronka sighs but she changes the subject. "Do you still love Johann?"

This is the last thing I expected her to say. Her drilling gaze doesn't leave my face, so I know there is no avoiding it. "How could I?"

She clears her throat. "I'm not asking you if you want to love him, I'm asking you if you love him."

Anger flushes through my body. "I loved him during the days in Władysławowo, or it's more that I was infatuated with him, but seeing him in Gdańsk took that illusion away from me. I realized his true nature and that before he only pretended. So no, I will not allow myself to love him. Never."

"Have you ever thought that it wasn't him that you saw that day?"

"It was him," I say, without any doubts. "I saw him well."

She answers with a small nod; her eyes reflect my own sadness. She understands me so well. After a sorrowful silence, she says, "You must be careful then and avoid him at any cost."

"That's the plan."

I'm grateful when she changes the subject. "Have you heard from Władek?"

"Nothing so far. I pray he's alive. The knowledge of his death would kill my mother-in-law."

"Oh, Netuś, you know nothing will kill that witch; I assure you of it. She'll not stop until she's done draining all your strength, unless you finally draw the line."

I sigh. "You're right. Anyway, I have a feeling that Władek is alive. He's always been so savvy and determined, but most of all incredibly strong. He'll survive whatever he has to. I adore him like he was my younger brother, so there is not a day I don't think of him."

"He always seemed shy whenever we visited and never cared to join our company."

*Because he was in love with you from the moment he saw*

*you for the first time,* I think but don't say so. She doesn't need to know this since her heart belongs to Roman. Bronka and Władek's paths are destined to run in opposite directions. My brother-in-law is a noble man, so it never even occurred to him to show his feelings for her. He respected the boundary and simply stayed away whenever she was near. I saw it all in his eyes but never confronted him about it. It just saddened me to know his pain for loving the wrong woman.

She looks around and for a moment longer her face focused as if she's making sure that no one else can hear our conversation. "What about the Steins now the Germans are next door from you? What if Johann decides to search your barn and finds them?"

"I had to move them to the attic because Johann announced that some of his soldiers will be sleeping in our barn. Poor Mrs. Stein at least had some fresh air at night when they could come outside to the orchard. Now it's like they are jailed within our four walls."

She sighs. "They are good people. I know you will do everything so they survive, but please, my friend, be careful. If they are discovered, the Germans will not have mercy on any of you."

# SEVEN
## ANETA

July 1943—Aneta's village

The next day I'm busy bringing hay in from the meadows. Keeping busy makes it easier not to think of Janek being away from me in another village, but at the same time, I'm relieved that there's no chance that Johann notices him.

My son resembles his father to the point that Johann would guess the truth within seconds of seeing him. But the most important thing now is that my Janek is safe and out of Johann's way.

I inhale the sweet, earthy aroma of sunbaked hay and nudge the horse, hitched to the wagon, toward the next haystack, the largest one. I'm about to dig my pitchfork to transfer a batch of hay into the wagon when a tiny sob causes my body to freeze.

I move away layers of hay and discover a little girl with dark hair wearing a shabby dress. I can't help but stare at her in confusion. There are many Jews hiding in forests and coming at night to villages to ask for food. I always give whatever I'm able to share when someone knocks at our door, but this is the first time that I find an abandoned child.

The moment the little girl sees me, she cries loudly, tears running down her cheeks.

"You're safe, sunshine. What's your name?"

Her frightened, black eyes stare at me, but she says no word. She looks no more than two.

I put my index finger to my lips. "Shhh, little one. Everything will be alright." When I touch her arm to console her, I notice a small scrap of paper in the hay beside her. I grab it and read it:

*I'm dying. Please, save my Hana. I beg you.*

I swallow the lump of emotion that forms in my throat and gaze around. But there are only dense forests encircling us, no sign of another human. Someone left their precious Hana here for me to save, probably when I went back home with the first wagon of hay. Is that someone still watching me from the forests? I don't know what to do. If I leave the poor child, I will be no better than the Nazi monsters. I must take her home and care like for my own, even if it means playing with a death sentence....

I decide to think of details later and after calming down the crying girl by giving her an apple, I settle her into a wagon and place piles of hay around her. She's so busy chewing on the fruit that she's ceased sobbing. Who knows when she ate something last?

"Please, Hana, stay silent. I will take you home, so you can fill your stomach with warm soup," I say and stroke her hair. I'm not sure if she understands because she's so focused on the apple that she doesn't even look at me.

I know it's best to leave now when she's not crying and since it's only three o'clock in the afternoon, Johann and his soldiers are most likely not back yet.

It takes about ten minutes to return home. Before lifting the girl from the wagon on which she's camouflaged within the hay, I carefully look around to make sure no one watches us.

Hana still sucks on the apple core, so I scoop her into my arms and scramble into the hut. When we are inside, I exhale with relief, praying that no one saw us. My mother-in-law isn't in the kitchen, so I sit Hana at the table and feed her with *krupnik*, a barley soup. The whole time, she devours the soup and every crumb from the chunk of bread I handed her.

In the meantime, I heat up some water on the stove, strip the filthy clothes from the girl and give her a bath. She squeals with delight when she's in the water, which makes things so much easier. After I dress her in Janek's old pajamas, I burn her filthy clothes inside the stove.

She's so tired that I decide to move her to my bed where she cries herself to sleep. The whole time, she doesn't utter any words, which makes me wonder if she knows Polish. I must dress her like other children in the village and tell everyone that my cousin died, so I decided to take care of her daughter. We will teach her Polish prayers and bring her to church with us on Sundays. She will pass as a Polish child.

I also consider bringing her to the Steins but that might be dangerous if the girl starts crying in the attic and someone hears her.

At night, the little one doesn't stop weeping even though I hug her and sing old lullabies. After long hours, the exhaustion and despair take a toll on me. I feel like I can't breathe anymore, afraid that my mother-in-law will wake and get angry. She wasn't pleased when she saw Hana this evening.

I cradle the precious girl into my arms and walk into the darkness outside. I know I might attract the soldiers' attention, but I would go insane if I stayed there any longer with her like this.

As if sensing the change in the air, she switches from her loud cries to a low sobbing. We perch on the bench and I point to the twinkling stars in the sky, while telling her about different constellations. For a moment she listens as if she understands me but then goes back to sobbing.

"What has happened to this little princess?" Johann's quiet voice comes from the side of the house, sending chills down my spine. I must get up and leave as soon as possible, before he realizes that she's Jewish.

"Just a bad dream," I say, hoping he will not get closer but by the time I finish the last word, he's already standing in front of us, holding a black kitten in his arms. He looks so different in the crisp white shirt, without the uniform jacket. Fear that Hana might say something in Yiddish shoots through my heart. She did utter a few words before in that language.

"Look at this fellow, little girl." He crouches and gently strokes the kitten. "I think she needs a hug." His voice is so soft that for a moment he reminds me of the boy I fell in love with all those years back.

Hana stops crying and peeks at Johann despite the fact that she doesn't understand what he says, then she reaches her hand to touch the kitten.

"Here, you can hold her," Johann says with encouragement in his voice. The kitten doesn't object but snuggles into Hana's lap while she chuckles in delight and keeps stroking her.

My hopes that the girl doesn't say anything are pumped with adrenaline that swirls in my head like a carousel on a blistering day.

Johann gazes at me. "Your daughter is precious."

I clear my throat. "She's my deceased cousin's daughter. She doesn't have any other family besides me." I feel hot and cold at the same time, unable to move, paralyzed by every passing second and that he questions if Hana is Jewish.

He nods in understanding. "What's her name."

I stop myself just when I'm about to say *Hana*. "Hania," I say the Polish version of her name.

"You've a good heart," he says and brings his hand to my face making my skin shiver. His thumb rubs my cheek in a circulating motion.

I hate the feeling of warmth that spreads through me; I hate that my body responds so strongly to his touch. "We'd better go to bed," I say before realizing how my words might sound.

"There is nothing else I dream of." His eyes are like two drifting crystals among the sea waves. "Fair enough, Netuś," he adds and brings my hand to his lips to kiss the knuckles while his daring gaze stays on me.

I don't react. I am overwhelmed by his kindness and sensuality, by hearing him say my pet name, which I told him about back then. Besides my mother, only Bronka calls me that. His gentle approach fleetingly assures me that he doesn't intend to harm us. But how long before he changes his mind and goes back to our tormentor?

"Well, I'd better get some shut eye before another busy day tomorrow." He strokes the girl's hair, then leaves while the kitten leaps away from Hana's embrace and follows him.

I feel so lost. Why is he like this? Is this all pretending, but then why would he even care enough to be like this?

I'm so confused about who the true Johann is, especially now after witnessing his softness with Hana. Can a man behaving like this be ruthless to others? Well, he proved back then that he could, when he didn't know that I was watching him.

But the seed of doubt has been planted in me tonight. Now it's going to be even more tormenting not knowing his true intentions. After all, I can't forget the stand he takes as a grown man, the uniform he puts on every day. He's my enemy.

# EIGHT

BRONKA

July 1943—Bronka's village

I open my eyes and wonder at the howling of dogs outside and a whiff of smoke in the air. The grandfather clock across from our bed shows nearly five in the morning. Not wanting to wake my baby boy, who's still asleep in his wooden cradle, I tiptoe to the window to investigate which way the smoke comes from. I gasp.

"Roman, wake up," I scream while shaking my husband. "Germans with rifles are coming down the hills."

I don't have to repeat myself because he leaps out of bed the same moment his mother in a white and long pajama-dress charges in. "The village is burning. We must save what we can."

"Your mother and I will let the animals out, and you bring Bronka and the children into the rye field across the road where you all wait," my father in-law says calmly and resolutely as always while putting on a felt hat, his deeply wrinkled face showing a sickly complexion. "It's not a good sign that *Szkopy* are burning the buildings."

A moment later, we run out the cottage but the shooting

from the hills makes us hover near the back wall on the other side of the hut.

"Damn it!" Roman utters and squeezes my hand. "We just need to cross the road to the field." His voice is feverish as if reality just hit him.

I hold my son close to my chest who's now awake and crying, while Roman cradles Janek in his strong arms. In my worst nightmares, I never imagined another human trying to hunt us down like animals.

"Half the village is already burning," Piotrek, the neighbor's teenage son with red hair and freckles, says after collapsing beside us. His eyes shine with a fever. "Pa sent me to warn you to hide in the rye if you can."

"Is your family safe?" Roman asks.

"Ma and the girls are already in the rye. *Szkopy* charge into houses, kill people and set everything into flames. I'm going back to my Pa to help him to free the horse and cows," he says before running toward his own courtyard that now is grazing in fire.

"Now," Roman shouts, "run!" We bolt from the wall and sprint across the dirt road. Luckily there are no shootings our way.

We settle in the tall and thick rye field, near Faustyna, Piotrek's mother.

"Stay here, darling. I will go find my parents and we'll get here in no time," Roman says, and wipes sweat from his forehead with the back of his hand.

"No," I whisper, my mouth feels so dry. "Don't leave us."

He kisses me on the mouth and gives me an assuring look. "I'll be back, my love. I promise."

I nod and let go of his hand, for a moment convinced by his strong gaze. "I love you," I whisper.

"I love you too," he says, rubs my chin with his forefinger and kisses my forehead. "Be strong for the children." Then he runs away, in the direction of the cottage, and closer to the hills crowded by the Germans.

For a moment longer my eyes follow my handsome man with broad shoulders, the man I've grown to love so fiercely. I nurse my baby and assure Janek that everything will be fine. How ironic that Aneta brought her son here for safety....

I pray that Roman comes back to us and that we'll all somehow survive this.

# NINE

## BRONKA

July 1943—Bronka's village

The last few days were quiet, while Janek settled in with us, his laughter spreading through the household like a rainbow above our village. He found delight in tickling Jordan's feet, making him giggle, and he enjoyed playing with the neighbor's children. I was so glad to help Aneta, my kind and brave friend who's been there for me through the years. But now it all has changed...

The fire spreads quickly and the roof of our cottage is in flames, eaten by the unstoppable beast ignited by another human. Horses, cows, pigs and dogs run all over the road making confused sounds, like some invisible tormentor smacks them with a whip. There're no people in our sight right now. The ones that were able to escape like us and hide in the fields, stay silent.

But there are also the ones that are still on the other side trying to save the cattle from burning alive or their most valuable belongings. My husband and his parents are among them. I'm so angry that they failed to put their lives first. I'm so angry at Roman for choosing his parents over us. I'm so angry but at the same time I'm more frightened that he will not come back to me, that the soldiers will murder us in cold blood. I'm so angry and so afraid that I choke on my own saliva...

I know that I shouldn't be angry but proud of my husband for his bravery and sacrifice, but I can't comprehend even the thought of losing him.

As I'm waiting for his return, I experience this awful hopelessness like that day when my aunt from Lublin, the big city in the area, took me to the cinema. We watched a movie about the Great War and there was a scene with a fire in which the main character perished. I wanted to get up and help until I remembered that it was just a film that I was there to only watch. I could do nothing about it. Now, I can't do anything too, just a pathetic spectator witnessing my world falling apart. But I must protect the children's lives at any cost.

Suddenly, Faustyna's husband runs out of his yard toward our field, but a series of bullets from behind strike him, and he collapses to the ground.

Faustyna gasps and extends her hand into the air as if wanting to touch her beloved in his last moments. Pain freezes on her face like icicles sticking out of the thatch of a barn on days of deadly frost.

"They killed Pa," Sabina, Piotrek's six-year-old sister, cries out, terror painted on her angelic face.

Her mother, with tears in her eyes, pulls her to herself and whispers, "Shush, little one, or the Germans will shoot us all too." Her other daughter Jasia, who's only three, clings to her mother like a newborn kitten. They all quietly cry.

What an incredibly strong woman. Even in a moment like this, she thinks of the good of her children. I've always liked her for her wisdom and good heart, but now I admire her resilience.

Janek begins to sob too. "I want Mama," he wails, tears streaming down his face.

I swallow hard and tell him to lie on his back and count the white clouds in the sky that keep moving undisturbed by what's happening down here. When he counts one hundred of them, it will be time to go to his mama. I also explain to him that it's important that he watches the sky for any sign of the rain that would help with the fire. To my relief he obeys. I do recall Aneta telling me with pride that he already learned counting that far.

Minutes later, I spot Roman and his parents hovering near the side of our cottage now fully inflamed by the fire. They must've let all the animals out and now are trying to cross to us but there's constant shooting from the woods. My mouth goes dry as I pray to the Virgin Mary that they get to us safely.

After the shooting dies out, Roman signals with his hand and they all leap forward as hope settles in my heart, but suddenly, two soldiers appear from the left and shoot their rifles.

My beloved sways but he still moves forward to crumple down when he reaches the road; his father follows.

My entire world stops, everything around me just a blur as shards of pain stab me from inside, straight into the center of my heart.

I yearn to run to him, to help him, so I turn to Faustyna and mumble, "Please, take care of the children. I must help my husband."

She holds my arm, her strong gaze on me. "They will kill you too. You need to live for your baby and your friend's son. Stay put."

I know she's right but everything in me screams. "I can't sit here and do nothing when he needs my help."

"Too late," she whispers and motions her head to the road. The two Germans now stand beside my husband and his father and finish them by firing their guns.

There is a scream stuck in my throat, and I feel like I'm

suffocating. I can't breathe or swallow the pain in my every fiber. Nothing matters anymore, nothing... my life is over.

Then, I watch in horror as a German soldier lifts Roman's mother, who's kneeling and sobbing, and throws her into the flames of the cottage. He releases a demonic laugh and barks something to his company before they move onto the next courtyard.

I vomit and get swept over by dizziness. My muscles feel numb as I keep shaking my head in denial. This hasn't happened. No, no, no... Roman is only pretending to be dead and will run to me once it's clear. But he doesn't move. I close my eyes and rock back and forth. "He's gone," I whisper.

Faustyna slaps my cheeks and shakes me, her glassy eyes meeting mine. "Think of the children, nothing else. Forget for now what has just happened. Right now, think only of your baby and survival. Do you understand what I'm saying?"

I swallow the painful lump and nod, tears streaming down my cheeks. "Yes."

Janek counts out loud the clouds and now he's at twenty-three. It took twenty-three clouds for my life to come to a stop.

"We all must be very quiet," Faustyna whispers, "so they don't know that we're hiding here, or at least forget about us."

I cease thinking and ignore the unbearable pain in my heart. "We should move further into the rye," I say, feeling numb inside but refusing to give up for the sake of the children.

As we do it, I spot a wooden wagon settled on the border of the grass field and filled with manure that Roman left here yesterday. He joked that sometimes unfinished jobs might turn out to be blessings. He's still here with me, even now. Suddenly, it feels like getting under that wagon would be like running into Roman's embrace.

"We should hide under it," I say and point to it, "it's long enough to give protection to all of us."

"If it sets on fire, we will be trapped under it and burn

alive," Faustyna says and fixes her head covering. "It's wiser to stay here, especially as my Piotrek might be looking for us."

Piotrek. What has happened to him?

I have this strong urge to go under it and become invisible to the entire world, so I don't have to pretend to be so brave when I'm terrified and broken. "If you change your mind, please join us," I say. "Janek, darling, come with me."

He shakes his head; his eyes betray fear. "But I've only counted to thirty-three, so we can't go to Mama yet." His large blue eyes set trustingly on my face, but I can't feel any more pain than I already have.

"Sunshine, right now we must hide from the bad soldiers, so we can go to your mama soon."

"Mama said to always listen to you, Aunt Bronka."

We move on our knees toward the wagon and crawl under it. I position Jordan at my breast, so when he wakes up, I can nurse him, so he doesn't cry; with my other hand I cradle Janek to me. "It's important that we stay silent, sunshine," I say. "The bad soldiers cannot find us. After that I promise, we will go to your mama, but you must not cry now."

The rotten egg stench of manure gnaws on my nose and takes my breath away. I can't believe the baby has slept through all this ruckus, even when his daddy was murdered. I do everything not to sob. I can't think of or say that word. I just can't.

Soon, the sound of boots makes me go still. I stroke Janek's arm and whisper to him not to make any noise or move. Just when I thought I could not feel anything else, a hand of fear squeezes my heart.

I open my eyes and hopelessly wait for the oppressors to come and shoot us too. It's why they're here.

A soldier shouts something at Faustyna and then he grabs the sweet Jasia from her embrace and throws her to the side like a sack of potatoes. Faustyna drops to her knees, begging him to spare her daughters but he shoots her. Then he fires his rifle at the terrified girls...

I dig my nails into my skin and fight not to scream, unable to control my body's trembling. How can this world go on like this? *God, why aren't you stopping this world from existing? Why?*

I swim in waves of shock, like in the sea overtaken by storm. My already shattered heart breaks into even smaller pieces. I turn my head to make sure that Janek hasn't witnessed the massacre, the last moments of his little friends. But his face is sheltered faithfully in my arm, just like I instructed him to do regardless of all the noises. He heard the shotguns and the screams and he knows that something terrible is happening because I can feel his little body shaking.

The murderer jumps further into the field, while we make no sound or move. I do everything not to think. I surround myself with a thick wall, or I'll break. That would be the end to my baby's life, or Janek's life. *God, please help my children stay alive.*

More booted steps, heavy breathing, someone collapses against the wooden wagon under which we're hiding. The man sobs and keeps whispering, *"Mein Gott, mein Gott."* He leans his back into the wagon as his body shakes like a rooster whose head was just cut by a hatchet.

He can't see us. *Virgin Mary, please leave it that way. Don't let him know we're here.*

My son wakes up and releases a single squeak before I manage to thrust my nipple into his mouth. I feel as if cold fingers run up my spine.

The soldier's back stops shivering and soon he kneels, and our eyes meet. He's visibly surprised as his gaze takes me in. He mumbles something in German.

"Please, don't kill my baby," I whisper in my tongue, not

knowing his, not caring to wipe away my tears. I know fighting him will not do a thing and I can't communicate with him, so I insert all my heart into my eyes.

# TEN

## BRONKA

July 1943—Bronka's village

"*Tu... siedzieć...*" He whispers in broken Polish for me to stay put and lifts his gaze. "*Sam-ol-ot.*" Plane. He jumps back to his feet and charges away.

I can't control the shakiness of my entire body as I swallow my salty tears. "Thank you," I whisper even though he can't hear me. There are decent people even among the worst. How is it that the other soldier turned to be a ruthless murderer while this one showed compassion?

His words prove to be right because soon there are rumblings from the sky followed by shootings and bomb explosions.

We stay close to the ground. I wonder if I'm not suffocating my baby. Bullets hit all over the wagon. I fret for the children, never stop praying. *Please, God, let them live. I will never turn my back on you, not even now when I want to die and join my Roman. Please, spare them...*

Then, I hear Roman's voice in my head telling me that it

must end, it can't go on forever, that we will be alright, that he will watch over us, that he never truly left, that he loves us.

I sob.

Everything has its end, just like my beloved husband's life. Just like my sanity that has perished along with him.

Then there is nothing. Only silence that comes after Armageddon, except, there was no fight here; we had no way to fight. I can't believe we somehow survived this...

We wait a long time making sure that the Germans don't come back before we crawl out from under the wagon. I know where we must go.

The air is hot and spoiled by smoke while the whole village cries in flames. I hear the moaning of the ones that managed to stay alive and the sickening sound of flames eating the whole village.

I find my husband and cradle his face between my trembling hands. My entire world... every breath of my soul... every muscle of my heart... is frozen. The back of my head tingles as I feel the invisible arms of my lover encircling me. "Please don't leave me," I whisper kissing his lips, his cheeks, his nose... "Please, love, don't leave me."

My world is like broken glass while I'm dancing on its sharpest particles. Still, everything goes on. Another minute passes, the birds sing, somewhere people go about their business.

The sudden thought of the children forces me to pull myself together. I put my hand over my mouth and bite my thumb. I can't give up. I must fight for the little ones. "Please, darling, help me. Bring strength to me."

After suppressing my sobs, I kiss Roman's lips for the last time and whisper, "I'll love you forever, darling." I wipe my tears with the back of my hand though they don't cease coming. "I must go now and save the children. You told me to be strong for them."

The sweetest little Janek, holds the baby in his arms, his head facing up. He's counting the clouds. I can't hear the words or numbers because of the constant hum in my head, but when I look up, there are no clouds, just darkness. The entire sky is gray and black. Still, the little boy continues counting the imaginary, fluffy and white clouds. Aneta has raised her son to be strong and resilient.

I've let him and the baby down, while succumbing to my despair, but now I will do everything to protect them.

We walk up the hill and into the forest. Aneta's village is ten kilometers from here. I've been doing everything to keep her son safe. Now I will bring him to her and we will rely on her kindness. I need her now more than ever. She's my hope in this darkest moment of my life, when my beloved husband is gone.

The whole time, I try to refuse letting the thoughts of losing Roman take over my mind, to sink in. I must only think of bringing the children to the safety of Aneta's home. Nothing beyond that. But I fail miserably because the moment when Roman dropped to the ground after being shot replays in my mind like a nightmare. Except, this is not a dream that I can just awaken from. This is my reality, a deadly one.

I whimper but quickly remind myself about the children. After a sharp intake of breath, I squeeze Janek's hand and pull the baby closer to my chest. I force my mind to good memories, like when Roman kissed me for the first time. That's all I have left now, the good memories to soothe my broken heart.

As we falter on the sandy road that will eventually lead us to Aneta, I carefully listen out for any noises. Soon enough, only the halfway through, we stumble at the sound of barking dogs and shouts in German.

# ELEVEN
## ANETA

July 1943—Aneta's village

"No Kostek all day yesterday and today," my mother-in-law says and fixes her glasses up her nose while crocheting at our oak table decorated with sunflower oilcloth fabric. "One day he's going to drink too much and bring only problems to us."

"Maybe he's left for good now because the Germans are here," I say while hustling at the stove making some *twaróg*, a white cheese. It's not the first time Kostek has disappeared without a word.

She shakes her head. "Neh. He's probably drinking like a pig, but he will be back. Where else is he going to have better? You're way too good to him and because of it he comes and goes whenever he wants."

I pretend to focus on my task, so she doesn't continue this conversation; her blaming purge will only get worse. I line a colander with white cloth and using a wooden spoon, I ladle the milk curds from the iron pot into the fabric, which I wrap around the mass and squeeze it gently for a long while, then I hang it and watch as milk droplets hit bottom of a steel bowl.

Once the white cheese is ready, I will take it down and put a small panel on it with glass jar filled with water on top of it for the night. This way the cheese will be more compact. Janek likes it with sugar on top and I enjoy making a cheesecake.

Just when I'm about to say good night to my mother-in-law, the squeaky sound of the front door makes me stumble over the chair. The sight of Kostek's red face peeking into the kitchen calms my shaking hands.

He takes his hat off and says, "Praised be Jesus Christ."

"Forever and ever," my mother-in-law says watching him with triumph. "We worried that the Germans did something bad to you."

I can see that he's not fully sober but also not that drunk either. There is this sadness emanating from his face that makes him look so much older.

He sighs while taking a seat on the bench across from my mother-in-law. "I'm alright but a lot has happened since yesterday."

She must've also noticed how ill he looks because she leaps to her feet and says, "Let me bring you supper, hun, so you can tell us what's on your mind."

He only nods. Normally he's a cheerful man ready to joke or tell stories, but now he seems too quiet.

"What is it, Kostek?" I ask, bracing myself for the worst news. "You are not being yourself."

She puts two small bowls before him, one filled halfway with curd milk and the other with mashed potatoes. He stares into it for a short moment. "One of the nearby villages was burned yesterday by the Germans."

I gasp and my mother-in-law makes a sign of the cross. "Any dead?"

He picks up a spoon, but his hand trembles so violently that he puts it down again. "Nearly two hundred people."

"What?" The cup filled with water that I held in my hand

drops to the floor releasing the sound of breaking glass, small particles all over the floor.

He spends the next minute telling us about the terrible and unthinkable events from yesterday.

"No one survived?" I whisper and swallow hard.

He wipes his tears away. "Over two dozen people did by a miracle. We took them to the hospital in Biłgoraj. But the bodies of the murdered remain in the village. There is an order from the Germans to bury them tomorrow in the mass graves at the edge of the forest."

For a moment longer we just sit without another word. Sometimes silence tells more than any words ever could.

"But why?" I finally say. "Why have been they doing this?"

"Rumors are that they did it to punish the villagers for helping the partisans. Some say that the village failed to pay the contingents too. No one knows the reason for sure, only the bloody murderers do." He spits to the floor but then glances apologetically at my mother-in-law, but she doesn't comment on it, clearly also affected by the horrible news.

"Which village?" she asks, her face drained of any color, making me realize that I was about to ask the same, though with a painful heart. I can't even imagine learning that someone I know was there.

He draws his eyebrows together and peeks at me with sorrow. "Bronka's."

I stop scooping up the particles of glass from the floor and stare at him in disbelief. "It can't be," I say as my voice goes weak and cracks. I leap to Kostek and grab his arms in a frenzy. I shake him and shout, "Janek is with Bronka."

His face momentarily turns white, but he stays silent, so I intensify my grip on his arms shaking him even more. "Please, tell me they went to Biłgoraj." My voice cracks and a series of sobs come out.

"Come here, daughter." My mother-in-law's strong voice

makes me freeze my grip on him. I swirl around, ready to scream at her that we must go look for my Janek, but her painful expression plants a seed of doubt in my heart. She pulls me into her arms where I cry and cry and cry while she strokes my hair.

Kostek's tearful voice makes my sobbing cease. "I didn't know our boy was there. He wasn't among the living that we took to the hospital in Biłgoraj, nor was Bronka or her baby. But I didn't see their bodies either." He clears his throat. "Though I saw the corpses of Roman and his father."

I free myself from her embrace and wipe my tears. "I have to go there."

"It's too dangerous. Tomorrow they will be burying the dead. It's best to stay away."

"You don't understand. Janek is alive, I just know it. I'm sure Bronka escaped with him and the baby, so it's why you didn't see them there. I'm going to her parents' village." I won't let any doubts enter my reasoning. My friend isn't one to accept the worst without fighting. She found a way to save the children, I just know it.

"It's not wise to do that now. We'll go there in the morning."

I form a fist, press it to my chest and say through my clenched teeth, "I'm going now. If my son is dead, I must know."

"You don't know what you're saying," my mother-in-law says. "You're in shock. You must listen to Kostek and go to bed before the Germans kill you too." Her voice breaks and a dreadful whimper emerges from her

I brace myself by listening to my gut, which tells me that Janek is alive. "Please, Mother, watch over Hania while I'm gone," I say quietly and without a glance at her, I walk out. I'm fueled not only by adrenaline shooting through my veins, but also by the stubborn belief that my sweet Janek is fine, and I must find him as soon as possible.

There are no soldiers in sight from the next door, but their laughter and loud conversations can't be ignored. I run through the yard and pass the wooden barn. Thankfully no Germans sleep in it so far despite Johann's declaration. I waddle through the tall grass of the orchard, then I enter the birch tree forest and navigate in the direction of Bronka's childhood village.

Then I realize that Kostek never left my side. I'm thankful for that. Before we even get to the village, we bump into one of the partisans who informs us that the Germans charged into Bronka's parents' village today and brought everyone to the camp in Zwierzyniec, though they didn't burn the households or kill anyone. His words are confirmed a moment later when we get there, and everything is in disarray; the houses are empty.

"You heard him," I say. "They took everyone to that camp in the town. Bronka and the children must be there too."

Kostek puts his hand on my shoulder. "Aneta, we don't even know if she was able to escape and come to her parents. I did not see their bodies but there were many that were burned inside the buildings. I'm sorry but it's better you face this now."

"You're heartless," I bark at him not caring to wipe at my tears. "How can you say this to me?" I point my finger to his drained face. "How dare you deny me that last sliver of hope? My gut has never betrayed me in the past and it's telling me now that they are alive." I get up and march back into the forest.

"Where are you going?"

"To Zwierzyniec."

"He leaps to me and shakes my arms. "Stop this, child, just stop." His voice cracks. "They are gone."

"No," I shout. "Get out of my way!"

For the next hour I risk everything by heading for the camp in Zwierzyniec, while Kostek stays by my side. I hate putting him in danger like this, but he doesn't react when I prompt him to go back home.

The good thing about summer is that it doesn't get dark

until late, and this is to my advantage, while we still have some time before the start of the curfew.

"Halt!" one of the two soldiers on guard barks when we near the camp's perimeter, his submachine gun pointed at us.

The surge of adrenaline pumping through my blood must be doing its job because I refuse to let fear overtake me. Instead, I summon all my courage and say in crisp German, "I need to find out my son's whereabouts. He was brought to this camp today."

"No Pole is allowed to enter unless arrested," he says in a dangerous voice, his steely eyes running me down as he lifts his weapon. "You look like one of those bandits from the forests."

# TWELVE
## ANETA

July 1943—Aneta's village

"I don't know what this soldier just said but we'd better leave," Kostek utters in a weak voice, taking my arm.

I know he's right. Pressing more will get us shot. "Fine, but we must come back tomorrow morning."

Visible relief sets in his features as we walk away. I feel the guard's cold stare on me but he doesn't stop us.

We stray back to our village without another word but when we near my favorite creek by our yard, I say, "Go get some sleep. I want to stay alone here for a few minutes."

He nods without a word and leaves.

I drop down and wash my face with the cold water from the stream. It's here where I will be able to put my thoughts together.

My son is alive. I've never felt my inner voice telling me something as strongly as it does now. Still, the doubt slowly stabs at my heart like my mother-in-law's harsh words. What if I'm only imagining it? Maybe it's my mind's way of coping with the loss. What if my precious son isn't here anymore, how can I live with this pain for the rest of my life?

"He's gone," I whisper, unable to control my sobs anymore. Just like that, he is gone... I feel all the strength leaving me like air from a burst balloon.

Sometime later, I freeze at the sudden realization that the birds still sing, the frogs chum and the creek gently murmurs as its water flows over the rocks. Maybe these are signs from the Creator that Janek is alive. *He's alive*, I think and give into crying my heart out. *He's alive...*

Someone's strong arms encircle me from the back, the touch soothing and protecting as if shielding me from the entire world. I feel deep in my heart that it's Johann, but I don't jump out and run like I should. For this one short minute I need to remain far deeper than my mind, because my mind right now can't deal with the pain, it can't deal with the reality that he's one of those murderers. Just for one minute I'll pretend that he's the man I thought he was years ago, and I want to feel again his warmth, have hope and faith. I want to love him again. I want to share with him that our son is surely alive and that we must fight for him.

But at the thought that he took part in the massacre in Bronka's village, my heart sinks. I slip away from his embrace and sit with my head between my knees. I don't want to look at him or talk to him, so I hope that he takes the hint and leaves me alone. I'm disgusted with myself for the moment of weakness I just experienced.

"What is it?" he asks, perching beside me.

"Just leave me alone."

"Not until you tell me." His voice is hoarse.

"Very well then," I howl at him. "You want to know what happened? Let's start with the fact that you and your peers murdered almost two hundred people in the nearby village. You didn't care about the children. You will all rot in hell." *You didn't care about your own child...*

"I had no part in burning that village. I swear."

I meet his painful gaze for the first time and the honesty in it makes me want to believe him. Should I tell him about Janek and beg him to help me get to the camp in Zwierzyniec and to find him? But what if all of this is pretense? How can I possibly trust this Nazi?

"I'm telling the truth." His voice is devoid of emotion.

"Why are you here then? Why do you wear this uniform, why are you in charge of the squad? You think I believe that you're only visiting me to play a soft-hearted hero? I saw what you're capable of all those years back."

"I don't know what you're talking about." He sighs and lights a cigarette, then offers one to me.

I don't move. I would never touch anything that belongs to him. Never.

"For a long time, I was busy managing my family's brewery in Danzig and we made sure to generously supply our beer to the Nazis, just so they'd leave us alone. I feel shameful about it but thanks to that I was able to stay away from joining Hitler's forces until February of this year when the Nazis threatened to take away the brewery and send my grandparents to the labor camp in Germany. So, I had no choice. They sent me to France where I was guarding one of the car factories. I hoped to spend the rest of the war like that, without killing anyone.

"One day I saved one of the generals who toured our factory, from an assassination attempt by a French worker. I was pronounced a *hero* and promoted to a much higher rank. Then last month I got an order to come to Poland and was sent to Zamość where I was put in charge of this small squad and sent to your village. At heart, I'm not one of them. You must trust me."

I know this is all a made-up story, but I should at least

pretend to believe him for the sake of my son. I will do that, but I will never again let him touch me. He seems to care a lot about making me believe how good he is. I must use it to my advantage.

"So, what's your assignment here?"

His blue eyes drill into mine as if he's trying to find at least a hint of proof that I believe him. "My main duty is to protect the nearby villages with the German colonists from the Polish partisans." He closes his eyes and winces. "There are several squads up there hunting for them, but this part was assigned to me." He takes a drag from his cigarette and releases clouds of smoke. "And we're to watch out for any remaining Jews in hiding."

I shiver but quickly brace for control. He's talking about this like it's a regular thing to do, like peeling potatoes or milking a cow. "There're no Jews here. They all were already arrested. You're wasting your time."

"So far all we've done since arriving here is guard those villages with the colonists. But hopefully I get demoted and sent to the east front where some Russian will slaughter me. I know it would make you happy."

How can he expect that I believe him? I leap to my feet and say, "I must go back; it's way past the curfew."

"You're safe with me. Stay."

If I stay any longer, I will end up vomiting. He disgusts me. "I must get some sleep as I have a lot to do tomorrow." I purposely don't tell him about Janek. I will find a way to save him and keep him away from this treacherous liar.

"I've noticed how hard you work. You transformed from a delicate city girl to a strong and beautiful woman."

"I'm a village woman now," I say proudly and march away.

I can't sleep at night, thinking of Janek, stubbornly believing that he's alright. I hug Hana who sleeps beside me and pray for my precious son and Bronka and her baby. Then my mind drifts to Johann and the fact that he likes to manipulate people. It's what he tried to do tonight by telling those silly stories, so I'd go to bed with him. Snake!

~

The next day we are unable to enter the camp again. They don't let anyone in, not even bribing the guards with vodka helps. They take it from us anyway and threaten to kill us if we don't leave.

We visit the Countess Róża Zamoyska, who's known for her kind heart and savviness, to ask for help or advise but she is away with her husband. There is no one to turn to for help...

I have no choice but to tell Johann the truth and beg him to go to the camp in search of our son, for my friend and her baby. I must take that risk even though I get goosebumps at just the thought of it.

A little hope rises in my chest at the reminder of his kindness last night, and all the other times since he arrived at my village. But can I truly trust him to help me?

# THIRTEEN
## BRONKA

July 1943—German temporary camp in Zwierzyniec, a town thirty kilometers from Zamość

I sit on a grimy floor beside my mama, feeling numb inside. Jordanek is asleep in my arms while Janek is in my mother's embrace. After crying the whole night, I'm drained of all strength. We were brought here after the German soldiers caught us in the forest.

Mama told me that everyone from my childhood village was yesterday dragged to the road and ordered to walk among other villagers to Zwierzyniec. Men were separated from women and children, so my mother hasn't seen my father and my brother Heniek since arriving here.

The camp barrack is overcrowded by people, mostly women with children and elderly. There are no bunks here, so people lay on the ground while being bitten by lice and fleas.

I can't afford to cry any longer. I must be strong and take all that comes my way while doing everything for my babies to survive this. It's what Roman wants me to do. I don't know from where I take the force to keep going. Maybe my husband never truly left my side, bringing the desire to fight for the children.

In the morning, each of us got a small piece of black bread and a cup of grain coffee and for dinner a bowl of watery soup made of overcooked carrots and millet.

"People swell from hunger here and die from exhaustion," an elderly lady in black head covering says.

"How long have you been here?" Mama asks.

"Today is the sixth day. How old is the little one?" She watches Jordan who's still asleep.

"One month," I say.

Her deeply wrinkled face grows somber. "Be careful. Sicknesses spread quickly here. They throw the dead onto the square every morning."

Her words tighten my stomach into a knot. If I continue nursing, then my baby will be fine, but to do so, I must eat and drink. I glance at Janek who's thankfully still asleep. Aneta must be going out her mind. If I only had a way of letting her know that we are here and that her son is alive. By now, she probably thinks that we died in the village among the others.

My mouth feels so dry and my throat scratchy. "They haven't given us any water," I say.

"Because there is no water here," the woman says and licks her parched lips. "The well in the camp is dry as desert. Sometimes they bring barrels from the Wieprz River, but not for days now." She waves her hand. "It's never enough for everyone anyway."

"What will they do with us?" Mama asks, her light-blue eyes betraying fear. I would give everything to get her out of here. She doesn't deserve this.

The lady sighs dejectedly. "Rumors say that people are being sent to camps or labor in Germany. And trust me, they will find ways to get rid of old folks like me and everyone else that can't work." She glances at Janek. "Though, I heard that some children with blond hair and blue eyes are being sent to be turned into Germans. We all—"

She stops talking because of a sudden commotion at the entrance. Beside the uniformed Germans, there is a group of people in civilian clothes. I quickly recognize the priest from the town's church and the young and tall Count Jan Zamoyski and his pretty wife Countess Róża Zamoyska, along with a group of other women from their orphanage.

Count Zamoyski informs us that he miraculously obtained a special permission from the head of the SS and German police in this district to take the children under six years old out of the camp and place them in the orphanage run by his wife, Countess Róża—on the condition that mothers agree to separate from their children.

The last words send chills down my spine. I bring my baby closer to my heart and remind myself that I swore to never cry again. How could I give my precious son away? This all is so unexpected, and I can see that other mothers hesitate as well. But isn't this the only way of saving them? I must do what's best for my child because I doubt he will be able to survive staying with me, especially if they send me to a labor camp.

Still, I struggle to find the strength to give him away. I can sense Mama's worried eyes on me, but I fight to suppress my tears, so I don't look up. I never thought that I would find myself in such an impossible predicament.

One thing is certain though: this is the only chance to get Janek out of this, back to Aneta.

It turns out that one of the mothers recognizes a lady from the delegation and decides to hand her daughter in, saying it's for her safety. Many others follow her suit, but I don't stir, paralyzed by the thought that I must do the same. There are also mothers who decide to keep the children with them despite persuasions from the delegation members. Should I be one of them? Will my son survive this with me? I'm so lost.

When I see Countess Róża walking by, I pull on the hem of her skirt. "Countess," I say shyly.

She turns my way and without hesitation leans toward me. "What a precious baby boy," she says, her warm eyes on my Jordanek.

I always liked looking at this good lady with her blonde hair and angelic face when I attended church on Sundays. I often thought that her name suited her so well. She does remind me of a white rose because of her gentle face and sincere smile.

I touch Janek's arm. "This boy needs to go back to his mother." I tell her quickly about him staying with us, Aneta's family name and where exactly she lives.

She nods and promises to get Janek to my friend. She calls her husband over who gently takes the sleeping Janek into his arms.

"Thank you," I whisper. Knowing that this precious boy is going into safety and hopefully back to the loving care of his mother is everything to me. At least my friend can be spared from loss.

Róża's sweet, compassionate gaze sweeps over me, and I instinctively know I can trust her. "I must be honest with you because it may save your baby's life," she whispers, "maybe even yours too. The Germans take children away from their mothers. Even if they let you keep the baby, which is unlikely, there's very little chance your son will survive with you, but we can make sure that he's well and stays alive."

"I still nurse," I say and swallow hard, unable to stop my tears.

"Listen to the countess," Mama says in a choked voice. "Give my grandson a chance to live."

The countess's soft eyes find mine, conveying encouragement. "We will make sure your son thrives, and you focus on surviving this, because he will be waiting for you."

I know she's right, so I must do it. I kiss his flushed cheeks and the sweet little nose, and I hug him to my heart. "Oh, my sweetheart, what will I do without you?" I whisper.

The countess touches my arm. "It's the only chance to keep him alive, trust me on that. You must make the decision now as this might be the only time they let us do this."

"The commandant wants us to leave now," one of the ladies from the orphanage says.

Her words bring panic to my heart and prompt me to hand my baby over to the countess. I can't stop sobbing.

"You're doing the right thing," she says. "Do you want me to bring your son to your friend as well?"

"Yes, please," I say and wipe my tears.

She nods and gazes at a teenage girl not far from us. "How old are you, sweety?"

"Fourteen."

She looks both ways and then at her mother before whispering, "We bribed the camp commandant, so they'll let us take some children older than six. Please, let your daughter come with me."

The woman pulls her child into her embrace and kisses her forehead. "Go with the good lady."

Everything happens fast and soon the delegation leaves, being rushed by the Germans, along with the children whose parents agreed to let go.

Now, when I don't hold my baby, I feel this emptiness within me. A painful lump forms in my throat and I'm unable to answer my mother who just asked me something.

She pulls me into her arms and we both cry for a long moment, until there are no more tears left.

"What will I do now?" I say, my voice breaking.

"You must be strong and stay alive for your baby," she says and brushes a strand of hair from my forehead. "Now when you know that he's safe, it's going to get easier for you, I promise. I know it hurts but in time you will realize that you did the right thing and saved his life. Remember that our countess will watch over him, and she will contact Aneta who will do everything in her power to protect him. It's a true blessing that she arrived here today."

"You're right, Mama, but it's just so hard without having him in my arms. I lost my husband and now my son."

"No, you secured your son's life, my daughter. You proved your love and strength as a mother."

"Now I know why some call her the angel of kindness," the lady with the black headscarf says. "She just managed to save so many little ones trapped in this terrible camp."

"She truly is our angel," Mama says. "God bless her."

May God bless us too, so that I can see my baby again one day. The thought that my dearest Aneta will see her boy soon and that she will take care of my baby, is my only consolation in this terrible predicament.

# FOURTEEN

## ANETA

July 1943—Aneta's village

As I rest on the bench beside the stove, inhaling the savory aroma from *kopytka*, potato dumplings topped with cracklings and onion, I listen to any noises from outside. The moment Johann arrives next door, I will go to beg him for help.

A knock on the door makes me straighten up. Who would be coming so late in the evening? Are these the Germans coming to search the house?

"Where is Hania?" I ask gazing at my mother-in-law who must be thinking the same because the crocheting lies forgotten in her hands.

"She fell asleep, so I brought her to your bedroom."

I walk on wooden legs and open the door. Instead of soldiers there is Marta, one of the orphanage caretakers from the town, holding a tiny bundle in her arms.

"I brought over Bronka's baby," she says. "The little boy miraculously survived the massacre."

I can't stop my mind from reeling as I stare at her. Is

Jordanek the only one that survived since Janek and Bronka aren't here? Does this mean that my son is gone for good?

The racing heartbeat causes pain in my chest. "Is he the only one that survived?" I ask in emotion-choked voice.

She shakes her head but looks past me. "Is it safe?" she whispers. "No Germans?"

I touch the base of my neck. "It's safe," I say looking for answers in her alerted face.

She takes a step back and says, "Come, sweetie, your mama is here."

Only seconds later Janek appears from the side of the house and runs into my embrace.

My heart is beating so fast that I'm feeling dizzy. "Janek, my sweetheart," I say and press him to me with relief. "I love you so much."

"Mama, I was so scared. The bad soldiers burned the village, but Aunt Bronka told me to count the clouds and that when I got to one hundred, she would bring me to you, but I wasn't able to count that far because other soldiers stopped us in the forest."

Hearing his chatting again is everything to me. He is here with me unharmed.

"Marta, thank you," I say hugging my son, "for bringing my Janek to me."

"I'm glad I could help. If it's too much for you to take Bronka's baby, we can keep that precious boy in the orphanage in Rózin."

I feel ashamed that in my worries about Janek, I'd forgotten all about the baby. The truth is that I would die before I let anyone hurt my godson. "Jordanek will be fine here with us. The Germans next door leave us alone most of the time." I gaze into her brown eyes. "Is Bronka in the camp in Zwierzyniec?"

She sighs. "She was yesterday and that's when she handed the children to us asking us to bring them to you, but the

Germans sent a lot of people away today, rumors say to that camp in Lublin. I'm sure that the baby wouldn't survive with her, so she made the right decision."

I must keep Jordanek safe until she is back. This is the least I can do for her after she saved my son.

Marta explains that when Bronka handed the children to the countess, she told her where I live, so they could be safely brought to me. I blink away the tears, focusing on the fact that my Janek is alive and fine, and Bronka wants me to watch over her son.

"We will have to get the old cradle from the attic," my mother-in-law says and takes the sleeping baby from Marta.

"Are you hungry?" I ask, still holding Janek in my arms, and motion to her to take a seat at our kitchen table.

"A little." She sighs and pulls off her headscarf revealing her dark and curly hair parted in the middle and gathered into a bun at the back of her head.

My mother-in-law keeps her small, calculating eyes on Marta while resting on the bench beside the stove with the little bundle in her arms. "How are things in Zwierzyniec?" she asks.

I place a bowl filled with *kopytka* in the middle of the table. Janek has already dashed away to play with his favorite wooden airplane after hugging my mother-in-law, declaring he's not hungry.

"It's hard with Germans all over the town but we're doing everything to survive," Marta says and transfers a spoonful of dumplings onto her plate.

The sucking in my stomach prompts me to follow suit. Overtaken by worries, I haven't been able to swallow a thing since Kostek brought the terrible news.

For the next minutes we chew on the soft and pillowy texture of the boiled dumplings made of mashed potatoes, egg and flour.

"How did you get to see Bronka?" my mother-in-law asks.

"Let me explain it all from the beginning to you, ladies." She spoon-cuts a dumpling into two even pieces and after munching on one of the halves, she continues, "Our countess has been doing everything to save the little ones from that German camp in the town."

Marta works for Countess Zamoyska who's known for her kindness and all the effort she puts in to save as many children as possible from the Nazis.

"She sent Count Zamoyski to some important German dignitary and by sheer luck, he got permission to enter the camp and rescue children under the age of six. It's a true miracle that this was granted to the count. I was sure that he would first get killed before this happened."

"The young count and countess are good people," my mother-in-law says and makes a sign of the cross.

"There is nothing more truthful than this. We saved so many children yesterday, some of them are still in our orphanage, some were picked up by relatives, some by other villagers, so they all can be well until their parents are back. All we can do is hope and pray for survival and return for as many as possible.

"It's God's will," my mother-in-law says softly, acting unusually for her.

∼

At night, I twist and turn wondering how I will manage to keep all these secrets from the Nazis next door. Now, when Janek is back and we are to take care of Bronka's baby, I need my mother-in-law's help more than ever. With all the mouths to feed, I must work hard so we have enough food on the table. At the same time, I will do everything to keep my son away from Johann and to assure that Hana's identity stays hidden, and the Steins stay out of sight. It's a lot to hold onto while sometimes I feel so drained, especially when I wasn't sure if Janek was still alive. How do I find the needed strength?

In the past, I always knew that out of the both of us, Bronka was the braver one, which she proved by saving the children despite losing her beloved husband. She's my inspiration and I will do everything to not disappoint her.

In all of this, I wonder if Johann is the decent man he claims to be, after all. What would he do if I asked him to try saving Bronka?

I quickly dismiss my thoughts, deciding to keep my secrets. He's in charge of the German squad next door. He can sentence us to death whenever he feels like it. I must remember that and refrain from trusting him despite his assuring words and soft approach. Though I have to admit that his presence here doesn't affect our village. There is no killing or stealing, instead they spent their nights next door and days out of the village. It's not what happened before when other squads were stationed here.

So, somewhere in the back of my mind and deep in my heart there is a tiny spark that he's a good human being and his explanations were truthful. Time will tell.

# FIFTEEN
## BRONKA

August 1943—Majdanek (KL Lublin, Konzentrationslager Lublin), a German concentration and extermination camp on the outskirts of the city of Lublin

"You have to get up, Mama, or they will send you to the gas chamber," I whisper, shaking my mother's arm.

Her glassy, unfocused eyes are closed again. "Go without me. I will catch up later."

"Get out." At the sound of Ursula's voice shaking with anger, I jump to my feet, my body feeling cold. This woman has no barriers and needs no excuses to beat someone to death. She's the Kapo in our barrack. Rumors are that she came from one of the prisons in Germany where she served a life sentence for murdering her own mother. In here, she does everything to please the German female guards and get special privileges.

She smacks my legs with a whip. "Someone from the infirmary will come to get her," she says without elaborating. "Get your ass outside to the roll call before I lose my patience."

At her words my legs feel weak. Not too many come back from one of those so-called hospital barracks, but what other choice do we have? At least Mama will have a slight chance of surviving over there. The sickness would eat her in this barrack anyway, if they don't drag her out first and murder her. It's what they do here—*dispose* of everyone unfit for labor, like we're nothing more than objects that aren't useful anymore.

I walk away with my jaws clenched, afraid to look back at my mother because if I show her too much attention, this woman will beat both of us. It wouldn't be the first time that she has done something like this.

Outside, I stand in line for black chicory coffee but when I hold the tin, battered cup, I struggle to bring it to my lips because of my shaking hands. Just the thought that I left Mama at the mercy of that cruel Ursula, unnerves me. What if she beats her to death instead of sending her to the infirmary? What if Mama ends up in *Gammelblocks*, the isolated barracks, deprived of food or any medical assistance? People go through slow agony there, and if they don't die within days, they are taken to the gas chambers.

I can't return inside because it will make things worse; I hate this powerlessness.

"What happened?" Krystyna, a small woman in her mid-fifties, asks while I watch the Jewish men prisoners in striped uniforms carry outside all the sick and dying women along with bodies of those who already died inside the barrack at night. According to the camp's rules everyone must be counted during the morning roll call, even the dead.

"My mother is ill, I mean she has been for days, and I hoped she would come out of this, but today she can't even move."

"What are her symptoms?" she asks, her face somber. She works in one of the hospital barracks for women where everyday duties are handled by prisoners like her but under the supervision of Germans.

I don't answer because when I see two men carrying my mother, I instinctively leap to my feet to run to her.

Krystyna holds my arm and whispers, "Ursula is right there, please stay or she will lash at you. That won't help you or your mother, trust me."

I nod, having a hard time controlling the shaking of my voice. "She's been constantly coughing and complaining of headaches and muscle aches and also has a rash," I choke out. "Yesterday she vomited blood."

"It's typhus. I will see if she can be brought where I work." She brushes my arm. "I will do everything I can to help her."

"Thank you. I can't lose her." For days, I was telling myself that it was just food poisoning, but Krystyna's words deprive me of any hope. My mother refused to go to the hospital, afraid of never returning, just like the ones who received a phenol injection.

Now, my greatest fears have come true. A typhus fever is a death sentence here, only few survive it. Because of the primitive sanitary conditions, lack of access to water, vermin and lice infested in swarms, it's an ongoing epidemic. It doesn't help that every Sunday when we are free from labor for the second part of the day, we spend hours crushing the lice between our fingernails. They're impossible to get rid of.

The roll call goes smoothly and soon I must join my working Kommando. Escorted by the SS guards, we scramble toward the camp's gardens as it's where we are assigned for labor. When I turn my head, I spot Krystyna leaning over my mother. I exhale with relief knowing she's in good hands.

When we arrive at the gardens, it turns out that there is a new Aufseherin assigned to us today, a dog at her side.

Once we all get busy digging up onions, carrots and beets, I glance at the German female guard hoping to find signs of humanity and culture in her face.

She watches us with her small eyes and chin up. I soon regret my move because the only thing I see there is hostility. I quickly look down and focus on my task of pulling carrots, which isn't easy considering that the soil is hard as rock.

The woman paces between us, occasionally shouting to be faster and smacking our backs with her whip. It's a relief she doesn't hit us with wooden boards like the other guard, which give dry and hard blows and with every strike hurts more and more. At the memory of it, I shiver inside.

I work quickly, so she doesn't have any reason to lash out at me. Dry earth digs under my nails, making them bleed and hurt, but I ignore it. This is nothing compared to the treatments from Ursula, who from the very first day of my arrival in this camp has tormented me by beating me on the head during roll calls, usually for no reason.

After hours of labor, we go back to the field with barracks for a meal. My mouth is dry like the Sahara Desert as we never get any water during work time.

Everyone receives a ladle of watered-down soup made of leaf cabbage, mixed with sand and dirt, and a small slice of bread that tastes like sawdust. Krystyna is nowhere in sight, so I'm not able to ask her about my mother. She must be busy at the hospital.

The break only lasts for half an hour, so by the time I'm done chewing on the bread, we are already going back to the gardens. It's no more than one o'clock in the afternoon, so we still have five long hours of labor before the six o'clock roll call.

I hope time goes fast because I can't stop worrying about Mama. I'm sure that Krystyna will do what she can, still, I need to hear from her that she's okay. It would be easier if I was the one suffering right now. It's so hard to see our loved ones going through pain and misery. If I only could, I would have saved my mother from this.

I work fast as this type of task isn't new for me, after all, I've spent my whole life working hard on my parents' farm and then on my husband's. My husband... There isn't a day when I don't think of him. He's on my mind constantly, just like our son. Fate took them both away from me, but I have faith that Jordanek is doing well; I have no doubts that my friend will not leave him.

That day when I handed him to the countess, I wasn't sure if I'd done the right thing. I felt so abandoned and empty, so incomplete. But when I arrived here and looked at all the children sitting against one of the barracks' walls, I knew I'd saved my son's life. My baby wouldn't survive here with me where typhus takes so many lives and where the food rations are meager and inedible.

I will do everything to stay alive for my son, so one day I can get out of this camp and reunite with him. This thought drives me through each day, and I know that there is no force in this world that will make me relent in my stubborn resolve to hang to the threads of life.

We report to the roll call around six where they count us, which takes longer than normal as someone is missing. I'm still not able to spot Krystyna, so I settle on going after the roll call to the hospital barrack where she works. For some reason, Ursula pays me no attention today, which I take with relief.

We receive a slice of bread and a small amount of beetroot marmalade along with a weak heather coffee for supper. I only take a few sips of the liquid, and the rest of the food I hide under my striped dress, so I can offer it later to Mama.

Afraid to not make it before the final gong, I edge toward the camp hospital and soon bump into Krystyna.

"I was coming to get you," she says. "Your mother may not make it through the night. I'm sorry."

All I feel right now is this dull pain in my heart and this awful resignation. "Where is she?"

Layers of empathy show in her sad eyes. "Come, I will take you to her. I already got approval from the Revierkapo, but she was clear that you must leave before the night gong."

We enter one of four stable-type like barracks in Field 5,

called Revier, for female patients. I wince at the stench of urine and unwashed bodies. The heartbreaking moaning from sick women is unbearable.

Krystyna told me that due to lack of medicines, they can't help much. Whatever they have at their disposal isn't enough, so they use their knowledge and wits to do what they can, to help the ones that they are able to. The only good thing about being here is that the patients don't have to work or stand for long hours at roll calls.

The misery of the sickness is so overwhelming that for a moment I want to turn and run far away from here. But I remind myself that I'm here to see my mama, for the last time. This so-called hospital is the final destination for so many after prolonged sufferings in the camp.

My mother lies motionless on a primitive bedtick, a headscarf compress on her head. She looks so fragile but, at the same time, there is this peace emanating from her, or maybe it's just because she doesn't make any noise betraying her agony.

I kneel and take my mother's hand in mine. The skin on her hand is as rough as it always has been from hard work. This little detail brings a drop of normalcy into my heart, the assurance that she's still here, still alive.

"Mamusia," I whisper and kiss her hand. "You can't leave me here by myself. What will I do without you, without your wisdom?" I wipe tears away with my trembling hand and lean forward to kiss her forehead.

She opens her eyes and smiles faintly. "Promise me that you will be strong for Jordanek. He needs you."

"I promise." The sobs that I desperately try to keep inside me, make it hard for me to talk.

She licks her dry lips. "Remember that I will always love you. We will meet again."

"We will meet again," I repeat after her as if I desperately want to believe it, for it to be the ultimate truth. "I love you."

My mother gives her last breath only minutes later. She had a peaceful expression while life was slowly leaving her body. It reminded me of a glowing lamp with someone screwing down the wick. My mother was always full of light and hope, always caring for her loved ones. Even when I closed myself to the world after my husband was murdered, I felt her gentle presence and support. I knew she was there for me, being my strength.

When I leave the Revier, I don't walk back to my barrack, instead I stand to the side with clenched fists while my nails dig into my skin. My mother will not be buried like others in our family. Those murderers will burn her body in their crematorium. They will mix her ashes with soil and waste and then use it as fertilizer. It's their evil way.

It's what they do with our bodies after they hang or shoot us as a form of entertainment; murder us in gas chambers or by firing squads; administer a phenol injection into our hearts; drown us in latrines or attack us with dogs; beat and torture us to death. This place is worse than hell.

When two prisoners in striped uniforms bring Mama outside and lay her on a cart, something breaks in me forever. I run to the men and say, "Where are you taking my mother?" I look from the face of one man to another and go back to the one with kind, soft eyes, eyes that remind me of someone.

"We will take care of her, Bronka," the one with the soft eyes says.

The moment he says my name, I know. The man before me is Aneta's brother-in-law, the one that always stayed quiet and away from sight when we visited my friend. He looks nothing like his old self with his malnourished body and shaved hair, but his eyes haven't changed.

I sniff my nose and wipe a fresh batch of tears. "What will happen to her, Władek?"

"We have to make a deal," he says, not taking his warm eyes

from mine. "You will pray for her soul, and I will take care of her body. I will make sure that it gets buried outside of the camp, so when we leave here, we can visit her grave. Deal?"

I sob and swallow the emotion blocking my throat. "Deal," I say, knowing that he only says this to make me feel better and that in reality my mother's body will never get buried. But just hearing these words from someone else makes me feel not alone in all of this.

A small smile touches his lips. "What barrack are you in?" he asks.

When I tell him, he says, "I will find you," before walking away with my mama on top of the cart.

The coming days go on, and I feel like a machine fulfilling tasks, lacking heart or soul. While I feel so alone without my mother, I'm even more determined to find a way to go back to my son. This is my entire purpose from now on.

# SIXTEEN
## ANETA

August 1943—Aneta's village

"We've done enough today," I say to Kostek as we stand together the last two sheafs of rye. We have been working in the field since the early morning.

I grab a wicker basket from under the rowanberry tree as we walk toward a dirt road. "Anything new from the forests?"

He fixes the scythe on his shoulder, and we navigate the field road with a strip of green grass in the middle. "The Resistance burned one of the villages with German colonists in retaliation for the massacre in Bronka's village."

Maybe the one guarded by Johann and his squad... I stop my chin from trembling and say, "More children and women dead. When will this end?"

His face reddens and his nostrils flare. "We must fight them, or they will wipe out our entire nation," he snaps averting my gaze.

"Yes, I agree that we must fight, but I also think that women and children should be protected, it doesn't matter if they are Jewish, Polish or German."

"I'm not going to argue with you on this." He sighs. "But war is war. Germans are the ones who've started this war and have proved over and over their cruelty and ruthlessness by murdering and mistreating innocent people. They've created hell on earth, and we must fight back to stop them."

For the rest of the way, we stay silent.

"I will take care of the farm chores today," Kostek says when we near the cottage. "You get some rest. I wasn't much help lately, so let me make it up to you now."

We pause at the wooden fence, and he pushes the gate open, gesturing for me to walk first.

But I stay still and look at him. "Are you sure?"

"Yes, I need to get back into a routine again. Too much thinking isn't good."

"You've changed, Kostek. It's good you don't drink that much anymore but you also don't laugh."

He sighs. "I can't. Not after what I saw in the burned village. All the people I knew from there are dead now."

I put my hand on his shoulder. "All this madness will end one day. For now, we must get through it together."

His features soften but he remains silent.

I take my hand away and walk through the gate into the courtyard. The neighboring property is empty, which indicates that Johann and his soldiers aren't back for the day. This knowledge makes me relax. Whenever they are here, I feel like I'm under constant watch and that something bad might happen at any moment. Though, so far Johann has kept his crew away from us and no soldiers have moved to our barn.

When I enter the hut, my mother-in-law is in the midst of plucking the hen's feathers.

Watching her brings a bitter tang to my mouth. This is one thing that I have never been able to do since I've lived here: to take away life from one of the animals.

I watch Janek and Hania play with wooden blocks on the

rug. The little girl still doesn't say much but she also doesn't cry for her mother anymore. We've been teaching her Polish words along with prayers and forbade her from using Yiddish ever again. One of the ladies in the village gifted us a lot of clothes, so Hania looks just like all the other children in the village. People believe my story about my cousin and her daughter. We also make sure to call her Hania instead of Hana.

"Baby is asleep?" I ask my mother-in-law.

"Yes, I just put him down into the cradle," she says not stopping the task of pulling on the tiniest feathers from the chicken's skin, then she ignites the desaturated alcohol in a dish and holds and moves the dead bird above it.

"Thank you," I say.

"It's only a matter of time when those Germans next door will throw more demands on us and steal our food. With so many mouths to feed, we will all starve and get killed."

I'm aware of all the dangers. Our village could be burned any day, or we could be taken away like so many others, but I choose to have hope that we will be spared, and this war will end soon. After all, we get the uplifting news from underground gazettes from partisans about Hitler suffering more and more defeats, but hearing my mother-in-law's complaints, puts my mind in a dark state when I doubt everything.

∼

The next day, after taking care of the farm chores and bringing breakfast to the Steins, we set out on the journey to Zwierzyniec. I perch on the front bench of the horse-ridden wagon, right beside Kostek who holds the reins in his hands and a pipe in his mouth. In the back portion of the wagon, we put a large sock filled with young potatoes, the ones I dug a few days ago, another sock with carrots and beets, a block of white cheese, five jars with apple marmalade and a loaf of bread. We put a sheepskin coat over it, hoping to bring it to the orphanage safely without encountering any problems.

I owe thanks to Countess Zamoyska for saving Janek and Jordanek, so bringing food is the least we can do.

We've only three kilometers to Zwierzyniec, while the straight road leads mostly through woods. The knowledge that there are partisans hiding in the nearby forests who do everything to fight the Germans, brings a sliver of security.

When we reach the end of the village, we pass the statue of the Virgin Mary surrounded by white and blue gladiolus flowers with tall spikes, large blossoms, and sword-shaped leaves. I make a sign of cross praying for Bronka and her family, and for Władek to come back safely home.

Kostek releases a blanket of smoke from his pipe. "Are we going straight to Rózin?" he asks.

"Yes. I just hope that we will not be stopped by a German patrol." I have papers, but still, you never know with them. They often decide to kill or arrest for trivial reasons.

Kostek only nods.

Soon we enter the town now marked with Nazi swastikas, the symbol I hate with my entire being. Signs and posters in German are everywhere. Streets are crowded with soldiers, gendarmes and Ukrainian nationalists. Polish civilians walk with their heads down.

I've grown fond of this town through the years, so it's hard to look at its transformation.

As we navigate through the streets, I glance at a small white church inside the park, situated on the pond. To access it, we would need to cross a bridge. It's where I met Bronka for the first time and knew right away that we would be fast friends for the rest of our lives. That was before the war though. Now we head for Rózin, the home of Count and Countess Zamoyski.

Soon we navigate through the shady alley that leads slightly upwards toward the Folwarczna Hill and then to the front of the white Rózin villa with large stairs, prominent portico with Ionic columns, and sloping roof covered with shingles. The villa received its name from Countess Róża.

The gate through the majestic spruce trees gives us a view of the courtyard. There are gardens around the villa with juicy grass and stunning flowers but also rows of hedges and bushes, and avenues of trees.

The house is on a hill, so I admire a view of the surrounding forests and the fields of the farm, as we drive toward the orphanage situated on the property.

Count Jan Zamoyski became the sixteenth Ordinant after the death of his father Maurycy in May of 1939. He took over the administration of the Zamoyski Ordinance, but times are hard since the start of the war, and Jan and his wife chose to act and fight for others, instead of just waiting out the war in the safety of their home, with their own children.

As Marta mentioned, Róża and Jan have managed to save hundreds of children from the camp and now they run the orphanage and hospital for the little ones. Besides that, she, as a representative of the Polish Protective Committee, is permitted to enter the camp in Zwierzyniec, dressed in a white apron with the Red Cross on her sleeve. Every day she brings milk for the youngest in the camp that couldn't be removed, and bread and soup for others. But she's allowed only in the first field where the camp's administration resides. Marta told us how the countess saw the dying children behind the barbed wire. This breaks my heart.

When we near the orphanage, we are greeted by Marta. "The countess went to Zamość but she will be so thankful when she sees all the goods you brought over," she says.

We help her unload the food and get back on the road as our little ones at home are waiting for us.

There is a commotion at the town's main square, so we are halted by a German soldier who instructs us to park the carriage to the side and join the crowds of people as there is an important announcement for everyone to hear.

We know well how to obey without putting ourselves on their radar.

"What's this about?" Kostek asks one of the men in the crowd, whose face seems familiar. Then I realize that he's the town's butcher whose white apron stained by pig's blood proves my observations right. I rarely come to town, especially since the war started. I found my solitude in that little village between forests... it's where I feel more at home than I ever did in Gdańsk.

When the butcher glances at Kostek, his face registers instant recognition but also a flash of pain. He leans and whispers, "Damn *Szwaby* have caught three partisans and now are about to execute them."

I swallow hard wishing to run far away from this madness. I don't want to see these brave men being murdered while I'm unable to help them. This place is heavily guarded by armed soldiers, they are everywhere. This is so unfair.

Soon the partisans are being brought into the center of the square, their hands tied behind their backs. My attention goes to the one in the middle who is in his late teenage years. His eyes betray fear. The other two men are much older, calmer, as if they are already reconciled with their fate.

My mouth is dry. Just like that, they will shoot them. I desperately hope that the Germans will stop on only making their announcement. The way the men look betrays that they've been through harsh interrogations. Their clothes are soiled with blood and dirt, their beaten faces swollen.

One of the soldiers speaks through a metal megaphone and informs us that the three men are the worst bandits and that they were given a death sentence, which will be fulfilled today. He also urges all of us not to engage in any activities against the

Third Reich or aid anyone who already does, or we all will be given these men's fate.

I feel weak and my vision becomes foggy as a rush of adrenaline tingles in my veins. They can't do this, but I don't find enough courage in me to say it aloud.

The young man in the middle sobs, tears running down his cheeks. "I don't want to die," he cries out over and over. "I don't want to die."

A lined-up squad marches in and halts across from the partisans. The leading soldier steps forward and shouts out for his soldiers to prepare their rifles.

My heart freezes when I realize that the man giving those instructions is none other than Johann.

He stands sideways and I have a clear view of his face on which every muscle is as tight as a bowstring. The thought that he doesn't want to do this crosses my mind. He behaves so differently now than five years ago when he was a predator hungry for his victim's blood. Now, there is torment written on his face, like he can't avoid doing something terrible. Or is this my imagination and it's how I want to see him?

For a moment, I hope that he indeed won't do it, that he will spare the men, but he closes his eyes and shouts something that I refuse to understand.

The soldiers fire their rifles; the three men crumple down. The boy in the middle doesn't cry or sob anymore; his body just lies motionless on the cobblestone.

"No!" I wail and take a step back as my knees feel weak, but Kostek's hand supports me and he whispers, "Shush, Aneta, before they kill you too."

I nod and lift my gaze, which is when I meet Johann's eyes filled with shame as he marches through with his squad. No, this is not a shame; he only pretends. I turn away from him.

# SEVENTEEN
## ANETA

September 1943—Aneta's village

Jordanek laughs as I tickle his feet. He gets chubbier with each day, a healthy baby. I wish I could return him to his mother's arms. I hug him for a longer moment thinking of Bronka. There is not a day when I don't try to find a way of getting in touch with her. I've sent letters to the camp but never heard back from her.

She saved my son's life by keeping him safe through the hardest moments in her life, when she lost the love of her life, her in-laws, her neighbors... And she gave up her child to keep him safe. So, I'm determined to do more for her than just take care of her son.

As per those who were able to escape, Majdanek is the most primitive and deadly place on Earth, or at least it's what Kostek had told me. He seems to know a lot thanks to his involvement with the Resistance. I dread Bronka won't survive... I wish I could just hug her and remind her to be strong and never give up because this little boy is waiting for his mama.

My mother-in-law is busy crocheting, just like every other

evening. In those moments of solitude, her mind seems to travel somewhere else. I never ask but I guess she's thinking of Władek or remembers her husband and Zygmunt. She has endured all these losses but keeps going the best she can. Even though she has a harsh attitude toward me, I notice that in the hardest moments she never fails to provide support. While we will never reach mutual understanding nor will we genuinely like each other, I feel more respect for her now. I shouldn't judge her so easily, though there are moments when I want to strangle her.

"Mamusia, I have a question," Janek says after catching his breath. He's been running all over the house with Hania. They like to play the catch game, as they call it.

Hania has been with us for two months already. She's got used to the Polish version of her name. For the first weeks she kept crying for her mother but with time the tears dried. Now we often hear her contagious laughter, especially when she plays with Janek. She entered our lives in such an unexpected way but now she is like sunshine on rainy days. We all adore her.

It's been a good move to have Hania live with us openly like she's a non-Jewish Polish child instead of hiding her with the Steins. She mostly stays with Janek inside. I only allow them out to the yard in the late morning when Johann and his soldiers are away. I will do everything to keep my secret from him, and so far, things are going fine.

"What is it, darling?" I ask as Janek's face grows more and more somber. It's been like that since his return. He can stop in the middle of playing or eating and look like he's pondering over something very sad. Occasionally he also has nightmares when he wakes up drenched in sweat. He always tells me about his dreams or the traumatic memories, though I think that my friend managed to shield him from seeing the worst.

"When I was holding Jordanek and counting the clouds, I

saw that Aunt Bronka was talking to Uncle Roman, but he only lay down without answering her or even moving. Why is that?"

I swallow the sudden emotion that has formed in my throat. "Do you remember how I told you about Daddy going to Heaven to God? Uncle Roman joined Daddy there." Janek only knows Zygmunt from the pictures that my mother-in-law religiously shows him. He doesn't know that Zygmunt wasn't his biological father, but he's only four, so he wouldn't understand anyway. It's easier that way.

He frowns as if he's trying to process this in his brain, making sense of it. "But Uncle's body was there on the ground when we left."

"Well, only his soul went to Heaven, his body was buried at the cemetery. Just like we visit the graves on the first day of November when we pray, bring flowers and light candles." He doesn't need to know that Roman's body was thrown with others into the mass grave at the edge of the forest, or that we don't know what happened with Zygmunt and his father's bodies. Something so terrible would confuse him even more.

"He was the best uncle and even took me fishing." He thinks for a while squinting. "What's the soul?"

"The soul is a special light inside you that you can't see or touch but you can feel it. Thanks to it you're unique, happy, kind, loving or even sad. You are yourself. And when our bodies die, the soul parts away and travels to Heaven."

"But why do our bodies die? And what's it like in Heaven?"

I think for a moment about how to explain it to him in the easiest way but just when I'm about to open my mouth, the rumbling on the door makes me jerk from my seat.

"Open," an ear-piercing voice barks in German.

Why would the Germans next door suddenly decide to come here like this? Then the thought that maybe this is the Gestapo agents causes my heartbeat to rise painfully in my chest.

I hand the baby to my mother-in-law and instruct the children to sit on the bench beside the stove. "Don't move from here," I say and gaze at Hania whose large eyes are painted with fear. "Sweetie, remember to only say Polish words. If they ask you something, you recite one of the prayers."

"*Öffnen!*" a voice in German barks for the third time to open the door.

After glancing achingly at my children, I lift my trembling hand to turn the key in the lock. Within a strike of a match, sets of black boots stomp on a hard floor.

"We're ordered to search this hut," a soldier in a steel helmet snarls while his rifle shoves me to the side, then four of them surge forward.

I clutch my hand to my throat, overwhelmed by the sensation of choking on the sickening acrid odor that they leave.

My mind races like a bullet from a fired pistol. They can't discover my secret, not now, when I've been able to hide it from them for so long and keep my children alive.

"No reason to fret," Johann says, making me aware of his sudden presence, his pale blue eyes fixed on my lips. He stands in the door frame looking wickedly handsome in his Nazi uniform. "You have nothing to hide, so it will end faster than it started," he adds and smiles. "Your family is safe."

This coward ordered his soldiers to search my home while playing friendly since his arrival in our village last month. "Yes, of course," I say, forcing myself to return his fake smile. If he only knew the truth, we all would have been dead a long time now.

"Commander, I spotted a hidden entrance to an attic in one of the bedrooms." The soldier's out of breath voice reverberates along my nerves, stiffening my spine.

The reality that they're about to discover the very secret that will bring death upon my children, rips my heart out of my chest.

Johann nods and follows his soldier without another glance at me. It's like he has anticipated this moment.

Everything in me screams while I run after him... My stomach hardens as I follow them to my bedroom with my heart on my sleeve. *Breathe. I must breathe.*

"Here, the ladder is under the bed," the same soldier says to Johann while crouching to retrieve it.

Standing in the door, not knowing what to do as a cold shiver runs all the way down my spine, I know that my only hope is to somehow convince Johann not to do the search. I can only pray there is a sliver of the man I fell in love with still in there.

I reach my shaky and fluttery hand to pull on Johann's sleeve.

When he turns my way, I give him a pleading look, fearing he might disregard my attempts.

His questioning gaze takes me in. "What is it?" he whispers.

I glance at the soldier who's busy taking out the ladder to make sure he isn't watching us. "Don't do it," I whisper, inserting my entire heart into my eyes, silently asking for his mercy.

Without betraying any emotions on his face, he turns away from me.

Despair and failure set in, taking my breath away.

Johann suddenly says to the soldier who's now propping the ladder against the wall, "Good job. I will take it from here and check the attic. Please make sure all other rooms are searched, then move to the barn and outbuildings." His authoritative voice brooks no opposition.

The soldier salutes and leaves the room.

I want to exhale with relief, until it dawns on me that I've made myself vulnerable to him. It was that, or we'd all die at the hands of his soldiers.

As he stands in front of me studying me with his pale blue

eyes, I know I must play my cards right. "There is nothing in the attic, just old junk," I say.

"I hope so, Netuś, because I do have to look there. I don't need to tell you what would happen if you hid someone..." With a composed face he puts his foot on the first rung of the ladder. "Everyone in this home would have to die." His voice is shaky.

In this very moment I wish that I had a weapon I could strike him with, but even that would prove fatal because his soldiers are here. There is only one thing that could stop him from discovering the Steins.

"Johann," my voice comes out strangled even to my own ears, "I must tell you something."

# EIGHTEEN
## ANETA

September 1943—Aneta's village

"You have a son. He's right now in the kitchen. His name is Janek, and he turned four in May. So please don't go to that attic." I spit all the words without breathing, then I close my eyes and wait for his final verdict.

I can feel his eyes burning into my face, but I keep mine shut. There is nothing else I can do to save us. Our lives are now in his hands.

To my relief, he removes his foot from the ladder. "I knew you were hiding something," he says, a cynical smile twists his lips.

"I had no way of informing you."

He brushes a strand of hair back from my forehead. "I'm expecting you tomorrow night at my quarters. There is a lot we need to discuss."

I nod and swallow hard.

He walks away but stops by the kitchen where my mother-in-law still sits with the children on the stove bench. The other soldiers have already departed leaving disarray behind.

"How are you, little Hania?" he says and kneels before the children.

To my dismay our girl smiles hesitantly at him but says nothing. She must remember the kitten he brought to her. My mother-in-law looks like she was just bitten by a snake.

Then his gaze travels to Janek whose chin is trembling now. "And you must be Janek," he says looking over my son. "It's obvious that for once your mother is truthful."

I clear my throat. "He doesn't understand or speak your tongue."

He nods and glances at my mother-in-law, Jordanek in her arms. "I didn't know that you have a baby," he says, turning and drilling his intense eyes into mine.

"Not mine, but I promised my friend to care for it," I say quietly, refusing to move my gaze away first.

"So merciful of you." He leaps to his feet but before walking out he says, "Don't make me wait on you tomorrow. Promptly at seven o'clock."

"What did this German want?" my mother-in-law asks, her face white.

In this very moment I'm thankful she doesn't understand German. "He raved how beautiful our children are."

She snarls. "The last thing we need is for him to take them away from us."

Janek whimpers and runs into my arms. "No, Mamusia."

"Please, Mother, don't say nonsense like this. You are scaring them."

She waves her hand in the air. "It's a miracle that they didn't find the Steins." She wipes the sweat from her forehead and leaves to come back a minute later with two glasses along with a bottle of homemade cherry tincture. "We need this now more than ever," she says and pours into the glasses. I gulp mine down, enjoying the soothing heat unrolling through my blood.

"What's this celebration about?" Kostek says when he enters a minute later. "Have I missed something?"

The way he sways tells me that he's been drinking the whole evening while we feared for our lives. "Oh, Kostek, you seem to always miss out on the most fearful times here," I say and swig another portion of tincture.

# NINETEEN
## ANETA

September 1943—Aneta's village

When I wake up the next morning, the first thought that comes to my mind is that I must go to Johann tonight. Is this just a talk like he said, or is he planning something else? I wouldn't put it past him to force me to go to bed with him. What if he tries to take Janek away from me? I put my hands over my face and refuse to get up.

Jordanek babbles something from his cradle, and I know I should feed him. Janek and Hania share the bedroom with my mother-in-law since I have to get up in the middle of the night to feed the baby.

Hugging the little boy is what I need this morning, it makes me relax and believe again that everything will be fine. What matters is that the children are alive. Tears come to my eyes when I think of the danger they were in last night. Thankfully it was Johann and not any other soldier, or we would all be gone now.

∼

After I'm done with the evening chores, I put on a sea-green dress and let my hair down, which falls into waves on my shoulders. From the days spent with Johann at the beach, I remember that he appreciates simplicity, and right now, I will do everything to please him. I'm disgusted with myself, but I have no choice. If it comes to it, I will close my eyes and just let him use my body, then I will scrub myself raw from his touch.

I don't tell my mother-in-law the truth, I just say that Lucyna, one of the younger ladies in the village, needs help making sauerkraut, and that I will be back in two hours. I ask Kostek to help her with the children.

While I walk through the next-door courtyard, some soldiers whistle and laugh, calling me a pretty girl. I'm ashamed to be in this predicament but I keep my head up and knock. A short and bulky soldier opens the door and gestures for me to get inside.

I obey, but now my cheeks must be crimson from all the humiliation I just endured. He leads me to the guest room where Johann stands facing the window. He turns when the soldier announces my arrival and orders him to leave.

To my surprise the room hasn't changed much. Still the same round, oak table in the center, now set for two people. Along the walls there is the old wardrobe adjoined by a settee with a pillow and comforter on top. He couldn't make this more suggestive...

His eyes seem softened by heart stealing tenderness, or it's just my twisted imagination again... "I'm sorry you had to walk like this. I will reprimand my soldiers to show more respect next time."

I hope there will be no next time. "I'm here as you requested," I say, failing to remove regret from my voice.

The smile that sweeps me is lazily amused. Just a glance at his handsome face with a proud chin gives a nervous jolt to my betraying heart.

I look at the settee and blink my pitiful tears away. "Is one time enough, or do you expect more?"

He follows my gaze but rolls his eyes. "Don't flatter yourself. You are here to confess, and the only thing I'm willing to share with you is the meal that my soldier prepared."

Blood runs flaming hot to my cheeks. I stand with my gaze drilling into the floor rug and bite on my lip. I just made a fool of myself in front of him, but it's so hard to figure him out.

"You've a terrible opinion of me." His voice is quiet. "Please have a seat."

I do as he says, avoiding his gaze when he pours red wine into two glasses. The savory smell of schnitzel makes my mouth water as I couldn't swallow anything today.

I take a few sips of wine for courage. He adds a generous portion of food to our plates. We eat in silence while I still can't bring myself to meet his gaze.

"You don't need to be afraid of me. I promise that you're safe and I would never harm you or my son. I'm glad you trusted me last night before my soldiers were able to discover your secret. Though I do not want to know who you are hiding there. I will pretend that I know nothing, for both our sakes. I'm only asking you to be cautious and do not trust others," he says in a deep voice that vibrates along my nerves. "I'm still the same Johann you knew back then."

I'm confused by his behavior and straightforwardness; it's not what I expected when I came here.

When I stay silent, he continues, "I was angry with you all those years back when you rejected me without a word, but with time I grew to understand that you must have had strong reasons for it because as much as there are many things in this lifetime that I haven't been sure of, the fact that you loved me as fiercely as I've loved you, is not one of them. I trust one day when the right time comes, you will tell me your reasons and we will clear the air between us." He reaches his hand and takes mine sending jolts of sparkles up my arm. "I dream that one day you will open your heart to me again. There was never another woman for me. Ever."

His words awaken the old feelings inside me, the ones that I never was able to let go of. But I don't tell him that. "How can you say these things? Now, when you stand on this side..."

He exhales loud, then says, "That day when you saw me in the town, I went there with my squad to give the usual report as my platoon is settled there. The lieutenant expressed how unhappy he was with my lack of any progress in catching the Polish *bandits* as we are to call your partisans. I tried explaining that I've been focusing on guarding the villages with the German colonists and that it consumes all my time, but he wouldn't listen. It's all senseless to me, this entire Nazi ideology. I only joined the army to save my grandparents from the concentration camp. I would not care if they wanted to punish only me for not supporting them, but I couldn't stand my folks going through this fate in their old years.

"Anyway, the lieutenant ordered my squad to perform the execution on the three partisans." His voice breaks, but a moment later he clears his throat. "I tried convincing him that we had to go back to our duties, but he was clear that if I didn't do it, I would be executed after them."

My hands freeze as I gaze at him. His words stir something painful in me, something hopeless.

The tears in his eyes make me realize that he's either a skilled actor or he tells the truth. "I killed them." His voice breaks again, this time transforming into a few sobs as he wipes tears with the back of his hand.

I don't move, telling myself that it's all just a game of pretend.

"I will never forget the fear in the young boy's eyes. I will never forgive myself. It will haunt me for the rest of my days." He brings a cigarette to his lips, his hand trembles. "I know you don't believe a word I say, but I wanted to tell you this anyway because I could not stand for you to think that I'm a damn sadist."

"How can I believe in all of this when I saw you back then in Danzig cutting the neck of the elderly man just because he was Jewish? And you did it with obvious pleasure." I delve my eyes into his, our pains search each other. "I don't know, maybe you have changed because you decided to listen to your consciousness. I really don't know. But I know what I saw. So now you have your answer why I never wanted to see you again."

"You confused me with someone else because I've never committed such slaughter."

I sigh. "Stop it. You did it after I gave you all my trust." I shake my head. "And now you prefer to lie instead of admitting to it."

"It wasn't me." His voice is hoarse, almost pleading. "Maybe you saw my brother."

"I saw you, Johann." I feel such disappointment because for a moment I wanted to believe that he had changed, until he just lied.

"I must go." I get up and walk away from the table, feeling so empty inside. But before I reach the door, I pause and without turning his way, I say, "Thank you for not harming us. I decide to trust you with our lives."

"I want to spend some time with my son." His voice is warm but dangerous at the same time.

When I swirl, I almost collide with him. "I don't think it's a good idea. He thinks his father is dead. Besides, it might be a traumatic experience for him considering your position and the uniform you wear."

"You said you chose to trust me but at the first turn, you prove otherwise." His gaze is challenging, but also soft. This man is defined by so many contradictions

"There must be a boundary set, and my son is everything to me. I'm ready to die for him."

He lifts his hand and caresses the contour of my bottom lip. "Still so stubborn. You must remember he's my son too and I've lost so many years with him. You took them away from me, so the least you can do now is let me to get to know him, without telling him the truth about me."

"You can't do this." My voice comes out weak.

His thumb travels to my cheek and then my ear, rubbing and caressing, making me more and more hungry for his touch, just like back then. I shiver involuntarily as his mouth nears mine, then he kisses me. At first, there is almost no pressure as if he expects that I will reject him. But I stay still, paralyzed by how much I crave him. Soon he deepens the kiss.

I close my eyes and let the pleasure circulate through every end of my nerves. The warmth travels down my stomach, entangles my heart with a web of twinkles. I moan.

"Johann," I whisper when his mouth moves to my neck, his one hand travels to my breast while the other one delves into my hair. "I don't want this, please."

He sighs but steps away, making me feel cold so suddenly, incomplete without his touch.

I clear my throat. "I wanted to ask you for a favor."

"If I can help you, I will."

"My friend, the mother of the baby that I take care for, is at the camp in Lublin. Is there a way that you can help me deliver a letter to her?"

"Of course. Consider it done."

At home, I drop into my bed, relieved that the baby is asleep in the cradle. I'm ashamed that my body responded like this to Johann. It's like he unruffled the loneliness stored within me for so long. His heart-stealing kisses felt as sensual as before... but all those years back I thought I was with an honest man. I don't understand why my gut doesn't warn me about him like any other time when there is danger. Being touched and held by him felt so right, and only my mind knew that it was terribly wrong. My body wanted his.

Why must it be so confusing and complicated? The only right way is to keep my distance from him. I hope he changes his mind about spending time with Janek. He must know it's not going to work, not in this reality, not when he's one of them.

But he promised to deliver my letter to Bronka, and that means the world to me.

Maybe he truly has changed.

# TWENTY
## ANETA

September 1943—Aneta's village

September this year has been hotter than a blister bug in a pepper patch, at least so far. It's in favor with the field chores, especially that there are no helping hands with digging potatoes before the winter comes.

I drive a hoe into the soil, paying attention not to scrape the potato tubers. After lifting the plant, I shake the dangling potatoes onto the ground. I place them into a wicker basket and plunge my hand deep into the soil to check for more. Thankfully, it rained at night, so the earth isn't that hard, though I feel like I've been roasting in the sun all day today.

I repeat this task over and over for hours and every time the basket gets filled, I transfer the potatoes to a linen sock, so I can continue digging for more. But my mind is far away from this field surrounded by forests.

Since the end of August, the Germans have stopped their displacement actions of the villages in our region. I read in the underground paper that it's because of their worsening situation at the front. Now it seems like the German troops here focus on defending the colonists and fighting partisans. Or at least it seems like what Johann has been doing anyway. Since that dinner, I haven't seen him much and when we encounter each other, I avoid his gaze. To my surprise, he hasn't inquired about spending time with Janek. Maybe he realized it's not a good idea. I can't wait until he finally leaves our village. I don't want to see him ever again.

I'm angry with myself for giving in to his charms and letting him kiss me. Worse, I enjoyed his every touch. I cherished his masculine scent, the way his eyes beamed light when he looked at me. It's because I felt that very sparkle of light in my heart while being with him and that is very wrong. I'm a damn traitor, worth nothing more but to be shunned.

I straight up and inhale an earthy air mixed with a pinewood scent from the nearby forest. It's so quiet here. The only sounds come from chirping birds and buzzing bees, overrun by geese honk. It's the happiest place for me while being immersed in the stillness of this world. So much simpler, filled with harmony, to the point it brings at least a little hope into my heart.

The fact that Himmler gave the order to cease displacements in our area, is good news for my village and all the others that weren't displaced or destroyed by the Germans, though they might resume this at any moment. But hundreds of other villages were affected by them, and nothing will ever change that. So many tragedies of innocent people.

The partisans have done everything to resist and organize self-defense and often retaliated against crimes and cruelty. Same with the regular villagers: when they suspected that their village would be next, they ran away from their homes and hid, firstly making sure they left behind no farm animals or any sort of harvest for the Germans. I was prepared to do the same, if it came to it, but thankfully we've avoided it so far.

I recall reading in one of the underground gazettes about

the Germans planning the eviction of the Slovians in favor of the so-called Aryans and how the region of Zamość is to become one of the first "bastions of Germannes". Our area was chosen because of its favorable location and fertile soil, which, according to them, are more deserved by the German colonists than us Poles.

As per their plan, all of Central Europe is to become a new place to live for the "master race", like the Germans who, according to them, are racially nobler and deserve the best conditions. We Slovians are only "subhumans" and it's why they must remove us from here or murder us.

This is such a sick ideology. Just thinking of it brings nausea to my stomach, so I chase all the thoughts away and glance at a line of linen socks filled with potatoes.

"As always, hard at work," Johann says, getting off his horse.

I turn my head to him but make sure not to meet his eyes before returning to my chore. I was so lost in my thoughts that I hadn't heard him coming. For a moment I fight with myself not wanting to respond at all, and just to ignore him. But I force myself to act friendly, while cultivating in me the need to spit at him.

"Someone has to," I say without even glancing his way.

"Well, I'm not here to interrupt your hard work. I only wanted to tell you that I was able to deliver the letter to your friend. She's alive and seems fine. I thought you would like to hear that."

"Thank you," I say and slam the hoe into the soil. I act indifferently in front of him but it's a huge relief to know that Bronka got my letter. I can only imagine what she's going through in that camp...

When he's gone, I throw the hoe aside and cover my face with my hands. I was so afraid that he would ask to see Janek. I can't live like this.

When I'm back home after Kostek drove over to pick up the

potato socks, I can't help but glance at the yard with the German soldiers. They all sit around a bonfire near our wooden fence. As always, they talk and laugh loudly, but I don't see Johann anywhere.

I'm angry with myself that I was so harsh toward him. My stepfather often said that it's important to keep our enemies close. This should be my approach with him, so he protects us.

When a moment later I step into the orchard, I spot my son with Johann. They both laugh.

A rush of fear storms through my body. Without thinking twice, I leap to them and put my hand on Janek's shoulder. "Darling, it's time to go back home," I say, making sure to sound calm.

They both look at me, but Janek says, "Mamusia, look, the soldier gave me a little puppy. Can we keep him? Pretty please, Mamusia." Because of his eyes on me, I have no heart to let him down. "I named him Szarik," he adds.

The black puppy in his embrace wags his tail. Our old dog Azor was shot by a German soldier last year and we never replaced him with another. "You must give it back as it's not ours."

"It's for Janek," Johann says in his crisp German, and I'm thankful that at least Janek doesn't know his language, so they can't communicate easily. Still, it baffles me that they were laughing together before.

I don't have the energy to argue with my son, so I say, "Fine, but now please go home." He jumps up, gives me a kiss and waves at Johann before running away.

"We found the puppy in the forest. Someone left him there to die in the closed bag."

"Terrible," I whisper, relieved he saved the poor creature. At the same time, I wonder how they have more mercy for a puppy than for a human being while they chase partisans through the forests or search cottages for Jews. But I keep my thoughts to myself. "Thank you for making my son happy."

"Don't forget he's my son too," he says and gives me a knowing look while my stomach feels rock hard.

"Yes, he is, and it's why you should protect him from yourself," I say, pointing my index finger at him. "You are a soldier of the evil ruler."

A sudden look of rage passes across his chiseled face. "You forget yourself," he says through his clenched teeth and switches to a whisper. "I already told you that I intend to get to know him more, whether you like it or not." The approaching voices of soldiers nearing us make him step back. "Go back to your duties, Fräulein, before I lose my patience," he adds loud and walks away without another word or glance at me.

I swallow hard; my legs shake like jelly. Could he have said that because he heard the men, and wanted to protect me? Or was this his true, and deadly, face showing again? I can't tell anymore. When will all this end? I'm so drained.

# TWENTY-ONE

## BRONKA

September 1943—Majdanek

In September, they move us from the fifth field to the first, but the primitive conditions stay the same. The barrack also doesn't have any kind of sewage system or basic sanitation. We still deal with a lack of water, which makes it impossible for us to wash ourselves or clean our clothes. Some women use the coffee or tea that we get for breakfast for washing, since we are not allowed to keep any cleaning items.

For some time, I've been smuggling one vegetable a day, and today I was able to exchange it for a piece of paper and pen. I want to write back to Aneta. It was a relief to get her letter and learn that my baby boy is healthy. He's on my mind all the time, just like I dream every night of my Roman being alive and waiting over there for me.

I will never stop dreaming because it helps me to cope with my grief and the horrid reality of this camp. I know that Roman wants me to be strong, that Mama wants me to be strong, but I don't know how this world without them will ever be alright. I miss them while trying to survive another minute, hour, day, week, month...

I don't cry anymore, it's as if I've cried out all my tears. Instead, I focus on breathing and moving forward in this nightmare, while my heart aches for my loved ones. I feel so lonely... but I try to remember day after day that they are in a better place and that one day we will all meet again, or it's at least what our faith tells us. I just must believe it...

Today is Sunday, so we only worked half of the day. The weather is gorgeous, so most women prefer to be outside while I find solitude inside, despite the stench. The good thing is Ursula is out too, so I don't have to dread her lashing at me for no reason, like when, according to her, I wasn't carrying the pallet fast enough. I can't understand why she has picked me to be her punching bag, but this only hardens me and makes to be even more determined to survive and seek justice when we live in a normal world again.

I've learned to tame the pain and to be thankful when she stops at one or two strikes. At the same time, I can't cease thinking that at least my mother doesn't have to go through this cruelty. The moment we first arrived at the camp and heard guns, shouts and barking dogs, I understood that we had entered hell.

"Don't waste your time being sad," a quiet voice says, bringing me back to reality. Janina, the pregnant woman from our barrack. "You are still alive."

"One can't help it," I say.

"Do you have children?"

"Yes, a son back at home."

"Then you have someone to live for."

"There is nothing else I long more for than hold my baby in my arms," I say. "How far are you?"

"I think twenty-six weeks." There is this unspoken sadness in her eyes, her features, in the way she moves. She takes a seat on the bunk bed beside me, hunching forward just as I'm doing. There is very little space between the three-level bunk beds. "For a long time, I was able to hide it, but lately it's harder and harder."

She looks like she's at the beginning of her pregnancy. It's because of the poor food rations here. With the typhus all over the place, it's a miracle that she's doing fine so far. "God bless you," I say, unable to even imagine how hard this must be for her. When I was expecting, I felt constantly tired and went through mood swings. But it was easy to cope while having a loving and caring husband like Roman. His parents were supportive too. Good people. Bless their souls.

"As you know, I'm Jewish, so they will murder my baby upon birth." Her eyes get glassy from unshed tears.

"I'm sorry," I say knowing damn well that she's right. I witnessed when the other Jewish lady in the barrack gave birth to her son and Ursula put the precious little boy into a bag and took him to the crematorium... or when an SS man took a little baby girl by her legs and, in front of her mother, he hit the baby's head against the wall of the barrack...

That day I lost my belief in the goodness of humans, and so did my mother. She couldn't forget it; I saw it in her eyes. It will haunt me for the rest of my life.

With every new transport of Jews, Germans send the elderly and children along with anyone else not fit for work straight to gas chambers where they get poisoned to death. How much chance does a Jewish newborn baby have when it comes to surviving? Zero.

All people should be treated fairly and with respect regardless of their beliefs. The Nazi Germans keep committing the worst crime against humanity and civilization by ruthlessly murdering them. But they also murder us, non-Jewish Poles when they want to get rid of us, and my village is the perfect example of it.

So yes—my faith in humanity is lost for good...

"My mother was Polish catholic, and my father Polish Jewish. She converted to Papa's religion after they married, but I grew up between two traditions and love both. Anyway, I look more like my mother."

I notice how she talks about her mother in the past tense, but I don't ask. Some things are hard to talk about, maybe she isn't ready for it. Just like I'm not when it comes to my mama.

"Both my parents were sent straight to the gas chamber upon our arrival here. Somehow, they deemed me fit for work not realizing that I'm pregnant." She wipes her tears that now roll down her cheeks like the most painful, unspoken words. "My husband is in the men's part of the camp, but I've only seen him once since our arrival."

"I'm so so sorry." I can't chase away the awful truth that if there are complications during the labor, they'll murder her along with the baby. This is so cruel and unfair. "Is your husband Jewish too?"

She puts her hands on her abdomen. "Yes."

I get this sudden determination to save her and the baby at any cost, but how can I accomplish something so impossible in this terrible place? I look around and lean back to reach for a carrot from under my pallet. "Here, take it. It will give some needed vitamins for your child."

"Thank you," she says with emotion echoing through her voice. "I never get enough courage to hide one when we work in those gardens. I feel like the guards watch us like hawks."

"They do," I say. "What did you do before being brought here?"

"I was a teacher."

Our conversation is interrupted by the arrival of other women and Ursula, but just before Janina walks away, I manage to whisper into her ear, "It all will be fine. Just be strong."

I can't even imagine what this poor woman is going through

knowing that the baby she holds under her heart has no right to live in this world shaped by the believers and executors of Hitler's mental sickness. Yet, she finds enough strength every day to keep moving forward, maybe even having hope that fate will change.

It pains me to even think of it and for the millionth time I thank God that I found enough strength in me to hand in my baby to the Countess Róża. By doing it, I protected his life. Now, I need to write a letter and give it to one of the civilian workers from Lublin who enter the camp and smuggle letters. I need to make sure that my son is still doing well, that Aneta and the family are still alive.

～

The next day we are sent to harvest pumpkins which are so big that we have a hard time lifting them. Because of this, the work progress is slow even though the guards keep smacking us with their whips and shouting to move quicker.

Finally, they must realize the pumpkins are too heavy for us because they bring over Jewish boys. They are supervised by the SS guards who talk loudly and laugh a lot today.

The malnourished teenage boys struggle with carrying the pumpkins as much as we do. To my astonishment some of the SS guards push sticks between boys' legs, so they fall and when they do, the pumpkins break. As a punishment, the SS men then beat the boys unconscious or even to death.

They throw the unconscious and dead to the side into piles and continue tormenting the ones that still move.

Why is something so awful and heartbreaking happening? We all try to focus on our own tasks because we simply can't do anything to stop those murderers. They disgust me so much that I force myself not to vomit.

That evening, I walk to the latrine before we are ordered to stay in the barrack for the night. There is also a man's latrine on the other side, so I wonder if my father and brother are there. I haven't seen or heard from them at all. I'm sure that if they could, they would've sent word. They don't even know that Mama departed this world...

The line is long and there is no way that I'll make it before the first gong, so I resign myself, my stomach revolting at the thought that I will have to use a bucket in the barrack.

But just when I turn around and pass the other women standing behind me, a familiar voice to the left calls my name. Władek stands in shadows of the latrine. "I have to tell you something."

Without thinking twice, I look around and not spotting any guards watching me, I edge his way, where we're now both out of sight.

I haven't seen him since the day my mother passed, so at first, I don't feel comfortable, but his warm eyes calm my nerves.

For a moment longer his deep gaze delves into mine, pulling on something fragile in my heart. I didn't know that I'm still capable of feeling something like this.

"How are you?" he asks, and I don't know why but because of the way he observes me, I feel adored.

This thought is so absurd that I scold myself in my mind for it. "Poorly," I say. "How are you doing?"

He shrugs. "Trying to survive this hell."

"I got a letter from Aneta. They all are fine."

"Good. I don't want to give false hope to my mother by sending mine to her. It's better she thinks that I'm gone, so when it happens in fact, she will be prepared. Where's Roman?"

I swallow hard and continue blinking, so there are no tears. "Dead." I refuse to keep looking him in the eye. "The Germans burned our village and killed almost everyone."

"I'm so sorry." He pulls me into an embrace. I don't fight it because any gesture of kindness brings strength. I feel it in my barrack or during the labor in the gardens when we support each other. There are no words or actions needed. We feel that we are there for each other. Of course, there are a few women who choose to be mean and do everything to please those monsters.

"Have you seen my father and brother? I'm not sure if they were even brought here, maybe they are somewhere else."

When I say it, he pulls me even closer and whispers, "Listen, Bronka, I didn't want to tell you this the other day because you were so devastated about your mother, but it's just fair that you know."

I freeze. His words are filled with so much sorrow that I dread the worst.

"Your father and brother were executed by the squad on the second day of their arrival here."

If he didn't hold me, I would drop to the ground because my legs go weak. Once more I break my promise and cry, but he puts his fingers to my lips.

"Shush, little one, or they will hear you. You must find strength for your son. Think only of him now."

I give in to this unbearable pain in my heart and soul. "Why? You are fine, so why them?"

"They were accused of aiding the Resistance. There is no justice in this world, and nothing makes sense."

After Roman and my mother died, I thought I could not survive any more losses...

"Were you able to talk to them?"

"No, we didn't share the same barrack, but those bastards made us watch the execution."

He takes my face between his bony hands. "You must have hope, so you can survive this. We must fight and get through this. From now on, you are my strength, and I want to be yours. Understand?"

"I have nothing left in me." I feel like a puppet on a stick.

"You have that little boy waiting for your return. Never forget that."

I sigh. "It's what keeps me going. I would give everything to hold my son again."

"I've been trying to find a way to escape for a while now, especially as there were successful escapes in the past. Trust me, there is nothing else more on my mind than this."

I pull on his sleeve and meet his eyes with pleading. "Please, don't forget about me. I'm willing to take on any risk to run away from here."

He pulls me into his arm and whispers in my hair, "I wouldn't leave you here, but remember that I will only make a move when I'm sure it's possible to escape. If we were caught, they would hang or execute both of us."

# TWENTY-TWO
## ANETA

September 1943—Aneta's village

"Please, Mamusia, can we go with you?" Janek says, as always melting my heart. "It's so sunny outside and you always say that Hania and I need fresh air."

"Please," little Hania echoes and sends me a heart-stealing smile.

"It's too dangerous," I say grabbing up a wicker basket. It's Sunday afternoon, so I decided to pick some apples from the orchard to make marmalade later. The children insist on joining me.

"You should take them with you," my mother-in-law says and kisses Jordanek's cheek who is sucking on his thumb.

I shake my head. "The Germans next door are in all day today. What if they decide to bother us?" On top of that, I don't want to give Johann the opportunity to get near Janek.

She shrugs and waves at me dismissively. "If they wanted to bother us, they would find us here." Her face muscles harden while her squint eyes appear even smaller. "Besides, their commander will eat from your hand if you would let him. I saw the way he looked at you when they searched our home."

I snort and roll my eyes. "Nonsense, Mother. It's your imagination. If they find something on us, they will have no mercy, including that man in charge of them."

"Alright, alright, though there is no reason to keep the children home when it's so warm outside."

I sigh in defeat. "Fine but only for an hour, not a minute longer."

Ignoring the laughter and loud talking next door, we walk around the hut to cross the courtyard, then enter the orchard. The whole time, I pray that Johann doesn't spot us, but I have no courage to look that way.

The sweet and tart scent of ripe apples basking in the sun is so welcoming that I smile, exposing my face with delight to the touch of the sun rays. The children run freely around the trees while I contemplate if I should pick some of the yellowish *Krąselki* with a sweet flavor or the greenish *Antonówki* defined by sourness. Then, I realize my stupidity because if I was to choose the latter, I would need tons of sugar to make marmalade, and we have none right now.

"Children," I say and near the tree in the middle of the orchard, "lets pick some of the *Krąselki*."

In the end, I'm the one reaching for the apples while they take each one from my hand and gently place it in the basket. Throughout the whole time Janek keeps telling Hania about little dwarfs that hide under the trees.

"I bet those fruits are as sweet as the girl picking them," Johann's voice from behind makes me quiver and drop one of the apples. My hopes that we would avoid him are in vain now.

"Hello," I say folding my mouth into a faint smile. The children hide behind me.

"I didn't mean to scare you," he says apologetically, and extends his hand with a leather-bound book. I brought this collection of fairy tales with me from Danzig, and I wondered if the children would like to listen to my favorite story. His eyes are filled with hope.

What man takes with him a book like this to the war? Well, Johann, obviously. "The children don't understand German."

"I meant to ask you if you would be able to provide translations."

"We need to go back," I say and pick up the basket from the grass.

"It's not much I'm asking for." There is an edge to his tone, instilled to remind me who's the ruler here.

I crouch before Hania and Janek. "Darlings, this soldier would like to read you a story. I'm going to allow him but only because I'm here with you. Any other time, you cannot talk to strangers."

"But how we will understand what he reads?" Janek's large eyes hold wonder and curiosity.

"He asked me to translate it for you." I rise to a standing position and nod at Johann.

"Here, I brought over a blanket." He spreads the gingham throw under the tree and perches on one side of it.

I look around but since we are in the middle of the orchard, there is no one watching us, so I take the other part of the blanket with Hania on my lap and Janek between Johann and me.

"I hope the story is not long as we have to be back home soon."

"Well, if the children don't like it, we can stop any time." He winks at Janek but gets no reaction from him.

I'm glad my son listens to me and keeps a wary attitude toward outsiders.

Johann opens the book releasing a whiff of vanilla-like and musty scent, so familiar for older books. "The story I want to read to you was written by Mr. Hoffmann and it's entitled *Nussknacker und Mausekönig*".

"The man here will read you a story entitled *The Nutcracker and the Mouse King*," I say in Polish the shorter version of what he said. I will be careful to translate only what I feel is right for their little ears.

"The mouse king," Janek exclaims and claps his hands together.

"This is so exciting," Hania adds, her smile reaches her black eyes.

If I hoped for the children to get bored and not wanting to listen for too long, I was disappointed. They listen carefully as Johann reads and stops after every few sentences for me to translate.

Hania never moves from my lap while Janek gets closer and closer to look at the pages and at some point, Johann lifts him and settles on his lap. Janek doesn't protest at all but stares with wonder into the book.

If someone didn't know better, we would look like a perfect, happy family sitting together like this. The irony of it chokes me from inside. We're in this situation because I had to tell him about our son, but at least we are alive and so are the Steins.

The story he chose is sweet as it's a tale of a young girl named Marie who has a soldier-shaped nutcracker toy. Johann vividly reads, altering his tone of voice as he describes the soldier coming alive and leading the other toys against the evil mouse king.

As he keeps flipping the pages, we learn that the soldier-toy was once a young man who was destined to marry a princess. But he was cursed by the mouse queen and turned into a nutcracker, and he's proclaimed too ugly to marry.

When Marie tells the soldier that she would love him regardless of his looks, the curse gets broken, and love prevails.

After Johann closes the book, our eyes meet and the tenderness in his sends a gush of fire to my cheeks, but I quickly move my gaze away.

"I wish I knew the right words to thaw your heart," he says and smells Janek's hair who now strokes the leather-bound book, awe painted on his face.

As much as I hate to admit it, and I will never say it loud, Janek is Johann's replica. It makes me wonder if my mother-in-law hasn't still realized that. It's probably because she's so overwhelmed by the Germans' presence that she fails to notice it.

Anyway, I must protect my son from him. He is still an enemy soldier—even if I can't tell how bad a person he is.

# TWENTY-THREE
## ANETA

September 1943—Aneta's village

When I'm done feeding milk to Jordanek, he's almost asleep, so I put him into his cradle rocker. Janek and Hania play on the floor with wooden soldiers, their little puppy sleeping right beside them. I kiss Jordan's forehead and rock him gently while singing a lullaby that my mother sang to me when I was little.

"A-a-a, a-a-a,

there were two little kittens.

A-a-a, two little kittens,

Both grayish brown.

Oh, sleep, darling—"

I'm interrupted by Kostek who charges into the guest room, his face pallid. "The German next door brought two Jewish girls into the village."

Adrenaline shoots through my system as I leap to my feet. "Stay here. Keep rocking the baby and make sure that the children don't come outside."

When he nods, I run out of the cottage and when I reach the middle of the village, I gasp. Johann aims his pistol at two hugging teenage girls in shabby dresses who stand before him weeping.

There are so many German soldiers that I wonder if Johann's squad had been expanded. I'm among other villagers watching the scene, whispers of sorrow hanging in the air.

An overwhelming dread paralyzes me. So, he's decided to finally reveal his true face and stop playing a good man. He hasn't approached me at all since our last encounter a week ago when he read to the children. Deep in me I hoped that the softness he presented in front of us was genuine and every word he said was truthful. I hoped that he changed when he learned about his son and is a different person now. But I was so foolish to even consider it. From now on I refuse to listen to my stupid heart.

"Kneel down, you ugly rabbits," Johann says in a malicious voice, and for a moment I wonder if it's even his voice. It sounds so different. But this is obviously Johann.

When they obey, both trembling, he presses the gun to one of the girls' head. They both whimper.

I can't take it anymore, so without thinking I step forward. "Please, spare them."

He snaps his head my way and takes me in, then he gives a small derisive laugh. "Who do you think you are, Polish whore?" He leaps my way, his gun now pointed at me.

His eyes are empty and venomous, with no trace of the softness that has lingered there since the day he arrived in our village. How can this be? How can one person go from being decent to this hostile?

My mouth feels painfully dry, but I manage to say, "These are innocent girls, they haven't done any harm."

He says through his clenched teeth, his hard gaze drilling into mine, "Anyone who even attempts to help those parasites must share their deadly fate. Go on your knees and I may show you mercy, Polish slut." He laughs in self-appreciating amusement.

Hearing him calling me those names hurts, but seeing his malicious side scares me to death, it strips me from all hope I've nestled so faithfully in my heart. So, this is the ultimate truth about him: he's the worst henchman and he played me into believing in his kindness. But it all makes no sense; the things he did in the past make no sense. I hope so desperately that his face changes back to the softer one from before, but that's just proof of how naïve I am. He's just the same criminal from Gdańsk.

Suddenly, nothing makes sense anymore. I feel like I just lost the biggest part of my heart as his treachery comes to light. The good Johann never existed; he's just this imaginary creature, the product of my naivety. I straighten up and say, "I only kneel before God."

He strikes his hand into my face, "Get on your knees, bitch, or you will be dead in seconds," then presses his pistol to my forehead.

Everything before me becomes hazy, my cheek stings. The film of my life flushes before me and I don't hear anything anymore. The man to whom once I gave everything, now will kill me, not caring for his own son.

I close my eyes and await my ending, feeling so drained and unable to fight anymore. I know Kostek will not leave the children. He will watch over them.

"Put the gun down. This woman cooks for us, so we need her," a familiar voice rings out right beside me, softer but otherwise just like Johann's.

I open my eyes and to my astonishment, I see two Johanns; one keeps pressing pistol to my forehead while looking in a mocking way at the other Johann whose face is stern, every muscle strung tight.

# TWENTY-FOUR
## ANETA

September 1943—Aneta's village

What is going on here? Am I experiencing double vision, or is this just a dream?

"Fine, but you need to teach your slave woman manners because next time I will not be so merciful." He puts his gun away and steps back.

"What are you doing here, brother?" the softer Johann asks.

Identical twins? He told me he had a brother, but not a twin. No wonder he rose through the ranks of soldiers so quickly. The Nazis have an obsession with twins.

"Well, since I'm in Zamość and you forgot all about me, I thought to pay you a little visit." He chuckles and motions to the Jewish girls. "I went hunting on the way here and it turns out that I killed two hares with one stone."

Johann glances at the girls and claps his brother on the back. "Well done, Erich. I will take care of them. Let's go to my hut, so we can talk." He winks. "I have something special."

Erich beams. "That's my brother."

"Tell your soldiers to station at the second courtyard to the left," Johann says and when his brother turns away to do as he suggested, his worrisome gaze takes me in as if making sure that I'm fine, stopping on my cheek that must now be swollen.

His warm eyes make this huge mark on my soul, just like all those years back. And I have this weird feeling as if my Johann is truly back.

"It's best you go home," he whispers softly and turns away to catch up to the other man.

People gossip but soon everyone leaves, while the two girls are brought to the Ramniwskis' courtyard.

It's not until I sit at my kitchen table that I get some clarity in my thinking and the initial shock wears off. I feel like I just came back from the biggest battle of my life. The boy that I saw in the Hitler-Jugend uniform five years ago was not Johann but his twin brother. It sounds so surreal that I need time to digest it fully. But it all now makes sense.

That man I fell in love with was not the same man I saw doing terrible things in Gdańsk. The man I fell in love with is the man I met in Władysławowo, and is now here, in this village for the last few months.

I'm glad that my mother-in-law went to lie down as she complained earlier about a bad headache. I could not stand her judging and accusing gaze.

Is it possible that everything he told me about his grandparents and his work in France is the truth? As I sit at this table, I can't chase away this shy feeling that I never truly lost my Johann. My heart feels so light like it got rid of a heavy stone that put my life on hold. I was right to love him because he is a good man, despite all, despite the uniform he puts on every day.

I pray that I'm right about him and that he will not kill those innocent girls that I saw his soldiers escorting to the cowshed. We need to free them.

Since his stay here, there has not been one execution in our village, he kept his soldiers away, not even stealing food like when other squads stationed in out village.

His brother, though, is another story. I have this strong feeling in the pit of my stomach that Erich will cause a lot of trouble. He almost killed me today.

# TWENTY-FIVE
## ANETA

September 1943—Aneta's village

At night, I'm having a hard time falling asleep as raindrops hit the window glass with the same stupor as Erich smacked my cheek today. There are too many spinning thoughts in my head, and I miss Johann. At my insistence, the baby sleeps in my mother-in-law's bedroom tonight. I hoped to see Johann somehow and talk to him but despite my frequent peeking out the windows, he never showed up.

I have this sudden thirst to feel the freshness of raindrops on my skin. Before Johann came here, I often sneaked out to the spring at night. Lately, I was afraid I'd meet him there, so I ceased going all together.

I change into my dress and slip outside. Cold raindrops have this restoring effect on my spirit. I smile and run through the orchard's long grass, then meadows to reach the edge of the forest. I don't care that I'm getting drenched; I need this. I inhale the earthly and pleasant scent of the forest and listen to the sound of rain falling on trees, combined with chirping of frogs.

When I approach the opening with a creek, I notice a silhouette of a uniformed man in the moonlight. For a second, I freeze, wondering if it's Erich, but I remind myself that I saw him leaving the village with his soldiers.

At the thought that Johann is here, my senses heighten. I yearn to look at him again in the same way I did back then, when I trusted him. I'm afraid that I'm rushing things. Maybe I don't know everything and he's not who I think he is, but I decide to listen to my heart, despite all.

"Johann," I say in a weak voice, doubting that he hears me because of the thumping rain.

But he rapidly turns around causing my heart to flutter wildly in my chest. Then, a smile plays about his lips as he bounds forward and takes me into his embrace.

But I stay still and ask, "Please, tell me what will happen with the two girls that your brother arrested today."

"Don't fret, darling." His voice is filled with emotion. "I let them go back to the forest after Erich left."

Relieved, I give into enjoying his touch and warmth. It doesn't matter that we are both drenched because our hearts have found each other again.

"I was hoping you would come. I've missed you," he whispers and caresses my lips with his. He frowns as he gently brushes my swollen cheek with the tips of his fingers. "Does it hurt?"

We act like we haven't seen each other for so many years and the last two months never happened. "I forgot all about it." I laugh before adding, "I've missed you too." I kiss him on the mouth with such yearning that I haven't realized I had in me. We cherish each other as if to make up for the lost years. I enjoy running my hand through his wet hair while his hand strokes my back.

"Do you have someone waiting for you in Danzig or

France?" I must know this before I let things between us progress any further.

"Netuś," he murmurs, "I never stopped loving you. There is no one."

"Come with me," I say and take his hand in mine. There is only one place where I want to be with him now.

He doesn't protest even when we enter the wooded area around swamps. "Stay close to me," I whisper, "I know how to go so as not to fall into the swamp." Fifteen minutes later we near a small shack that I had fixed up.

"What's this place?" he asks while holding my hand strongly.

"It's where we are prepared to run and hide if the Nazis decide to displace or burn our village. Locals don't come here because according to the old legend the swamp is cursed."

He laughs. "And I would never let my soldiers to enter it being unsure of the soft marshy ground that could pull us in."

"Exactly." I smirk and pull him inside the cabin. I find a carbide lamp and light it, then I remain in the same position without turning back to him. I smell the masculine, woodsy scent of his skin and dump hair. My senses anticipate his touch, and when it comes, I shiver.

"Are you still afraid of me?" he whispers and kisses the nape of my neck. "You shiver."

"No," I whisper back. "I want you as much I wanted you that night we made love."

My words have an instant effect on him because he turns and pulls me against the length of his body. The bliss of the moment wraps around us as we keep finding each other after so long.

Later, I lie in his arms, enjoying the warmth radiating from his sturdy arms. If someone asked what it means to be fulfilled, I would say it's being held by the man who you love without barriers, with everything you have, while knowing that he feels the same about you.

"I'm sorry that I doubted you," I say, caressing his cheek.

"You didn't know me that well, but you never fully clarified why you didn't show up at the Neptune Fountain like you promised. You accused me at the dinner of mistreating someone?"

"I thought I saw you that day in the Hitler-Jugend uniform mistreating an elderly Jewish man. But now I know it was your brother, not you. He cut the man's throat and ran away with his peers while laughing." I shiver at the painful memories. "The man survived only thanks to the doctor that happened to be near."

He pulls me so close that I can hear the chaotic beating of his heart. "I'm so sorry. Unfortunately, my brother has done much worse. I'm disgusted with his stand." I can sense that talking about Erich isn't easy for him. "I never belonged to the Hitler-Jugend. My grandfather obtained special papers stating that I was not fit for it because of my health issues."

"Why didn't you mention to me back then that you have an identical twin brother? I told you about my sisters."

He sighs. "It's been always painful talking about Erich. But I will tell you all another time. I don't want to ruin our brief time together here and now. Besides, we only had a few stolen moments back then in Władysławowo. Maybe that's another reason I never got the courage to mention my rebellious brother to you."

I place a feathery kiss on his mouth, still not having enough of his tantalizing touch. "You know, when I think more about it, your brother has a small scar in the center of his forehead, which you don't, and his tone of voice is a lot different from yours." I noticed it when I saw Erich earlier.

He nods. "That day, when I returned from Władysławowo, I didn't even stop at home but went straight to the Neptune

Fountain, but you never came. I kept returning every day at the same time for a week. I tried looking for you but encountered no luck. I couldn't get you out of my mind and then one day in December I saw a lady that somehow reminded me of you. I guessed it was your mother, so I followed her and later went to your family's boutique. A teenage girl with blonde bids blurted out that you got married and moved to this village, she even named it without hesitation, after I lied that we're school friends. That's when I realized I'd lost you."

"It must have been my sister Anna. Anyway, I refused to kill the unborn baby, so my stepfather forced me to marry a widower who owned the farm and was willing to help out a lost girl with a child on the way. I was only seventeen and afraid of being on my own. I was lucky though because Zygmunt turned to be a good man. He treated me and Janek with kindness. We slept in one bed, but he never even touched me. His wife passed away a year prior, and he was still grieving her, while I couldn't get you out of my mind. It was hard to accept the news of his death with the coming war."

He sighs. "War brings so much death and misery. There is not a night when I don't see the face of that boy that died in this senseless execution in the town. I hate myself for it. I allowed my soldiers to kill innocent men, just to save my own skin." His voice is distant now, as if something dark and heavy entered his soul.

I take his face between my hands. "You had no choice. Remember that."

"I did but I'm a damn coward," he says and moves into a sitting position.

"I press the side of my face to his back. "It's war, so the choices are impossible. We must focus on what's now, so we can survive, so our son stays alive."

He reaches to bring me back into his arms. "You're right. I can't go on like this. For a long time, I just took care of the brewery and the paperwork proving my medical problems kept me away from enlisting. But in February, since Hitler lost in Stalingrad, things changed. The Nazis needed more men to fight, so they threatened me."

"What health conditions do you suffer from?"

"None, my grandfather paid a fortune to obtain a special document."

"That's good."

His hand brushes away a lose string of hair from my face. "I can't get enough of you," he whispers. "That day when I saw you watching me while I was fishing, I felt like I'd found the missing light within my heart. I didn't even understand it, I just felt that way about you."

"I felt the same." I sigh. "But our feelings have no right to survive in this world."

"I will fight for you, my love, and for our son."

I want to believe in his words and that we can be together, but I know better. "It's why you are here? Because you knew where I live?"

He smiles. "I'm afraid I don't have that much power. It's just that my brother was already in Zamość, and he recommended me to be transferred here as they needed more soldiers in this area. Well, the Polish Resistance here is stronger than anywhere else. When they sent me to Zwierzyniec, at first, I didn't realize it's where you live, but when I looked at the map while the commander was assigning villages to us, I saw yours and the memory flashed back at me; I knew it was the same place your sister told me. You're surrounded by forests, so when I pointed out to your village on the map and said that it would be a good base for my squad, he agreed."

"It's hard to believe that of all the places, they sent you to Zwierzyniec."

"Fate wanted us together."

"Why is your brother here?" It's painful to even mention that ruthless man.

"Who knows?" His features are tightening. He truly doesn't enjoy talking about him. "In reality, he wants to find something to doom me. He hates me with a passion. It's why he used his connections to bring me here from France."

I nestle my face into his chest. "That's a strong statement."

"It's the truth. When we spoke today, he took delight in sharing about his years working in Warsaw. His words made me realize that my brother is nothing but a damn henchman and I don't want to see him ever again."

I don't ask for details because I can only imagine the atrocities he committed. I've had a taste of it already. "I hope he will not visit you often."

We talk until three o'clock in the morning as if we have a desperate need to learn as much as possible about each other and our stories. Maybe it's our way of making up for the fact that we are practically strangers because of the years of separation. Besides the moments from five years ago, this is the only time we've truly trusted one another. The months he spent in the village were filled with wrong assumptions, hate and miscommunication.

Yet, I feel like I've known him my entire life. Love at first sight does exist. We are proof of it.

# TWENTY-SIX
## ANETA

October 1943—Aneta's village

*My dearest friend,*

*It's been so long since I saw you last. As you know, so much has changed. You wrote in your letter that you know about my village, about my husband and his parents. I don't know if I will ever be able to get over the shock I experienced that day. I'm still not able to even think of it, so writing is even harder, but I sense you understand. I've cried out all my tears, and am now just trying to survive every day.*

*I will not be writing details in this letter; I will tell you all when I'm back. Because, my friend, I want to believe this ends one day, and I will be back to my son.*

*How are the children? I truly hope they are fine but know that I trust you more than myself.*

*My parents and my brother left this world...*

*I see W. once in a while though. He's doing fine and keeps strong. You were right about him. He brings so much strength to my heart.*

*I love you and miss you,*

*Your friend.*

I fold Bronka's letter and wipe my tears away. Just knowing that she is alive, brings so much peace to my heart. *Thank you, God, thank you for keeping her alive. Please give her strength, so one day she returns to us.*

∼

At night I meet Johann in the shack.

"Are you alright?" he asks, holding me close while we are lying down entangled within the blankets.

"I'm just thinking about my friend. I got a letter from her today."

"Jordan's mother?"

"Yes. I would do anything to get her out of there, but there is nothing I can do."

After a prolonged silence, he says, "I can try but can't promise anything."

I switch to a sitting position. "How? Do you know someone who works there?"

"I know one guard in there from Danzig. He delivered your letter to your friend, of course, after I bribed him with vodka."

"But this is so much more serious. Do you think he would risk helping you now too?"

"I'm not sure."

I sigh and press my head into his chest. "If there was only a way."

"There is and I will find it."

His words make the hairs at the nape of my neck rise. "It's too dangerous. If they caught you trying to take her out of the camp, they will kill you both."

"Don't forget that they think I'm one of them. I just have to figure out the safest way."

A shy spark of hope initiates in my heart but I say, "Still, it's too risky."

"We must try. That place is one of the deadliest and cruelest, so she has only a slight chance of survival if she stays there. Her only hope is for us to get her out."

"But how can you do it without being caught?"

"Leave that to me," he says and engages us in a powerful kiss, one that conveys his love.

# TWENTY-SEVEN
## BRONKA

November 1943—Majdanek

Today is All Souls' Day. We would be going to the church in Zwierzyniec and visiting the graves of family members who are no longer here... We would bring chrysanthemums and candles, and we would pray for their souls...

These times seem so distant now, more like a fantasy. That world doesn't exist anymore, replaced by a nightmare, for which I still fail to find the right words.

Based on what I overheard in the camp in Zwierzyniec, my Roman was dumped into one of the mass graves at the edge of the forest with his parents and other villagers. Like his life meant nothing... But I know his soul is free as I feel his presence not only in my dreams, but also throughout the days.

My parents and my brother will never have their graves; their bodies were burned in a crematorium.

Dreaming every night of meeting them brings so much comfort to me. The reality that they are no longer here is so surreal. I still refuse to believe it. In those dreams I keep asking them how they are doing, but they don't answer, they just look so peaceful. But every dream comes to an end and I miss them again. I take all the strength I need from those nights.

Every morning, I wonder how I will make it through without my husband. How to come to terms with the fact that he died so young? We'd only just begun our lives together, for things to end in such a cruel way.

I often think of my beloved brother who was only twenty and madly in love with his fiancée from another village. He was so brave and smart, doing everything to aid partisans. Now, he will never marry and have children, or simply enjoy ordinary things, like drinking his favorite beer or eating *bigos*, cabbage stew. But Heaven gained another angel, a special one.

At the same time, I feel that my loved ones up there want me to be strong, so I fight through every day. In the toughest moments, I think of my precious son. For him, I will sustain every struggle...

Now, it's two or three o'clock in the morning, I don't know exactly, I can only guess from the length of my sleepless night. The woman who shares a bed with me doesn't snore for once. There's something cold in the air, not exactly because of the low temperatures of November, there is something else that I can't grasp.

I don't really know her much because we speak rarely. She always seems distanced from everything here while I succumb to my pain and grief.

The sudden thought that she's dead crawls at me like an unwanted leech, sucking on my nerves. No, she is alive because she was fine yesterday. I want to touch her to confirm that there is still warmth in her body but I'm afraid of waking her up.

I listen to detect breathing or any noise from her for long minutes, sensing that something is terribly wrong. When I hear nothing, I move my trembling hand in the darkness to realize that her hand is very cold to touch. I move my hand up and feel her face which is also cold.

After checking her pulse, I find none and when I press my ear to her chest, there is no heartbeat. She's been dead for hours.

This shouldn't surprise me because every night more and more women and children die. There is no exception. Still, she didn't have any signs of typhus or other sickness. Is it possible to die of a broken heart? The woman lost her husband and only daughter, so she lived in constant pain, just like I do. But I have a little son who's waiting for me and that prevents my heart from giving up.

I pray for her soul and think that dying on All Souls' Day is more of a blessing than on any other day through the year. It's a sign from God, is how I see it.

In the morning, they will take her body and send her to the crematorium, it's their usual practice here. Maybe even Władek will be one of the prisoners who come to get the corpses after the night. What an awful reality we all live in.

He came yesterday morning, when he whispered that the Germans have the Jewish prisoners dig long and deep ditches in the fifth field. He heard rumors that the Nazis are preparing to murder all Jews in the camp. Just at the thought of it, I can't stop shivering. What if they take Janina out of here and do something terrible to her and the unborn baby?

Through the last month, we've grown to be friends. We support each other as much as we can, even with warm glances during hours of labor in the gardens or while standing on prolonged roll calls. We're there for each other because just the thought of not being alone in a place like this is worth its weight in gold.

The bizarre idea that I should take off the striped dress from the dead woman and bring it to Janina is so irrational, but I know this might be the only chance for my friend to stay alive. While my entire focus in this place is to survive to be able to one day go back to my son, Janina should have the same chance. I could never look in the mirror if I didn't do what I could to help her, so she has a chance of one day leaving this place with me, so, she can give a good life to her child.

If I tiptoe, no one will hear me. Ursula and her helpers sleep in the front part of the barrack with access to more air, while Janina is only three bunks away from me. I'm sure that even if any other women see me, they will not react. We have an unspoken solidarity in this barrack between us women. Only Ursula and the other two are the exception here.

This might work because since we arrived at the camp, we are only numbers to them. Our names don't exist here. The deceased woman is close to Janina's age.

I listen to my heart and when I feel the roughness of the woman's striped dress in my hands and the coldness of her metal tag with her camp number engraved into it, I know that I'm doing the right thing, despite the risk that comes with it.

The dress has a sewn-on patch with the woman's number and a red triangle with a letter P in the middle. It's the same one that I have on mine, and it indicates that we are Polish political prisoners. I will take Janina's dress with the patch of two overlapping triangles of red and yellow, which indicates that she's Jewish, and put it on the woman.

I know that this is all wrong and disrespectful to the deceased lady, but what she needs now are prayers. *I promise to pray for your soul for a long time.* After making this vow in my mind, I feel less guilty. Janina needs help and there might not be better opportunities than this one. How ironic: thanks to the fact that one human died, the other can have a chance to stay alive.

Besides, knowing that I helped her would give me more strength and resilience to survive another day.

I slip in the darkness between the bunk beds. Only three along to reach Janina's. Thankfully, she takes the lowest level.

At a sudden noise from the other side of the barrack, I freeze but soon the night silence takes over again. I touch my hand to every end of each bed, to make sure that I don't go too far as I can't see a thing in this pitch-darkness.

When I know for sure that I've passed all three bunks, I go to my knees and try to recognize any sign that I'm beside Janina. The woman that shared a bed with her was moved to another barrack and so far, her spot hasn't been taken.

"Janina," I whisper as low as I can, at the same time making sure that she can hear me.

I don't have to wait long because she responds, "You can't sleep too?"

"Yes," I say and tune my ears to any noise, but there is nothing. "The woman who shared the bunk with me has died. She was Polish. I have her dress and number tag. Please take yours off and put these on."

"What," she whispers in obvious shock. "Isn't that too risky?"

"I heard that the Germans are planning to..." I don't finish because the words would not come. It's one thing to have them in my mind, another to say them loud. "Please, this might be the only chance to save you and the baby," I choke out. "But you must hurry."

When I was assembling this plan, it didn't even occur to me that Janina wouldn't agree to the ploy. Now, I'm not so sure.

"At least we will try," she whispers.

After she switches into the other gown and replaces the metal tag with her own number, I slide back to my bunk and put Janina's clothes on the woman, not forgetting about the tag.

As I lie down, a sudden worry that Ursula will discover our little deception paralyzes me. There are around two hundred women in this barrack, but still, maybe Ursula has noticed Janina as much as she notices me? Though I never saw her paying any visible attention to my friend. The only difference in her look will be the patch with the number and new symbol. What if Ursula remembers that Janina is Jewish? If yes, she will kill her without second thought, and it will be all because of me.

In devising my plan, I failed to think of that. What if she dies because of me? I will never forgive myself. I get this urgent pull to go back to Janina and reverse everything but it's getting lighter and lighter, and I feel more fear with every passing minute. *What have I done...?*

The wake-up gong sounds out at five o'clock and I'm so clumsy because of the shakiness in my limbs that I keep dropping everything I touch. *Our Lady of Częstochowa, please help us with this. Please.*

We go through the normal morning routine and when I stand next to Janina during the roll call, I realize that no one has noticed anything so far. If any woman heard what happened at night, no one shows it. Surely, many know that Janina is Jewish, but no one glances her way or looks visibly surprised.

Ursula slogs between the rows of women glaring at each one, and if she doesn't like something, she strikes with her whip. In the other hand she has a wooden panel, which she hasn't used this morning so far. But she will, we all know, and every single heart in this roll call fears it.

If she somehow spares me today and moves to Janina, she might notice her new tag, or she might not. With that number of women, all in striped dresses and white headscarves, details like this can go unnoticed but she must get distracted by something else, just as precaution.

She enters our row and passes the first three women without as much as a sneer. Her small eyes stop on my face, a scornful smile touches her lips, but for some reason she's moving forward to Janina.

Without thinking, I pull on her sleeve but quickly take my hand away, knowing well that it's enough to receive a severe beating.

She turns my way and hits me in the head with the whip

while shouting words in German. "Stupid... whore... you Poles..."

I stop catching her words but put my hands over my head and haunch down, then I feel the so familiar dull pain, the one that unmistakably comes from the wood panel. Bouts of throbbing course through my body like poison into blood, but I clench my teeth and stay put. If I move or beg her to stop, it will infuriate her even more and my misery will be for so much longer.

When the beating stops, she keeps yelling two words, "Stand... death... stand... death."

I know that if I don't find enough strength in me to rise, she will finish me and send me to the other world.

# TWENTY-EIGHT
## BRONKA

November 1943—Majdanek

Aneta's encouraging voice plays in my mind, just like when she cared for me when I had pneumonia. "You must fight, Bronka, fight!" A stubborn thought that this doesn't have to be my end and that I can still return to my son, brings a surge of energy to my lungs. I release a long cough and force myself to get on my feet, while every bone and every muscle in my thrashed body is on fire.

She releases a malicious laugh before saying something in German, but this time I don't try to understand a single word. Instead, I focus on calming down the soreness that takes away my breath.

She passes Janina without even glancing her way. That's all that matters.

After the roll call, we head to the sewing shed, where my working Kommando was recently moved since there are no duties in the gardens right now.

I spend all day fixing German uniforms, trying to forget about the pain that shoots through my miserable body. I feel like a fish in water when it comes to sewing as I always liked to fix everyone's clothing in our home.

Janina, on the other hand, struggles, but with each day she's doing better. To my relief, no one pays attention that she has another patch. The good thing is that the deceased woman was assigned to work here too. With so many people and never-ending commotion in the camp, I begin to believe that it will work, after all. I urged her to memorize her new number as quickly as possible. When they talk to us, they call us by our numbers, not names, and in this situation, this is very helpful to Janina. But the truth is that the day we were made into numbers, we were stripped of our humanity.

I often wonder how two women from different worlds can understand each other so well. She is from an intellectual and wealthy family, well at least before the war, and I'm just a simple village girl with only five school years completed. Then I realize that Aneta is educated too, still, the bond between us is unbreakable. Circumstances shape people and their characters, not education.

During a break we're given turnip soup, which tastes like slop. There are small fiber strips in it, and for a very nerve-stirring moment I have this awful thought that these might be parts of another human's body. I quickly dismiss this, reminding myself that their deadly practice is to permanently remove our existence in this world by burning our bodies.

I can't swallow a thing anymore, instead I stare into streams of smoke from the crematorium that operates day and night. The odor of burning bodies is everywhere, there isn't a single spot in the entire camp and around where you can't smell it.

The shadow of the crematorium haunts us with fear and terror. It looks especially hellish at night. Anyone looking at it can easily go insane because of the extent of their atrocities.

The rest of the day is uneventful, and when the gong sounds for everyone to stay in the barracks for the night, I embrace it. This day turned out to be nerve wracking for me, plus my beaten body needs rest. I used the weak tea, which tastes like it's made of weeds found in the fields outside of the camp, to wash my wounds. It's not bad, it could have ended up much worse, like broken bones or damaged organs, if she hadn't stopped when she did.

This woman has been tormenting me for so long now, but I must admit that she always stops at a certain point. It's like I'm her *entertainment* that she wants to keep handy.

∽

One day Ursula is gone, which we realize when we are back from all day of labor. It's so sudden that I want to cry and laugh at the same time. What a huge surprise to all of us, and a huge relief to me. Her duties are handed to a Czech woman-prisoner who seems harmless. So far, she doesn't shout or strike us with a whip. Even the two helpers to Ursula behave in a decent way near her.

Janina takes advantage of the commotion and moves to my bed, which makes me feel less lonely. Together we can get through this hell and be free one day. This very hope keeps us on our feet.

∽

One morning at dawn, the SS men enter our barrack and order all Jewish women and children to come outside. They check every bunk bed if there isn't anyone left, then they order us to stay inside for the rest of the day. No roll call or work. They warn us that anyone who dares to look through the window, will receive an immediate death sentence.

"This is not good," Janina whispers as we sit on top of the

mattress, pressing her hand to her belly. "Where are they taking them?"

I rest my head on her shoulder. When we are closer it's easier to stay warmer as the barrack is like an igloo. There is only one iron heater here that doesn't generate much heat. "I don't know but don't have a good feeling about it."

"You saved me from whatever it is," she whispers, "but what does my life mean compared to so many others? I should be with them now."

"You must think about your baby," I say. I have been wondering every night what to do to keep it alive after its birth. If their procedures don't change, the newborn will not be murdered as now Janina is treated as a non-Jewish woman thanks to the switch, though I keep worrying that one day the wrong set of eyes realizes and reports Janina to the camp authorities.

Still, even the non-Jewish newborn babies almost all die here because the malnourished mothers don't produce enough milk or have means to feed them any other way in this primitive camp.

She sighs but stays silent, her face drained of any life.

The cold cuts through my bones, making me shiver, so I pull the filthy, lice infested blanket over my back. What other choice do I have?

Soon I forget about the coldness because the camp speakers release very loud operetta melodies, soon accompanied by constant machine gun bursts.

"What are they doing?" Janina's voice shakes, her eyes closed, and face strained with agony.

I take her hand in mine. We all know what that means for the Jewish women and children taken out from our barrack, and for so many others. "Bastards," I whisper.

"What if my husband is over there?" She sobs, so I hug her. There is nothing else I can do.

Throughout the whole day we aren't allowed to leave the barrack. The festive music and gunshots roar non-stop. All day long, while we sit paralyzed by fear and sorrow for the people up there. The whole barrack is silent; even Eva, the Czech Kapo, isn't anywhere in sight.

I could try looking through the window, but I have no courage. My head hurts and I feel terribly broken. At some point, one of the women quietly walks to our bed and touches Janina's shoulder in a gesture of solidarity. She whispers in my ear that I did the right thing by saving Janina and her unborn baby. It makes me realize how naïve I was thinking that no one heard us that night when we shifted the dress and the number tag.

The next day, the smoke from crematoria is so much more intense that I have this constant feeling of choking. My nostrils and mouth burn. My eyes fill with unshed tears, but not because of the smoke. I feel like hiding somewhere to cry out all this sorrow which has accumulated in me.

The familiar, excruciating pain in my heart deepens. It never really stopped after I lost my husband, then my parents and brother. I've been slowly learning to live with it and tame it, but now the scab has broken again, making me lose control of my emotions. Thankfully, the German female guard in the sewing factory acts decently toward us. Something so rare to encounter in this camp.

During a break, I overhear one of the women whispering about yesterday. It turns out that the Germans gathered all the Jews from the camp into the fifth field and ordered them to undress. Then they shoveled the innocent people into the ditches where they were executed.

One group after another, all day long.

The joyous music played all day to drown out the shootings.

I decide not to tell Janina. It would kill her and the baby.

But later there is more and more horrifying news of the Nazis murdering thousands of people that day.

The oppressors are calling it *Aktion Erntefest*, The Harvest Festival....

How to describe this? Evil? Demonic? The truth is, there is not one word in the dictionary which would be enough to describe their *deed*. I will let the silence speak....

It's harder and harder to survive in this place but the stubborn thought of seeing my son again never dies. To hug him at least one more time before departing this world....

# TWENTY-NINE
## ANETA

November 1943—Aneta's village

"Hello, darling," Johann says, approaching me from the back while I rake leaves in the vegetable garden. He stands at a safe distance as he knows that his soldiers or the villagers may look our way.

"No one should see us together in the open like this," I say and keep my face somber like I'm discussing my fate with my tormentor.

"Well, we're only talking," he says quietly, scanning the ground like he's inspecting my work.

I look around to make sure no one can hear us. "You're right, it's just not easy to not feel your touch when you're so close."

"You have no idea what I'm going through right now." He lowers his voice even more. "Though I'm here to tell you that I'm going to Lublin tomorrow."

I support the rake against the wooden fence and wipe my clammy hands on my skirt to rid them of sweat. "Why?" I ask even though I suspect he's going to Bronka.

"I've been in contact with the friend from the camp I told you about. It has cost me my gold watch, but he found out for me that your friend is assigned to work in the sewing and cloth-fixing factory in the camp."

I swallow nervously. "Are you planning to go inside that camp?"

He shakes his head. "While getting in is possible for me, taking your friend on the way out would prove fatal to both of us."

"Oh, Johann, I don't want this. I know she will do everything to survive. We shouldn't put her at risk like this. Besides, if something happened to you, I could not go on."

"I wouldn't do it if I thought this couldn't work. It's all planned well, and you must trust me."

"What will you do then?"

"There are regular transports from the factory where your friend works. They load a truck with stolen clothing from the arriving prisoners and drive it to the train station, so it can be sent out west, most likely. Anyway, my friend bribed the driver to switch their duties for one day. Horst will be driving the truck tomorrow. They routinely take a couple of women-prisoners to help with unloading. He will just have to make sure that Bronka is among the chosen ones."

"It's hard to believe he's doing all of this for the watch."

He smirks. "Well, there is more involved here that in the end will benefit him greatly if things go right. Let's say that I found a way to motivate him."

"But if he betrays you?"

"Well, then I will kill him."

The hardness in his jaw sends cold sweat up my back. "I take it you will meet your friend at the train station then?" My voice comes out shrill, but I can't control it.

"Precisely. With Horst's help, I will take your friend to my car and bring her here."

I overcome my trembling hands and grab the rake to drive it through the soil, in case someone might be looking. "What if someone sees you?"

"Pray that it all will go smoothly, and the little boy will have his mother back by tomorrow night."

"I'm afraid I will lose you both. I just have this feeling in my gut that it might not work."

"It will all be fine." His tone of voice is so assuring that I instinctively dismiss my worries and decide to put it all in his hands.

"Thank you for doing this," I say wishing I could run into his arms and feel his calming touch.

∽

The following day I can't focus on the simplest of tasks. My mind is distracted by the thought of Johann bringing Bronka safely home.

I've always considered myself a brave woman, especially since the war started, but now I'm not so sure. Instead of encouraging Johann to action, I begged him to pull back from this courageous mission. I'm officially a coward. If only it weren't for the gnawing pull of fear on my heart...

When night comes and they are still not back, I know something is terribly wrong. I picture both of them shot, lying in puddles of blood. I don't sleep at all but keep walking to the window and listening. As morning arrives, there is still no sign of Johann or Bronka.

Close to noon, a sudden commotion next door makes me jump to the window. I watch as a four-wheel motorbike arrives with an officer who must hold a high rank because everyone salutes him. Then, at some point Johann's soldiers run and yell about packing, to depart an hour later. The property is free from Germans at last but my entire world breaks. Johann and Bronka must have been caught.

# THIRTY

## BRONKA

November 1943—Majdanek

There is not a night since the terrible shootings when Janina doesn't quietly cry. She hasn't said it aloud, but I sense she dreads that her husband was among the murdered, but she's determined to be strong for her unborn baby.

Today our duties at the warehouse are to segregate clothes. I prefer sewing and fixing uniforms, it's easier to distract myself, to think of the past. I always revisit the few years I was given with my Roman, cherishing every sparkle of memory.

I blink my tears away and focus on separating cardigans and sweaters from lighter shirts. While touching these fine fabrics, I feel goosebumps all over my skin and pain soaring through my heart. These belong to people like me who were stripped from all their clothes and valuables and were given rugs to wear instead. But the saddest part is that most of these were once worn by the Jews like Janina who were brought to this camp and murdered. It's a pure miracle that my friend is still alive.

Cheerful laughter brings me back to my surroundings. The beaming female guard engages in a conversation with a truck driver who just arrived. She's obviously charmed by his good looks and flirtatious demeanor because she keeps batting her lashes and smiling.

When I take a closer look at the uniformed man, I realize it's the same guard who once handed me a letter from Aneta. It's the first time that he's driven the delivery truck.

While he chats with the German woman, he keeps glancing around, like he's looking for something or someone. When his eyes meet mine, instant relief appears on his face.

This brings me a surge of panic. Why would he react in such a manner? Did he take notice of me that day when he handed over the letter and has decided now to hurt me?

Soon they both walk among us and select two middle-aged women for loading clothes into the lorry. Usually there are four picked, so there is dread in the air among us. No one wants to be chosen because the other driver was always violent and brutal toward the helping women. I'm sure this man will show no exception too.

To my astonishment, he stops right before Janina and points at her, then grabs my arm and hurls us forward. We join the other two women in another part of the factory and get busy loading the truck with bags full of clothing.

The whole time, he smokes his cigarette and shouts, "Schnell!" The whip in his hand smacks our backs occasionally though I must admit he does it in a gentle way, as if for appearances.

I exhale with relief when he doesn't pay me any more attention than the other women. That look in his eyes from before was surely not directed at me. I'm just oversensitive. But who isn't here?

Halfway through the loading, another uniformed man charges in. He must be one of a higher rank because our guard drops his cigarette and salutes.

The officer shouts something I fail to understand then he

shakes the guard's arms and continues spitting out words in this harsh language.

The other man is obviously trying to explain something to him, but his face shows more terror with every passing second. When the officer presses a pistol to his forehead, the guard's voice turns high-pitched, and he releases a stream of sentences.

I manage to catch on some of his words, like "Johann—blackmailing—stealing—clothes—profit."

The tormentor barks something in response and two other uniformed men appear. One of them is the guard who normally drives the delivery truck, the cruel son of a bitch who hurts us easily. The smirk on his face and self-satisfaction that beams from him are not missed on me.

The high-ranking Nazi releases a series of howls, but I fail to understand anything as his speech is so fast. Though one word clearly stands out as it's repeated a few times: Gestapo.

All of this is unsettling, but we never stop performing our duties. When we are done, the two guards shove the two middle-aged women inside the lorry and push Janina and me away with their rifles. The message is clear: we are staying in the warehouse.

Without any resistance, we walk back but I manage to steal a glance, long enough to realize that the new guard drove away with them.

I don't know what just happened, but it's clear the new truck driver is in deep trouble. What a huge relief that we don't have to be on that transport with them. A tiny part of me feels sorry for the man as he seemed gentler than other guards here. When he brought the letter to my barrack, he didn't utter a word but smiled encouragingly. Maybe he got in trouble for not being ruthless toward us.

But there is one detail that lingers on my mind for the rest of the day: the fact that he said the name *Johann*. There are so many men up there with that name, and he surely didn't mean

Aneta's Johann. No, this can't be. So, why do I have this uneasy feeling within me, like something is wrong?

The next day, there is the usual driver and not sign of the new one, but weeks later I spot him passing near our barrack while supervising a line of skin and bones men-prisoners. It seems that he wasn't punished too severely for whatever he did. Maybe it was just a misunderstanding and since he is German, things were resolved.

If any sort of misunderstanding happens to one of us, we are shot on the spot. They are here to use us as free labor and murder us once we aren't able to work.

# THIRTY-ONE
## ANETA

November 1943—Aneta's village

I refuse to accept that I will not see Johann ever again. He will surely find a way of getting out of this. And what about Bronka? Is she in danger because of it too?

Jordanek sleeps peacefully in his crib, and I can't help but wonder if because of me he will never see his mother again. After all, I didn't stop Johann from doing this. Then the thought that they both might be already dead makes me sob uncontrollably.

All prayers are forgotten while a cold hand of despair wraps around my heart. An object hitting a windowpane makes me freeze. In another minute the same noise returns, so I know it's not a bird. I leap to the window and slowly open it. After listening for a few minutes, a whispering comes from the outside, "Come to the orchard."

Johann... He's here...

Pumped by adrenaline and the mixture of relief and fear, I put on my coat before slipping into darkness. The crisp night air makes me shiver but I swirl around the trees in the orchard to find Johann behind the last one.

He's by himself.

I run into his embrace and say, "Bronka?" My voice carries layers of horror.

He strokes my hair with his trembling hand. "I'm convinced she is fine, though it looks like Horst betrayed me."

"What happened?"

"It's all good now, darling. They tried arresting me at the train station, but I was able to escape."

"How?" Fear freezes my heart as I struggle to catch my breath, still reeling with the thrill of having him back and the awfulness of not having Bronka here.

"I was right by not trusting Horst completely, after all." Sadness sips from his voice. "I went to the train station wearing civilian clothes knowing that my uniform would give me away. I mixed with the crowds on the platform where I knew I would be able to see the truck with the clothing from the camp. When I approached it, I realized that something wasn't right. There were only two middle-aged women prisoners working, so obviously your friend wasn't there. Then when I looked at Horst, he was nervously looking around, another uniformed guard beside him, while they both supervised the women. What caught my attention the most were the Gestapo agents in leather jackets swarming nearby. It's when I knew that he either betrayed me or perhaps the driver he switched with started suspecting something and Horst was questioned. I realized damn well that I could not go back to my squad. They're looking for me everywhere now. In their eyes, I'm a traitor."

I swallow hard and ask with desperation of a haunted animal. "But how do you know they will not hurt Bronka?"

"Horst knows she had no idea of my ploy. I also never mentioned you to him, keeping him in the dark. But there was one thing he swore on the life of his daughter: if it got to me being caught, it doesn't matter what, he will keep Bronka out of it. We agreed he would tell them that I forced him by threatening the safety of his family to help me and I did this to steal clothes to resell for profit. So, they are after me. I also told him a lie that Bronka's mother was the dearest friend of my grandmother, and that's why I wanted her out of the camp. You see, my grandma was always good to him, and he treated her like the mother he never had. I pray he has kept his word and Bronka wasn't affected by this at all." He strokes my hair with his fingers.

"Your words bring hope to my heart. I thought that I'd lost you."

He kisses my forehead. "You must know that my soul feels like my old one again when I don't have to wear the damn uniform and pretend to serve this murderous machinery. I couldn't go on like this, but the only thing that worries me is that they will retaliate against my grandparents. I can't protect them anymore."

"You should hide in the swamps," I say and touch my hand to his cold cheek. "I will bring food to you every day, until the war ends."

"This is the perfect solution but I will get my own food. I don't want you to risk your life by coming to me every day while the village might be under observation because of me. Though I wish to find a way of helping the partisans."

"They will not trust you, but I will see if Kostek can help you somehow." There is more to our farm helper than just being out drinking. He is devoted to supporting the partisans, but this piece of information would give my mother-in-law heart palpitations, so we keep it away from her.

"What an outcast I've turned out to be. I must hide not only from the Nazis but also from your partisans." He draws in air between his teeth. "It's flattering they all want my neck."

# THIRTY-TWO
## ANETA

Christmas Eve 1943—Aneta's village

We're sitting at night beside a small bonfire near the shack, his arms around me. "Are you sure it's safe for you to see the partisans tomorrow? Maybe it's a set-up?" I say, and lift my gaze to meet his, feeling like I'm in heaven again. Just as every other time, when our eyes swim into each other's, the world around us ceases to exist.

"I must do this. I can't spend the rest of this war doing nothing beside running away from damn Nazi henchmen. And I will not leave you." He takes my face between his hands and places a gentle kiss on my mouth, "Remember that you're always on my mind. Never doubt my feelings because you and Janek are my entire world." He smiles. "And the sweetest Hania."

"I don't want to lose you." He's so set on doing the right thing that I know there is no stopping him. It's his way of trying to make up for that execution when he had signaled his soldiers to shoot the three partisans. It's been weighing on his conscience.

He kisses the tip of my nose. "I will be fine." Then he changes the subject, "Do you have any contact with your family from Danzig?"

I'm relieved he does or next I would be sobbing and begging him to stay in the hideout. That would only make harder for both of us. "I get letters from my mother once in a while. They still live in Gdańsk. My stepfather supports the Nazis. I know that she doesn't agree with it but she's afraid of him. I wish I could help her."

"Do you miss your sisters?"

"We were never close; we don't even look the same as you saw when you met Anna. My father was a fisherman. He died in a sea storm. I know Mama never stopped hurting because of losing him but she didn't want to be alone. Unfortunately, she didn't have luck with her second husband because he is a mean person and doesn't treat her right." I don't know why I volunteer all of this, but I have this bizarre need to tell him about myself as much as possible.

"Do you remember him?" His voice is quiet.

"No, I was only nine months when he died. What about your family? Are they all like your brother?"

"No, not at all. My parents died in an automobile accident when we were ten. Our grandparents took us in, so we had to move from Hamburg to Danzig. My brother didn't take it well. He became rebellious and with the years it got worse. We drifted apart, then he joined Hitler Youth, and the NSDAP."

"He became so ruthless because your parents died, and he felt abandoned?"

He sighs. "There is more to it. You see, when we were nine, our parents sent us for a couple of weeks for the summer vacation to our uncle, our father's brother. Our cousins were close to our age, so we looked forward to it, and I admit that I had a great time. Later, when we returned, I realized how wrong I was. Mutti noticed that Erich was quieter and sadder, I on the other hand didn't think much of it. My brother was known to have mood swings, but when he confessed to her that our uncle was coming at night to his room and—" he breaks, clearly unable to finish.

I gently pat his back.

"He did terrible things to my brother while I slept peacefully in the other room. When we were there, Erich never said anything to me." He sniffs his nose and continues, "Later, my father beat my uncle unconscious and didn't want to see him ever again. A month later we learned that our uncle hanged himself. He left a letter in which he begged for forgiveness."

"But the trauma stayed with your brother..."

"Yes, my parents were guiding him through it and his nightmares were less frequent. Though when it came to our relationship, something changed permanently. He became more competitive and jealous of me for no reason. It all got worse when our parents died, and our grandparents took us in. We drifted more apart."

"I'm so sorry," I say, letting the silence take over before speaking again. "How are your grandparents now?"

"A month after I enlisted, the Nazis took over their brewery and forced my grandparents to move back to Hamburg. Now they live with my aunt, so they are fine."

"At least they are alive," I say, "thanks to you."

For a moment longer we listen to the crackling fire in the primitive hearth.

"You mentioned that the swamp is cursed?" he asks.

I pick a tiny stick from the ground and throw it into the fire, watching it get eaten by flames. It's the same with us humans when our lives are so fragile. Every minute or hour might be our last, but we never know. Especially now with the war roaring around, there are so many innocent lives being taken away every day.

I live like the same thing might happen to us too, so I stay extremely alert to be able to run the moment we absolutely must. But I'm only a tiny piece in all of this, and when the worst day comes, I might not be able to save my loved ones and the people whose lives I'm responsible for.

"You drifted away from me," Johann says and kisses the inside of my hand. "What were you thinking of?"

"I was wondering whether to tell you the old legend about this place being cursed," I say, not wanting to ruin our last moments together by my worries. "It seems so irrelevant right now."

"Tell me. I have been curious about it for a while now but never got a chance to ask you."

"Well, it's just a legend, but the oldest people in the village swear it to be the truth."

"Who did you hear it from? You aren't from here."

"Zygmunt told me. He was an excellent storyteller." A familiar surge of pain and regret enters my heart, like every time when I remember that he is no longer here.

"You always speak of him with great respect," he says. "Did you grow to love him?"

"Only as a friend. He was the kindest man I ever met. You would have liked him."

He seems to consider my words. "I don't know if he would like me if he knew that I'm in love with his wife."

"He's in a better place now and I'm sure he wouldn't look at it that way. I believe he's reunited with his beloved wife, Celina."

"I would still like to hear the legend."

"Over a hundred years ago in our village, there was a family with two daughters. Both were different as water and fire, one with red hair and a fair complexion, and the other was blonde and had the most beautifully angelic face.

"The redhead loved spending her time in the forests where she picked blueberries or mushrooms, but she felt most comfortable in this swamp where she hid from people. She sang with birds and talked to wild animals, and they must have sensed her good nature because they never harmed her, not even the wolves or brown bears.

"Her sister, on the other hand, spent all her time engaging with other villagers, she enjoyed flirting with young men in the village and she never missed any gathering or parties. Both sisters didn't feel any connection toward each other though they were only one year apart. It worried their mother who loved both of her daughters the same. She hoped that they would both get married and live happily.

"One Sunday, the little hut was visited by a handsome farmer from another village, who was known to be wealthy. Earlier, he saw the blonde sister at a fest near the church in Zwierzyniec, and he thought her very pretty. It was time for him to find a wife as his parents were getting older. When he came to court the pretty blonde, she was delighted and so were her parents. She thought the man was good looking and most of all, she was impressed by his wealth and good reputation. She knew that there were plenty of girls hoping to get his attention, so it flattered her that he chose to court her.

"The visit was rather pleasant, and the man left promising to come back soon. When he rode on his horse up the hill and reached the edge of the forest, he spotted the redhead hugging a birch tree, her eyes closed, her face dreamy. He couldn't take his eyes off her. It wasn't just about the way she looked, it was more about the feelings she stirred inside him. He didn't understand it but it was as if he'd found something he had been looking for his whole life.

"When she opened her eyes, she instantly felt the same about him, like there was this invisible thread that connected their lives, like they'd known each other through eternity, through centuries. From then on, they spent time together whenever they could. She took him to the swamp where she taught him where to step without falling in, introduced him to her collections of insects and butterflies, or rare stones where she had it in this very hut where you've stayed.

"But when he visited her parents to court her instead of her sister, the blonde became angry. She pretended to be happy for them, but she devised a plan. One day she followed her sister and plunged a knife into her back. She hid her body behind the shack, in the deepest part of the swamp. She knew it well because as a child she sometimes went there with her older sister.

"The lover searched, just as her parents, the entire village, and the blonde pretended to be looking too. She hoped that the man would want her now, but he didn't even look at her. One night the redhead visited him in his dreams and told him where to look for her body. The next morning, he went there and found her. He brought her into the shack, and after placing a kiss on her lips, he took his own life. The blonde found them like this, which was when she realized the extent of her deeds. She cried and cried and begged for forgiveness.

"When she left the shack wondering how to tell her parents what she had done, she got attacked by a horde of wolves who ate her alive. Since then, no one has the courage to come here. There are stories that it's a cursed place and whoever comes here will be eaten by the wolves, the friends of the redhead."

"Are we the only ones with enough courage to be here?" he asks.

"Yes, but you didn't know what you were getting yourself into when you let me take you here." I wink and laugh.

"Well, there is only one moral to this story."

"What's that?" I ask, curious about his thoughts.

"One should stay away from redheads," he says and smiles, revealing his white teeth.

I shake my head and roll my eyes.

"I love teasing you." He gently brushes a stray strand of hair away from my forehead, caressing me with the loving look in his eyes. "I think that your gorgeous chestnut hair protects us from any beasts. Besides, we should be afraid more of people than wolves," he adds and engages us in a heart-stealing kiss.

∼

The next day, on the way back from the farm chores, I thump my feet to shake off the snow before entering the cottage. After taking off my coat and boots, I leave it all in the entrance hall. I massage my still frozen cheeks using gentle upward motions with my fingertips, until I feel blood circulating again in my face. It's brutally cold, which brings me back to thinking for the thousandth time today about Johann.

The Germans keep searching the forests but so far, no other squad has stationed in our village. Johann's brother didn't return either which was what I feared the most, that he would come to search for him.

Right from the beginning, Kostek tried helping Johann to join the partisans but for long weeks, our fighters didn't trust him. Things changed after Johann helped them in an ambush on the German rail transport. If not for his savviness and quick acting, many would have died. It was a turning point and the Resistance leader agreed to talk to him today.

I sigh heavily and eye a clay jug with pickles. This is the coldest part of the cottage, so it's where we keep any food that should be cold, especially in the warmest months. I stand by the wall for a moment longer inhaling the strong, sour smell of pickles mixed with dill.

Then, I go inside to get lost in the preparations for Christmas dinner for my children.

# THIRTY-THREE
## BRONKA

Christmas Eve 1943—Majdanek

It's a surprise that there is no roll call at the end of the day. We're allowed to have a simple supper at the two long tables with benches situated near the entrance of the barrack. To our relief, Ursula never came back but someone saw her in a different field. Eva, the Czech prisoner, has the function of the Kapo in our barrack. She's a good woman, one of us.

I can't stop glancing at a Christmas tree that was brought here via the Polish Red Cross along with Christmas packages. I received one from Aneta too with a letter in which she tells me so much about my Jordanek. I've read it so many times, not believing that my baby boy is already seven months.

It pains me that he doesn't know me though Aneta wrote that she keeps showing him our wedding photo. According to her, he smiles every time he sees it. The awful reality that he will never meet his father brings tears to my eyes. He was only two weeks when Roman was killed.

I can't digest this sorrow that comes with my thoughts. It drains me, especially in moments like this. It's easier when I'm busy working. I keep living like my loved ones will come back one day and when I leave this camp, I will reunite with them.

Janina walks over and perches next to me on the pallet. "Overthinking is going to make it even harder. You must leave a sliver of hope in your heart, which will help you survive this misery. Your son is waiting for you and the fact that he's safe, far away from here, is your biggest blessing."

"You're right. Sometimes those thoughts crawl over me so unexpectedly that I don't have the strength to fight them off."

"It's understandable. You lost your loved ones." Sadness sips from her tone.

"And so, you. Maybe it's why we understand each other so well." She brought up something that I can't deny: that my son being safe is a blessing.

"We should join everyone at the tables before the SS men charge in and ruin this evening," she says and slowly gets to her feet. "Or before the baby decides to come to this world." She smiles but I know that she fears the worst.

We share what we have from the packages that some of us received. We even have dumplings with poppy seeds and *pierniki ze śliwką,* gingerbread cookies with plum.

This is the first decent moment since I've arrived at this camp. Everyone's spirits improve as we all try to feel at least a spark of normalcy.

When we sing *Bóg się rodzi,* God is born, it seems like the Christmas carol permeates the walls of the barrack. We sing with tears in our eyes and hope in our hearts that our silent prayers will reach Heaven.

At night, Janina's waters break, so I wake Krystyna who assists her labor. After long hours of her misery, a baby's choking cry cuts the air.

"You've a healthy daughter," Krystyna says and smiles, then she puts the baby on Janina's chest, who now sobs.

Emotion squeezes my throat.

A moment later, when Janina, exhausted after hours in labor, falls asleep with the baby in her arms, I say, "She's a miracle." It, indeed, is a true miracle that her mother hasn't lost her in this hell.

"That she is," Krystyna says. She already washed the baby girl in a tiny amount of water and dressed her in a linen outfit I smuggled from the sewing factory. I hid a few more things for her under the mattress, like a plush blanket.

"How will we keep this tiny little bundle alive?" Eva sighs. "They all die here."

"She can't bring it with her to the sewing factory," I say and gaze at Krystyna, "but is there a chance that the baby stays in the infirmary with you?"

She shakes her head. "With so many sicknesses circulating in there, the baby wouldn't survive. Besides, the Aufseherin in there is a cruel bitch. I watched her throwing a newborn into furnace and I couldn't stop her." Her voice breaks as she avoids my gaze.

We stay silent for minutes while the exhausting feeling of powerlessness and loss hangs heavily in the air.

"My daughter can watch the baby through the day," Wiesia, a middle-aged woman says. "My Irenka is only twelve but already responsible."

I picture the sweet, fragile girl with her long, fair braid, who's asleep now. "That would be so helpful," I say and treat Wiesia to a thankful look. Children that are younger than fourteen stay in the barrack for the day and are registered under their mothers as they don't get separate numbers. Anyone above that age has their own number and works along with adults.

The following week proves how truly powerless we are here. Janina produces very little milk, and the constantly hungry baby Ronia cries all the time. I give my friend most of my meager food rations and as a result, I feel weaker each day. Other women share with her as much as possible, especially when someone receives a package via the Polish Red Cross, but that's not enough.

Right from the day I arrived and saw children miserably sitting outside the barracks, I swore to do everything to help save the children. Any spare food I get always goes to them and I tell them stories whenever I'm able to. It's all I can do but I wish there was more.

Now I must focus on keeping Janina's baby alive, despite all the odds being against us.

She was ordered to go back to work on the second day after her labor, and that's when Irenka, the teenage girl, watches the baby through the day. The coldness and dampness of the barrack isn't good for the newborn, but Irenka keeps moving with the baby wrapped in the blanket.

Today the precious Ronia doesn't cry anymore and is looking pale and poor. Janina holds her little girl while streams of tears run down her cheeks as she whispers loving words. Maybe soon she won't be able to...

It's so hard to watch this tiny spark of life fade away before our eyes, yet there is nothing we can do.

The next evening after roll call, Eva approaches us. Janina seems to be asleep with the baby while I'm once more trying to think of something. We've tried giving the baby some cow's milk that one of the women, who helps in the food canteen's kitchen for Germans, brought in a tin cup. Ronia swallowed a little but not much, and Janina drank the rest in hopes of improving her breastmilk supply.

"I was informed today that some villagers are being released from the camp, including our barrack."

Her words make me stare at her in disbelief.

She gives me a knowing look. "You aren't on the list, but Wiesia and her daughter are."

"I'm happy for them."

"Wiesia agreed to take Janina's baby with her. You know

well that this precious girl will not stay alive here much longer. Outside she has a chance."

I close my eyes. "This is the only way. I will talk to Janina."

"I agree. But the final decision belongs to her. They're leaving tomorrow, so I need the answer before the gong tonight."

When Eva walks away, I gaze at Janina whose face is twisted with pain as she sways with the baby.

"You heard," I say, thinking that once I was in the same exactly situation. Well, not really, because my baby was well nourished, while Janina's barely survives each day.

But seeing her in a similar position to the one I was in strengthens my resolve even more. I must convince her to hand her baby to Wiesia. It's the only way to keep the little one alive.

"How can I give her away?"

"You must because you want her to live. Think only of her."

"It's a long way and Wiesia doesn't know what she will find when she returns home."

"I will tell her to bring Ronia to my friend Aneta. She will take good care of her."

"What if your friend realizes my baby is Jewish and reports her to the Germans."

"She is not like that. Your Ronia will be safe with her." It repulses me that someone would think like this of Aneta, but Janina doesn't know her. She's just trying to wrap her mind around sending away her baby. I, of all people, understand it so well.

"What if the SS men don't let Wiesia take my Ronia? What if they kill my little sunshine?"

"There is always risk and this is your decision to make. But I think you should give the baby a chance at living."

In the end, she hands her to Wiesia and Irenka early in the morning, before the roll call. She doesn't cry anymore, just seems absent all day, while busy fixing uniforms.

At night she suddenly whispers into darkness, "I learned that my husband was among the murdered in November."

"I'm so sorry," I say gently and pull her into a hug.

She sobs for a long time. "It's matter of time before they kill us too."

"Do you remember when you told me to not overthink but leave a sliver of hope to be able to survive? I'm sure your husband wants you to do that."

"Ronia was that sliver of hope for me. Now I have nothing."

"But she has a chance to live."

"I don't believe it."

# THIRTY-FOUR
## ANETA

New Year's Day 1944—Aneta's village

"I don't know how to save this poor baby," I say to my mother-in-law in the afternoon while holding the bundle with a little girl inside whose name is Ronia, according to Bronka's letter.

The rapid banging yesterday evening made me believe that it was Gestapo wanting to search our home, but when I opened the door, there was a gaunt lady standing with the baby in her arms.

Her speech was chaotic, but she gabbled that the baby is from Bronka. Confused, I took the little bundle and the letter but before I could ask anything, the woman uttered that her daughter was waiting for her in a farmer's wagon and that the good man agreed to bring them to their village.

Within seconds, she was gone, and I was left with the baby girl. I'm determined to do everything to keep her alive. Bronka trusts me with it. I read the short letter from her feeling at peace that she's fine, especially after what happened to Johann, the few sentences she wrote about the baby's mother are so heartbreaking.

My mother-in-law looks up from her knitting and says, "This baby is slowly dying. We've tried everything but it's just too late. Maybe if she was brought to us earlier..."

For a moment longer I watch Janek train Szarik to bark when he tells him to and to give him the paw. Hania sings to Jordanek while she's clapping their hands together:

*Mow mow paws*
*we'll got to grandma's*
*Grandma will give us candy*
*and grandpa kiełbasa.*

The moment she sings the last word, our little sunshine laughs so cutely that my heart melts. If we've managed to keep our Jordanek alive, then why can't we help this baby? But Bronka's son was well-nourished when Marta brought him to us.

My mother-in-law is right that we've tried everything today to feed the tiny girl. So far, Ronia's only accepted a very small amount of goat's milk we exchanged for eggs from another villager, and a mix of hot water and flour, which we cooled. We also tried cow's milk even though my mother-in-law strongly advises that it isn't gentle enough for the baby. But her heart still beats, and I will not give up. I just must find another way...

"Maybe if we keep trying—" I don't finish my sentence because my mother-in-law stands up, gazing at me with her small eyes like she just got a brilliant idea.

"There is only one way," she says with authority in her voice. "Honorata's son was born one day before Christmas Eve. You must convince her to try nursing this baby too. One or two mouths doesn't make much difference."

"You know she doesn't like me." Honorata lives at the other end of the village with her husband and parents-in-law. When Zygmunt's wife passed, she was still not married and lived in the neighboring village. Her parents hoped that Zygmunt would choose her for his second wife, so when he brought me home, a stranger from the far away city, they were upset.

"You must try; she's your only hope."

"She won't do it for me," I say, feeling sour taste in my mouth at the memories. From our first encounter she treated me with pity and actively engaged in spreading gossip about me, like that I was a prostitute and Zygmunt won me in poker. It's been better since the war started but we just avoid each other.

"Offer eggs and white cheese in return for her to nurse the baby once a day. It will help us a lot."

In this very moment, I realize how she cares for the little one too. Her face is troubled. She discusses the matter without the usual insults or blaming.

I stand up and cover my head with a scarf. "I'm going now but I'm taking Ronia with me," I say, unconvinced. Maybe if she sees the poor thing, she'll forget her animosity toward me and decide to help.

Outside, I inhale the crisp air mixed with a whiff of smoke from chimneys and admire the enchanted blanket of white snow that covers ground. It feels like I'm in the most peaceful place, despite dogs barking and kids' laughter in the distance.

I hide the tiny bundle under my sheepskin coat and lurch through the village road covered with snow. I make sure that the baby has just enough air to breathe, and at the same time, it doesn't get too cold.

I tilt my head up and catch falling snowflakes with my tongue, something I loved doing when I was a child. My sisters always copied me, later reporting to my stepfather with tears in their eyes that I forced them to eat snow, which gave them stomachaches. I never understood why they cared so much to get me in trouble. After all, we're half-sisters and I showed them patience and turned a blind eye to their pranks.

Their behavior became clear to me when I once overheard my stepfather telling them that I was just a slave in our home. Every single day, he skillfully turned them against me, making sure to look innocent to my mother, so she couldn't accuse him of his sinister intentions. Mama, on the other hand, has always loved me with all her heart, so when he proposed to place me in an orphanage when I was eight, she got so upset that she started packing our suitcases. She was ready to leave him, but of course, he apologized and promised to treat me like his own daughter. His assurance was filled with empty words though... I miss my mama so much.

When I enter Honorata's yard, I unbutton my coat and position the baby in my arms. I tap on the wooden hut's brown door with peeling paint, now with its thatched roof covered in snow. I try to calm my palpitations by reminding myself that the life of the sweet girl in my arms depends on this, but I would be less nervous if I was to meet with the king of England.

The door swings open and Honorata's round face shows an initial surprise which instantly transforms into displeasure. "What do you want?" she barks and folds her arms at her chest.

"I need help," I say knowing well that small talk will only make her shut the door much faster on me. I motion to the bundle in my arms. "This innocent baby is dying. It was brought to us from the German camp in Lublin and it won't take a bottle."

All negative emotions melt away from her face when she peeks at Ronia. She brings her plump hand to her mouth, then says, "Oh my goodness. And where is her mother?"

"Still in the camp. The baby wouldn't survive with her, so when she saw that another woman was released, she begged her to take the baby with her."

She brushes her finger of Ronia's cheek, which brings a surge of hope to my heart. "You want me to feed her, I assume?" Her gaze moves to me and the so familiar hardness slowly returns.

"Once a day, if you could. Her mother tried nursing her in the camp, but you can only imagine how sparse food is there, so she couldn't produce much milk. Still, the baby latched and managed to survive this far."

"I'm going to do this for this innocent bird, not you," she says and takes Ronia into her arms, then she backs off into the warmth of the hut.

I didn't expect her to agree so quickly, so I exhale with relief and close the door behind me, following her into the coziness of this home that smells of roasted nutmeg. Honorata is known for her hard work and cleanliness, so it doesn't surprise me that everything here is neat and organized.

She doesn't pay me any attention but settles into a wooden rocking chair not far from her own baby in a cradle and brings Ronia to her large blossom.

But I don't care because I get busy watching how the baby doesn't react to the touch of nipple. *Please, little sunshine, take it. It's your only hope.*

Honorata parts the baby's lips with her smallest finger and thrusts the nipple into the tiny mouth. "Come on, little bird, take it," she says and pats Ronia's back.

# THIRTY-FIVE
## ANETA

New Year's Day 1944—Aneta's village

"This little bird is so innocent; I can't do differently. I only hope that I have enough milk for both babies," Honorata says half an hour later after she offers to keep the baby with her for a couple of months, until it gets stronger and healthier.

"Are you sure that Lucjan will be fine with it?"

She shrugs. "Why not? It's not like my husband will be the one feeding her."

After I assure her that I will bring eggs and cheese the following day, I thank her again and leave. I know that staying with Honorata is best for Ronia right now, so on the way home I feel peaceful. Before I open the door to our hut, I pause and then smile at the familiar voice from the side of the building saying my name. I would recognize it anywhere.

Without hesitation, I dart through the snow with my racing pulse and get scooped into his arms. He's here, my beloved is here.

"I couldn't wait any longer to see you," he whispers.

I press my face to his chest, hungry to hear his reassuring heartbeat. "You are with the partisans now?"

"Yes. I finally feel like I'm doing something good in this lifetime. I'm sorry I haven't visited before, but the Nazis keep sniffing around the area, so I don't want to put you and the children at risk."

"I know, but so much has happened. The good thing is that Bronka is alive. She sent me a letter with the baby."

He lifts my chin up with his forefinger. "She was expecting another baby?"

"No, her friend was." I tell him what happened and how Honorata agreed to help.

"It's inspiring what you do, Netuś," he says, caressing my cheek.

"You make me blush and feel like I'm a heroine or something." I laugh and playfully nudge his arm. "I do what anyone would in my place. I wish there was more in my power."

"I value in you that you risk your life and sacrifice so much to care for the children. I love and admire your strength and that you always try to do everything you can, even in the hardest circumstances. I'm lucky to be calling you mine and privileged when you call me yours."

"Your words mean the world to me," I say, shaking from the freezing air.

"You are cold," he says, bringing me against the length of his body. "You should go back inside."

Panic rushes through my heart like a blind bow. "Let's go to the shack. We will make a fire there."

"I wish I could, darling, but I must go back to my base. I will be visiting you as often I can when it's safe." He kisses me with such fervency that I can't catch my breath, staying limply in his embrace. Our tongues dance in endless touch of love and longing, yearning to be together.

"I can't stop thinking of you," he whispers when he lifts his mouth from mine. "Every night I dream of making love to you."

An untamed fire soars to my face burning my cheeks. "Then we have the same dreams."

# THIRTY-SIX
## BRONKA

April 1944—Majdanek

*Dearest Bronka,*

*At the time I'm writing this letter our precious Ronia is already three months old and thriving. Please tell this to her mama. The first month was the toughest and there were moments when we thought that she wouldn't make it, but thanks to one of the village women whose son was born also in December, our Ronia survived. The woman took her in and has nursed her since. This proved to be the best we could do for the little girl as she wouldn't drink from the bottle.*

*I wanted to assure you that the baby girl is well. She likes to smile and take long naps.*

*Jordanek is thriving as well. I can't believe that he's already eleven months. He enjoys crawling all over the hut and is trying to access things he shouldn't. But don't worry, my friend, because my mother-in-law doesn't take her eyes off him. She's so motherly toward him. We expect him to start walking very soon. Whenever we show him your wedding picture, he says:*

*"Ma, Pa". These aren't the only words that he sounds out so far. He's so smart and happy, and the love and attention he gets from my mother-in-law warms my heart. Janek adores him as well, and so do I.*

*There is so much more I would like to share with you, and I can't wait for the day when I can finally hug you. We miss you and love you.*

*Stay strong, my friend.*

*A.*

"You see, I told you that Ronia would survive," I say to Janina who sits beside me on the bunk bed and sobs. It's almost time for a night gong but we have a few minutes to talk.

Tears roll down her cheeks, but she smiles. "Just to hear that my little one is alive and doing well, means everything. Thank you, my friend."

"I knew that Aneta would do everything to save her. Now you must survive this to come back to your princess."

"True, now I must."

At night I take a little violet flower from behind my mattress, which Władek gave me a couple of days ago. I don't know where he found it but thanks to this small gesture, for a moment I felt adored again. In this place, we are treated like we're less important than objects.

That little flower, now dried, not only brought warmth to me, but it also sent a surge of memories to my heart. Every spring Roman picked wildflowers from meadows and made bouquets for me. It made me feel so wanted and loved and beautiful.

As silent tears run down my face, the salty taste in my mouth is like a painful reminder that I lost the life I shared with my beloved. Even if I leave this camp alive, I will have to start from the beginning, without people I lost, people I love so dearly.

But I must do what I've been doing since arriving here: hide all memories and painful thinking into the most secluded areas of my soul, because if I let them surface while being here, I know I will not survive. I want to live for my son, I want to raise him, to make sure that he learns about his father.

In this very moment, I'm about to cross a thin line, which can only bring me to despair and mental collapsing. Now, I must only think of the current moment and how to stay alive. My only goal is survival and return to my son.

Janina touches my arm and whispers, "You're overthinking again. Remember what I told you."

"Yes," I whisper back, "I remember."

# THIRTY-SEVEN
## ANETA

June 1944—Aneta's village

"People in the village say that the Soviets will be here soon, and Poland will be free again," I say one evening to Dr. Stein and his wife. I've brought a light supper of mini apple cakes that my mother-in-law made.

Mrs. Stein puts her fork down and sighs. "It's so hard to believe in anything these days."

The doctor takes a sip of chicory coffee. "I have no doubts that they're coming though it might not be as fast as people think. I read an article in one of those underground gazettes you bring," he says arching his brow, "the name slips my mind. Anyway, I read that Hitler still thinks he's going to win this war and mobilizes all his forces to fight with everything they have."

"We must be patient. Although I can't wait for the day when we're free from those barbarians," I say and yawn, feeling exhausted after a full day of hard labor in the fields. Since spring has arrived, there is so much work on the farm. And now that Kostek isn't here, it's all on me. I do what I can, always handling things the way that Zygmunt taught me so patiently.

"You will be able to finally leave this attic," I add, folding my lips into gentle smile. "I can only imagine how hard it must be to be confined here."

"We're still alive, and that's what matters," the doctor says, his face expression is filled with sorrow. "So many were killed."

"So many lives taken away, indeed," I say with sadness that presses on my chest. "Bless their souls."

Mrs. Stein sighs but changes the subject, "We've kept busy here and enjoyed so many visits from Janek and Hania. You treat us so well."

"Please, don't be so modest, Mrs. Stein," I say. "You've knitted so many hats, mittens and scarfs that our whole village kept warm through the winter." I wink at her. "You deserve a special award."

A sudden roar of engines outside makes us cease talking. Without a word, I walk toward a tiny attic window with a view to the Ramniwskis' courtyard, now being crowded by German soldiers. Again.

"Looks like another German unit is going to station at the neighboring property," I say, then for a moment longer I listen to shouts and commands in German. One voice stands out and when I realize it's Johann's brother, I feel ice trickle down my spine. I hoped to never see him again.

Now we must deal with Johann's brother whose cruelty has no end. I dread the fate of my children. What will happen to all of us? How far will the bastard go to torment us before he slaughters us like pigs?

"Be careful down there," Dr. Stein says. "Keep the children away from the soldiers."

As I walk down the ladder, I have this uneasy feeling that Erich won't stop at just barking orders at us and treating us with his self-amused, evil glances. Then I think of my Johann and how he worried that his brother would decide to station in this village just to prove that he's better than Johann and try tracing him. After all these months, we'd started to believe that he was assigned somewhere else.

Since the beginning of the year, Johann and Kostek have visited once a month, at the least expected moments. While Kostek came over to our home, Johann stayed near the creek. Our every meeting over there was filled with such happiness at seeing each other. He always assured me of his feelings and that even though I don't see him, he often checks on us. He can't wait to see Janek again, but not until we are free.

"The Germans are here," my mother-in-law says when I enter the kitchen. She's holding Jordanek's hand; he started walking a few days ago. It's so hard to believe that he will be one next month. He has Bronka's nose and Roman's eyes. His sweetness brings so much light to our lives, and I wish that my friend could be back to hold him again.

"I know. The children need to stay inside, no more wandering into the orchard," I say, looking at Janek who likes to sneak out. Now he pats Szarik who's sleeping on his lap. Erich cannot see my son, and it's safer when Hania stays out of his way as well. He's a very suspicious and ruthless man.

My mother-in-law closes the curtain at the window. "I can't even look at those soldiers anymore without feeling sick. Did you tell the Steins?"

I nod. "Hopefully the Germans won't be here long," I say, but at a loud bang on our door, I swallow hard. "Stay here. I will go see what they want."

I don't have a good feeling about all of this, especially knowing Erich's cruelty. When I open, a group of soldiers with rifles in their hands ogle me.

"We are to live in this hut starting now," one with a hooked nose and freckles says, "everyone must leave immediately for the barn."

Stunned, I manage to say, "But I have little children here."

He lifts his rifle and aims at me. "Any resistance will be met with death. You must leave now and walk over to the barn." His breath reeks of rotten eggs.

He motions for me to step aside and when I do, they charge inside, leaving me alone at the door.

I struggle to breathe, not able to grasp at what they expect us to do. What will happen to the Steins? Then, the thought that they are about to traumatize my children, sends a surge of adrenaline through me. I rush into the kitchen where my mother-in-law hugs the children.

"Mother," I say, my voice shaking, "they will be staying here, and we are to move to the barn." I avoid her gaze, praying she doesn't make a scene.

But she only nods and instructs the scared children to sit down on the bench, then she helps me grab a few items, like Jordanek's bottle, but the soldiers rush us out by poking our backs with their rifles.

Only minutes later, we all sit on top of hay in the barn, inhaling the earthy scent mixed with dust and a whiff of manure from the adjoining pigsty. At least they can't take away that smell from us that defines this farm. I scold myself in my mind for having such absurd thoughts. Everything happened so fast that my mind is still spinning.

"Thanks to mighty God the Germans didn't kill us and burn everything," my mother-in-law says and crinkles her nose.

"True," I say, knowing well that this may change any moment, especially with Johann's brother in charge.

She gasps and presses a palm against her chest like she just realized something. "If they find the Steins they will kill us," she whispers.

"Please stop saying these things in front of the children," I scold her. "The Steins are intelligent people, and they will realize that something isn't right and stay quiet. Besides, the Germans will not find out they are there, because we'll get them out soon."

I say this to calm her, so we can have a decent night. The last thing I need is for her to have a panic attack when she thinks her heart is failing because she can't catch her breath. She has done it so many times in the past. We have already had enough trauma for today.

She doesn't look convinced by my words. "How can you get them out with Germans in there?"

"I'm sure they will not be here the whole time." I look at the children who now all are asleep between the softness of hay. If not for the encounter with the soldiers, there wouldn't be any harm in sleeping here, maybe even an adventure for them. And the night is so warm, even refreshing.

"We shouldn't be worrying in advance. We'll see how things go tomorrow. Let's get some shut eye."

Sleep doesn't come to me for a long time. Just the thought that one of the soldiers takes my bed right now repulses me. I hope that the Steins don't make any noise and the man that is in my bedroom right now doesn't spot the attic entrance in the ceiling or the ladder under the bed.

In the morning, I open my eyes thankful that we're still alive. It means that they didn't find the Steins, otherwise we would all be dead by now. It flashes through my mind that we should run away but we can't leave the Steins like this. Even if the Germans don't find them, they will die of starvation. I don't know what's worse.

I resolve to walk over to the cottage and ask them to let me cook a meal for the children. But first I feed the animals and milk the cow, and when I'm done, I summon all my courage and knock. This is so ridiculous that I'm knocking on my own door.

When I get no response, I walk to the kitchen window. Soldiers sit at our table and drink our chicory coffee while helping themselves to our bread. I form my hands into fists. Criminals!

I knock on the window glass, watching as they turn their

heads my way. The taller one that barked the orders yesterday walks over and opens the window.

"What do you want, Polish swine?"

*I'm outside my own home you idiot,* I think, but say, "I need to cook a warm meal for my children."

"It's not my concern. If you want your brats to stay alive, you must get out of my face before I lose my patience." He's about to close the window on me when the other soldier with blond hair and crusty, red skin face stops him.

"Let me take care of this, Bruno, go back to your coffee, brother," he says, a note of firmness in his voice.

"Suit yourself, Claus," the other one says, waves his hand and walks away.

"Thank you, officer," I say, purposely calling him this way to flatter his ego.

A spark of pride shines through his eyes as he puffs out his breasts. He looks no older than eighteen, still, he had enough spunk to oppose the other soldier who must be double his age.

"We will be reporting to our commander in about twenty minutes. You can use the stove in our absence today and on other days, but on condition that you clean the kitchen after us."

"Yes, officer." What a lazy scoundrel, then I remind myself to thank him for his *kindness*.

He nods. "I have two little sisters," he says. "I wouldn't want them to suffer of hunger."

*I'm sure you do worse,* I think but thank him again and walk away, relieved there is at least one soldier with a sliver of compassion in him, even if he's using me to clean their mess. I didn't believe for a second that they would let me use the wood-burning stove.

True to his words, twenty minutes later the soldiers walk out of our home and head to the Ramniwskis' courtyard.

"Mamusia, will we ever be back in our home?" Janek asks as

I watch the outside through gaps in wooden planks of the barn's door.

"We will, darling, we will. You just must be patient and stay far away from the soldiers."

"I'm hungry. Can you make *kluski lane na mleku?*" The earnest look on his face makes me emotional.

I scoop him into my arms and hold him close to me. "Yes, darling, I will make your favorite drop noodles in milk, but first I must tell you something very important and you must listen carefully."

"Yes, Mamusia."

"I know that you and Hania like Johann, the soldier that gave you Szarik."

"He's the good soldier."

"Yes, he indeed is, though he has a twin brother who looks just like him. You, see, sunshine, his brother is the bad soldier, so when you see him at the Ramniwskis' yard, you and Hania must stay away from him. He hurts people." I feel bad telling him this, but I feel that it's the only thing I can do to prevent him from running to Erich, thinking that he's Johann.

"Don't worry, Mamusia, we will not talk to him," he says and kisses my cheek.

"What's this about?" my mother-in-law asks, her accusing gaze burning into my face. She is holding Jordanek on her lap while he drinks milk from a bottle. We still have the cow, so I could do the early morning milking.

"I'm making sure that the children stay away from the Germans, that's all," I say avoiding her eyes. I can't deal with her now.

Once Jordanek is done with his milk, he giggles and Janek takes his hand. They run across the barn with Hania, while Szarik follows them wagging his tail. The barn has a lot of empty space as we haven't begun this year's harvesting. Conflicting emotions pull at my heart. Will we survive this?

Half an hour later we hear the roar of engines followed by hooves of horses, then the commotion dies down.

"They left," I say to my mother-in-law who's now staring into wooden planks in front of her. "I will go make a warm meal for us."

"Go, child, go," she says. "I will watch the children."

The gentle tone makes her sound so different. It's one of those rare moments when she speaks to me without harshness.

"You must be strong, Mother. It will all pass. I heard the Soviets are near."

"The Germans chased us away from our own home like dogs and who knows what the Soviets will do? I don't expect anything good from them. Remember my words."

"Let's focus on now. As you said yesterday, we're lucky they're keeping us alive and aren't burning everything," I say. "I'd better go before they come back."

As I walk through the yard, I realize that the Germans have left one soldier on guard in the Ramniwskis' property, who's right now marching back and forth. When I realize it's the one with the crusty face, I exhale with relief. He's aware that I will be using the stove and won't try stopping me.

When I enter the cottage, a whiff of sweat mixed with the aroma of grain coffee intensifies the air. Dirty plates and mugs on the table and pens on the stove are the proof of strangers eating our food, from our plates, not bothering to clean after themselves. It disgusts me.

The eggs that I had put away here were eaten too. Each and every one.

I walk quickly to my bedroom and take the ladder out, then after knocking onto the ceiling, I wait.

There is no commotion, so I knock again this time saying, "It's Aneta."

The panel moves and the doctor's face appears.

I hand him the leftover bread and pate I made the other day

and managed to store in the vestibule. "German soldiers are staying in the house. Please be ready as I will try to come for you as soon as possible."

He nods. "Thank you, we will be ready." There is no panic in his voice or his face, instead I detect calmness, which gives me a little more strength too.

After cleaning the kitchen, I go to the hen house to gather eggs. When I get back, I add three eggs into a tin bowl with flour and whisk until smooth. I boil milk diluted with water and a pinch of salt. Using a spoon I gradually pour the batter into the boiling milk with circular motion and let it cook for a few minutes while stirring.

I bring the whole pot into the barn and settle it on the floor along with wooden bowls and spoons. So far, the soldier on guard hasn't interfered.

After we're done eating, we set the leftovers aside, so my mother-in-law can feed the children with it when I work in the fields during the day.

"I'm going to check on our Ronia," I say. When I saw that the baby would be alright, I offered to take her, but Honorata reasoned that she should stay with them until their mother is back. She also sympathized with me having three mouths to feed while she only has one.

I noticed that she grew to treat her like her own. It warms my heart, but at the same time, I worry if she's going to be able to give her back when Janina returns. If she comes back. I pray daily that Bronka and her friend will survive the hell they have been going through in that camp. Although she doesn't say much in her letters, I've heard terrible things about this place.

But thanks to Aneta, we know that Władek is still alive. I wonder why he never sent a letter. It's strange.

When I stop at Honorata's to check on the baby, as always, she treats me rudely, and as always, I ignore it. I don't mind because our little Ronia thrives under her care. The whole family have been removed from their home and now inhabit their barn, along with a red-haired man in his sixties who was hired by Honorata's husband to help at the farm. I never paid him much attention because he always seemed to stay away and keep his head down. But the way he stares at me now while he chews on the straw, alarms me. It's as if he knows something about me that makes him arrogant.

I chase my thought away as I know that I've been oversensitive lately. The man picks up her little son and makes him giggle by throwing the boy up and catching him. This man is obviously decent and I'm just overtaken with my worries.

"Aneta," Honorata says and touches my arm right after I've said my goodbyes. I swirl around to meet her gaze, somehow softer now. "Be careful."

I nod. "Thank you, and you as well. Do everything not to get into the way of soldiers. It will all end soon, I hope so, anyway."

The way she spoke and looked at me brought a tiny amount of warmth into my heart. The past isn't important anymore. We're together in this, since she chose to help us keep Janina's daughter alive.

On the way back home, I observe the guard who keeps pacing along the perimeters of the property, mostly staying near the entrance. If I'm to leave the house with the Steins he must have his back to us, occupied with something, or he will spot us right away.

I know I must do this because leaving them there brings more danger to all of us, but I don't know how to without being caught.

Then an idea strikes me, a risky one, but it seems our only hope in this situation.

# THIRTY-EIGHT
## BRONKA

June 1944—Majdanek

Since April, our ordeal here is unbearable. There are constant transports with prisoners heading to other places. Executions have intensified even more and are now continuous.

"They are liquidating the camp because of the rapid advance of the Soviets," Władek says one evening. We hide in the shades of the lavatory, while there are lines of people to use the primitive hole in the ground. "Keep doing your duties in the gardens as best you can and pray. Looks like only the lucky ones will survive. The Germans are on a rampage of executions. We must have hope that they will include us in one of those transports. At least it will give us a chance to survive." He lifts my chin with his fingers. "It's important that you focus on being strong and careful, so you can win this battle."

I try to smile but even that small gesture feels painful because my mouth is dry and the pain in my heart and soul is so unbearable. "It's hard to have hope. No one knows who will be taken next. What if they stop the transports and kill us all?" I haven't said anything to him, but with each day I'm feeling weaker and weaker, as if all my strength slowly abandons me, and I can't do anything about it. It's like the year of malnourishment and murderous labor is finally catching up with me. The mental and emotional misery is overwhelming, to the point I'm not able to take it anymore.

"You can't think like this. If you lose hope, you will have nothing. Remember your son."

"It seems like it doesn't matter what people do, they get killed or sent out to who knows where, maybe somewhere to be murdered."

"Please," he squeezes my hand, "be strong. You just must be strong."

I sigh. "And so, you. Please be strong too."

"I promise." His eyes reflect layers of tenderness and resilience, while his will to fight through the worst lifts my spirits. Men like him are rare jewels among ordinary stones, at least in my eyes.

That night I can't stop wondering if we will be lucky enough to survive. Every morning after opening my eyes, I go over my life like it's my last day, like I would be soon placed under the firing squad and executed like my papa and brother.

How fragile our existence is in the face of all of this. Is there anything beyond this? Is there a world where there is no more pain or worries, just this fulfilling love? I like to think that there is such a place that Heaven does exist. My faith tells me so, but there are also doubts creeping up on me from those dark spots of my soul. My soul—isn't that enough proof that it all doesn't end when our bodies die?

At the end of June, the strong headaches take the best out of me with each coming day, making it impossible to function. I have this constant nausea while all my muscles hurt so badly. Only when I realize that I have a persistent high fever and the same skin rash that Mama had on her chest and stomach, do I know that I've contracted typhus. It's going to get even worse, and I will die, like my mother, and so many others. I will never get to see my son.

I feel so empty as I lie there one night. I never said anything to Janina, so as not to worry her. I dread going to the camp's hospital where people drop like flies. I've decided to die here in this barrack, or during the labor in gardens instead of succumbing to the misery of the camp's so-called hospital.

But I get weaker every hour now, to the point that Janina starts noticing.

Then one morning, I have a hard time holding myself upright. I collapse during roll call and succumb to nothingness.

# THIRTY-NINE
## ANETA

June 1944—Aneta's village

I walk from the barn to the cottage while carrying a pot and soup bowls, so if the soldier questions me, I can tell him that I'm bringing it back. I can see out of the corner of my eye that he's peering at me but says nothing.

Once inside, I help the Steins get down. "When you see through the window that the soldier is standing with his back to you while I speak to him, you must go to the barn, but only when you're sure that he isn't looking." We agree that Dr. Stein will carry his wife. There is no other choice as she can't walk fast.

I make the sign of a cross and march out the house with my head held high.

When I approach the soldier, I clear my throat and say, "Hello, officer."

He turns around, his surprised gaze on me.

"I hate to interrupt you in this extremely important duty of protecting us from bandits, but I wondered if you have a cigarette to spare." I bat my lashes and fold my mouth into an innocent smile, then I walk around him, so he turns to see me. When he does it, I feel a sudden release of tension.

His serious face slowly transforms into a more relaxed one. "And if I do, how will you thank me?"

I treat him with a flirtatious look, the one reserved only for a sweetheart, while my stomach turns. "Why don't you find out?"

He chuckles but takes out his cigarette pack and offers one to me.

"Thank you, hun," I say and put it between my lips thanking Johann in my mind; he insisted a few times I join him smoking. At least I will not be coughing now like I did the first time.

He fishes out matches, and when I lean toward him, he lights up our cigarettes.

While exhaling clouds of smoke, I see in the corner of my eye that Dr. Stein is already walking around the hut with Mrs. Stein in his arms.

The soldier makes a movement like he wants to turn and look in that direction, but I quickly say, "Do you have a lover?"

My words hold him still as he looks at me carefully, lines of smoke coming out of his nostrils.

"I mean, do you have a girl back at home?"

"No, but there isn't anything wrong with getting one here." He winks at me.

"True. I'm sure there are some pretty girls in the nearby villages with the German colonists. And I can help you as I have a remedy for crusty skin, young man," I say in a motherly way and take out a small tube of cream. "Try this one and you will be thankful to me for the rest of your life. All German girls will be blushing at your sight."

For a moment he stays still, moving his hesitating gaze from the tube to me, but then he scratches his head and says, "Well, I guess it won't hurt trying it out."

"It will work, hun, just give it a time. Use it three times a day for a month; your skin will slowly improve." Władek used to have the same skin condition through his adolescence and this cream from a famous folk healer helped. Well, the solution is very old, but I'm sure natural remedies like this don't go bad. This soldier's approachable, so it's good to be on friendly terms with him. Who knows, one day we might need his help.

After I say goodbye, I go straight to the barn. The Steins are already consuming the milk soup from the two bowls we put aside for them.

"We must get going," I say. "Now, when only one soldier is on guard, is the best time to leave. We don't know when the others will return."

By the time I've taken them to the shack in the swamp and come back, it's late afternoon. Thankfully the good lady is as light as a feather, as the poor doctor had to carry her the whole way. I will make sure to visit them once a day with food.

Back in the barn, I exhale with relief when I notice the children taking their naps. "It looks like it's going to rain tonight, so I'd better head to the meadow for at least some of the hay," I say to my mother-in-law who holds rosary between her fingers, her eyes closed. "Can you make a barley soup, Mother? We should have all the ingredients for it."

She snaps her eyes open and stares at me with disbelief. "I will not leave this barn while the soldiers are still stationed here."

As stubborn as this woman is, I know there is no reasoning with her. "I can't do both."

"Even if it rains, the hay will dry later. You should stay here with us, to make sure the children are safe. Who knows what those Germans will decide to do?"

I sigh, knowing she's right, so I spend another hour preparing the soup and bringing it over to the barn. I even transferred a small amount of it to another pot and hide it in the barn, so I can bring it to the Steins later. Who knows what will happen tomorrow? I feel like I have been running from one place to another, all the while fearing the worst.

I manage to feed the animals and milk the cow before the soldiers next door come back. At least, at this point we don't need to worry about the Steins as they are safe in the swamp. They told me that they cleaned the attic making sure that even if the soldiers discover it, they will not realize that anyone was hiding in there.

Just when we hope to have a quiet evening, the wooden door of the barn swings wide open and two soldiers with rifles in their hands charge in.

"We need your hens," one of them barks. "Come outside." He nudges my arm with the weapon, so without further ego, I obey, telling my mother-in-law and the children to stay inside.

In the courtyard Erich walks back and forth with his hands behind his back near the chicken coop, his posture rigid and face cold. "How many hens do you have in there?" he asks when the soldiers prompt me toward him.

"Four," I say avoiding his gaze. It's hard to look into a face that looks just like Johann's, yet so different because of the harshness painted in every muscle.

He nods. "I want them all for our feast tonight. We deserve it after a whole day hard at work."

His words stun me. "All? But we need eggs—" I go silent because he takes out his pistol and cocks it.

"Do as I say, or you won't last another minute." His pale blue eyes rake mine of any sort of resistance. I must live for my children, and for Johann.

"Yes," I say obediently, washed out of any resilience, wondering how I will kill the poor birds. At just the thought of it, dread rolls through the pit of my stomach. I can't possibly ask my mother-in-law because it will only panic her, and she will do something foolish.

"I could use some help killing the hens," I say in a voice drained of any emotion.

He smirks. "Aren't you a village woman? You should know what to do."

"There are too many in here for me to handle all on my own," I say, keeping my demeanor calm. "Have your soldiers handle the killing and I will do the rest." It's not like it will be a big deal for them to cut the necks of the birds when they normally do the same to people.

His threatening eyes drill into my face making me feel a dropping sensation in my stomach.

# FORTY
## ANETA

June 1944—Aneta's village

Claus, the soldier with crusty face, says, "*Kommander*, should we bring other women from the village to help, so we can enjoy our feast faster?" There is this eagerness in his voice and posture. He's young and outspoken but with maniacs like Erich, it will only help him earn a bullet through his head.

Erich considers his orderly and curls his lips into sarcastic smile. "Fine. Go get the Polish sluts. Might as well get some use of them here."

The two soldiers bolt away while he remains in his rigid position across from me. "I remember you are the one trying to help the Jews." He points his finger at me, his eyes blazing. "My prodigal brother saved you."

I stare into the ground, wishing to run away from this intimidating man. I know what he's capable of and it scares me to death.

You don't strike me as a village woman," he says taking me in. "Those filthy rags don't do you justice. Besides, your

German is fluent, something so rare among the primitive villagers. Where did you learn it?"

Knowing I must answer him, I clear my throat and say, "I grew up in Danzig but married a farmer here."

He raises his brow making his scar look like a lightning bolt. "I lived in Danzig for many years but never met you there. What a beautiful city it's become now, so pure with our race." He seems to think hard at something. "Where's your husband?"

"He's dead."

"That's what happens to those who choose the wrong side. Just like my own brother. I remember him saying that you cooked for him. Have you seen him around lately?"

This conversation is so tiring to my frayed nerves but the fact that he expects answers, drains all energy out of me. Yet, I must be vigilant to stay alive and not provoke his short temper.

"No, officer, I haven't. I've been busy working fields and taking care of my farm, so I don't really pay attention to anything else."

"Well, I'm here because someone reported that my brother hides in those forests and helps those bandits in there." He chuckles, self-amusement written in his face. "Now I have orders to hunt him down like an animal."

I keep gazing down without showing any emotion. He might be saying this just to see my reaction.

"When we were little, I fell victim of a monster while my brother couldn't care less. Maybe I will at last get my long overdue justice."

So, he blames Johann for his uncle's actions. The raw truth that he plans to murder my Johann brings nausea to my stomach. This man has no lines.

"It's a pleasure talking with such a beautiful and cultured woman like yourself, but I find it rather disturbing that you avoid my gaze. Is there anything you find repulsive in my looks?" A dangerous hint of annoyance sounds through his words.

I look up. "I apologize, officer, I was just planning details in regard to preparing supper tonight for you." In reality, I just want to run away and never see him again.

He doesn't reply because the two soldiers arrive with Honorata, Jadwiga and Marysia.

"Get to work, women," Erich barks before walking away.

The women look panic-stricken, maybe except Honorata whose face is unreadable. "What does this *Szkop* want us to do?" she asks me.

"To kill all the hens and prepare a feast for them by eight o'clock tonight."

"Idiots," she says while smiling and winking at the two soldiers who watch us, knowing well they don't understand our language, especially that she uses the typical slang for the area, which I sometimes have trouble understanding.

"I've never killed a hen before," I admit, shyly.

None of the women laugh, they just look at me sympathetically.

"Bring the hatchet and I will take care of it, so we can go on preparing this feast for the bandits," Honorata says, pulling her sleeves up.

I exhale with relief and do as she says, then watch her cut the necks of all four birds, one after another, her face motionless.

I have this weighed-down feeling, but I help the women and by the eight o'clock, we get the meat fried on the stove. I manage to hide some pieces for the chicken soup I plan to make tomorrow.

When I'm back in the barn, everyone is asleep. I collapse on the hay right beside Janek, exhausted. Finally, some rest. I think of the poor hens and how we won't have eggs anymore. At the same time, I know we're fortunate to be still alive.

The following day, I make the chicken soup in the morning making sure it's enough for the whole day, maybe even the next. Then I hitch up the horse to a wooden wagon and pick up hay from meadows, since it didn't rain at night. I sneak into the swamp with food for the Steins who are doing fine, and in the evening, I take care of the farm. The same routine happens for another couple of days, when I try to find solace in everyday chores while watching over the children.

Most of the time, my mother-in-law just sits down and stares into one spot. I fail at convincing her that she must keep more active. She's closed herself to this world, her strained face folded into even deeper wrinkles, her small eyes seeping with sorrow.

On the third day, the German soldiers steal one of my pigs, but I can do nothing about it. They informed me that my duty is to feed the other two pigs well, so the meat is good quality. This time they didn't force me or other women to prepare the meat as one of the soldiers was a butcher before the war, and another one a chef in restaurant in Berlin. Claus told me all this one day during his guard duty while other soldiers were away. He also bragged that his skin has improved since he began using the cream. His face does look a little better.

I'm glad that my horse is old. Erich had already inspected and deemed my faithful mount as useless, which brought relief to me.

Erich and his soldiers keep sweeping the forest in search of partisans, but I know that he cares the most to find Johann.

I worry about him and Kostek. What if he does find them, indeed? It's hard to even think of it, so I pray that won't happen, especially now people in the village whisper more and more about Soviets getting closer. At the same time, there is this dreadful news about the Germans searching more and more forests through the entire region, but the partisans fight them bravely and organize skilled attacks, bringing hope into our hearts.

One evening, everyone in the village gets summoned to the grassy area near the pound where beaming Erich supervises his soldiers installing a thick, wooden pole into the ground. They drag a sturdy man in his forties and Erich announces to everyone that this "Polish bandit" will be punished in front of all of us. It's a lesson to all, a warning of what happens to the ones who go against them. Everyone is expected to watch until the man is dead. He orders me to translate his words into Polish.

When I'm done, my mouth feels so dry that I can't swallow. I'm glad that the soldier with a crusty face allowed me to leave the children in the barn, but my mother-in-law leans on me, staring ahead of her with the same glassy eyes. She must be in shock.

They tie the man's hands behind his back with chains attached to hooks and hang him by the wrists by pulling the chains up to a height that makes it impossible for him to touch his feet to the ground. The soldiers intensify his agony by rocking his body.

I can't look at his torment but whenever the soldiers notice someone turning his gaze away, they strike with rifles and bark at us.

When he loses consciousness, they pour a bucket of water on him and drop him to the ground. Erich snaps his pistol from his upholster and presses it to the back of man's head. "Do you regret your infidelity now?"

"Long live Poland," the man shouts right before the sound of the pistol rings out through the air, bringing metallic smell.

My mother-in-law whimpers but I press my hand to her lips. "Shush, Mother," I whisper, "or they will kill us too." My words make her close her eyes, but she stays silent.

I blink away my tears. How low Johann's brother has

stooped. I hope that after the war he will get justice and die in the same agony this brave man was put through.

The following days bring more terror, with constant executions of the captured partisans at the village square near the pond. And every time, he wants us, the villagers, to watch, while I must translate each word. I often find his amused eyes searching mine, as if expecting praise from me. It sickens me to the point that I struggle to breathe during those terrifying moments. It scares me like nothing else ever before.

# FORTY-ONE
## ANETA

July 1944—Aneta's village

"Sit down," Erich orders, pointing the chicken leg in his hand to the settee against the wall in the Ramniwskis' guest room. He continues chewing on the meat while sitting at the same table, Johann once invited me to have dinner. This man looks like he's enjoying the feast of his life with the stolen food from us villagers.

I obey and glue my gaze into the rugged floor. "How can I help, officer," I say after mustering my courage. This man terrifies me.

"I need you to translate something for me," he says, not taking his eyes off me for minutes that seem like hours.

His behavior is so awkward, but I pretend not to notice it by staring at my nails.

"How close were you with my brother? I do recall how adamant he was for me not to hurt you."

I make a surprised face like what he's saying is ridiculous. "How that could be? I'm only a Polish woman. I cooked for the officer once in a while, when his soldiers brought produce," I lie.

"His loss then." He smirks. "This fool can't even notice a beautiful woman right under his nose." For a moment longer his eyes seem darker, and I know that it's lust that flickers in them. "Your only fault is that you indeed belong to this pathetic nation, but I'm not a rule stickler. I do as I please and you will make a lovely mistress. I do find you cultured and attractive. Whenever you walk by me, you emanate pleasant scents unlike other village women who reek of sweat." He laughs with self-amusement. "And let me tell you, I'm damn starved for woman flesh in my bed. It's what happens in this forgotten pothole."

His rude remarks stun me, and bring fear to my heart because this man is unpredictable when comes to committing the worst crimes. I wish I was wearing a potato bag now and smell of something rotten because the fact that he finds me attractive is not flattering at all.

To my horror, he nears me and takes my chin between his fingers. "Gorgeous," he says smiling wide, a piece of chicken stuck between his teeth.

I feel nausea gripping my stomach and it takes a lot for me not to puke the sorrel soup that I had not long ago.

His face gets closer and closer.

I press my hand flirtatiously to his chest and smile lazily. "Can we toast with something stronger first?" I ask.

An amused smile clings to his lips but he nods and walks away.

While he pours liquid into two glasses, I fish out a small clove of garlic and chew on it. I was helping my mother in-law to peel it when a German soldier barged into the barn and dragged me out without a word. Not wanting to waste perfectly fine garlic, I hid it in my skirt's pocket. He strikes me as a pedant, so I suspect he would never kiss someone with that breath.

He walks back and handles one glass to me. I thank him and gulp it all in one sip, so he changes his mind about me being cultured. I must get him off my back at any cost. Then I exhale my garlicky breath.

He puts his hand on my cheek and caresses with his thumb. "With such rare beauty, I can even find pleasure in strong scents." He covers my mouth with his and aggressively works his lips against mine.

I feel paralyzed and nauseated as he forces his tongue inside my mouth. I don't respond to his urges but focus on surviving this disgusting act. I know that openly rejecting him would cost me my life.

"Don't be such a prude," he whispers. "I need some cooperation from you. Your touch makes me insane."

To my relief, there is a tap on the door. He swears under his breath but steps away.

I have this strong urge to wipe at my mouth but such a gesture on my side would be reckless. I just can't stand the lingering scent of him on me. His body might smell like lavender, but his mind, heart and soul are as ugly as loose piles of horse manure.

To my astonishment, Claus escorts Honorata's farm helper inside, the one who looked at me in the unsettling way when I visited them last. Why is he here? Did he get in trouble? I must try to help him.

The man bows at Erich with a servile expression while he still fails to notice me.

"What do you want, Polish dog?"

The man scratches his cheek in response which causes Erich to roll his eyes. Johann's brother turns his enraged gaze to me and barks, "Translate."

"The officer asks what you need, sir." I say in Polish to the man.

The man glances at me, then looks away. "This woman can't be translating this. She shouldn't even be here," he says looking intently at Erich who doesn't understand a word of Polish and glares at him with impatience.

The way the man opposes my presence is odd, but I keep a neutral expression waiting to see what happens next.

When the man stays silent, Erich walks toward him and grabs him by the collar. "I'm not going to waste my time on parasites like you, so you either say it or you will earn a bullet in your head," he says through his clenched teeth.

I translate his exact words, then I realize my mistake. If Honorata's helper is here to tell on her, it was wiser of me to omit the part with bullet, so maybe he would decide not to go ahead with his treachery. Now he's too scared not to tell him whatever he came with. I must be more cautious here.

"I will tell all," the man spits out and exhales with relief when Erich lets go of him and walks back to his chair.

The man turns my way and makes an ugly twist to his mouth. "This woman is hiding a Jewish child. The little girl was hiding with her family in the forests until this woman took her in and treats her like a Polish child. I know that family from Zwierzyniec."

The sound of my heartbeat trashing in my ears causes my pulse to race. What a pitiful scumbag! He's got to be the backstabber who reported the Ramniwski family. I should have listened to my gut...

I summon all my resolve to not show it on the outside because Erich's eyes pore over my face. In this very moment, there is only one thing that I must do to protect my family.

"This man says that your soldiers engage in crime by looting and stealing from the hardworking farmers in the village. He also says that if you don't stop them, he will go to Zwierzyniec to report you to your superiors," I falsely translate into German, while the foolish man stands with thrust-out chest, sure that I'm doomed.

Erich wipes at his mouth. "But he did say something about

Jews, I know the word 'Żyd'," he says with amusement in his voice.

"Oh, yes, he also stated that your soldiers should spend their time chasing the Jews in the forests instead of the pigs in our village," I say, for a moment acting like I'm at a loss of words, "I was rather hesitant to translate this insult to you, officer."

At first, Erich keeps moving his gaze from the man to me, making me feel like I'm going to suffocate on the tension of the moment. There is this malice hanging in the air but I'm not sure if it will be directed at the betrayer. Or was Erich smart enough to detect that my translations are untrue?

As for the man, I can sense from his shining eyes that he's sure I wouldn't dare try lying to the Germans. Idiot.

But Erich's furious eyes stop at the man. "How dare you telling us what to do, Polish bandit!" He slams his fist into the table, his nostrils flare, causing the *snake in the grass* to jump, and me to gasp. "Claus," he says through his clenched teeth, failing on controlling the rage that's now painted on his face, "take this filthy pig behind the barn and get the other bandit we caught yesterday." He pauses and releases a self-amused grin, before continuing, "Have them dig out a grave. We will teach them a lesson."

When Claus grabs the man, the rat screams, "You forgot to give me my reward." But when he's dragged not in a gentle manner, he yells this time at me, "I knew I couldn't trust you, bitch. Tell them the truth now or I will kill your brats."

I don't even glance his way, busy fixing my head covering. The fact that Erich didn't realize my little scam sends a soothing release of all tension. So ugly of me dooming this man but it was either him, or all of us. Especially as he would continue reporting on good people, just to get rewards from the Germans. Still, I feel terrible about what I had to do to save us.

Erich prompts me to follow him behind the barn where we

watch the two men dig a hole in the ground. A group of soldiers surround them shouting insults and laughing.

My heart breaks. When I was devising the lie, I made sure it wasn't anything terrible, but I guess I overdid it. I wish there was something I can do, so I try finding the courage to beg Erich to spare them. "Officer, please spare them. I'm sure they regret their sins. Besides, they can be useful to you."

"Useful to me they will be if I get rid of them." His laughter rings out and I feel like there are icicles forming around my heart. "Your habit of asking me to show mercy to those parasites is touching, my dear. First the Jews and now the arrogant villager and the bandit."

I know I shouldn't push because this time Johann will not save me from this maniac.

"Oh, don't be so sad, my mistress. I want to make you happy, so I will put them through a test. If they pass it, they will live. If they fail it, they will die."

Did he just call me a mistress? This is getting out of hand and that terrifies me. "What test?"

"Watch and you will find out soon." He winks, the arrogant smile never leaving his mouth.

When the men are done digging out the ditch, Erich orders his soldiers to force Honorata's helper inside it. Then he tells me to relay to the partisan that if he wants to stay alive, he must shovel dirt onto the man to bury him alive.

I blink away my tears and translate his words into Polish, avoiding the partisan's gaze. This is horrible.

But the man just shakes his head and refuses to obey, knowing full well that he just chose to die by taking his stand.

"Well, well," Erich says and chuckles. He barks at his soldiers to take the man out of the hole in the ground and throw the partisan inside it. Then, once more he tells me to relay to the traitor the same thing I did before to the other man.

Without delay, he picks up a shovel and begins to dump soil on the partisan.

Erich shoots me a satisfied glance. "You see, my mistress, how well my test works? The vermin always float to the surface." He takes his pistol out and shoots Honorata's helper straight in the heart.

Everything happens so fast that I feel dizzy and hopeless.

He turns to Claus and says, "Help the bandit come out of the grave and set him free."

# FORTY-TWO
## BRONKA

July 1944—Majdanek

I open my eyes and stare at wooden beams in the ceiling, confused about my surroundings. My mouth is painfully dry, and I would give everything for a drop of water. Hot and stuffy air burns my skin, or it feels like it. It's like there is no air here allowing me to take a breath, only the suffocating stench. No one comes. I try saying something but I'm not able to utter a sound.

I turn my head and watch the miserable, gaunt faces of other women who lie on wooden beds with poorly bedticks. Some have headscarf compresses on their heads, some moan absently, some yelp in pain.

I realize that I'm in the *hospital* in the fifth field. This is a place of suffering and inevitable death, and now I'm among the ones in agony.

"You're awake," the so familiar voice jerks me away from my thoughts. Krystyna leans and puts her hand on my forehead, a gentle smile tugs at her mouth.

I try to talk but I only make gurgling sounds.

"Let me get you some water, my friend. I will be back."

When she returns, she brings a tin cup to my lips.

I take a small sip and feel my throat and mouth slowly release the painful dryness. I take another sip and want to drink more and more, but she takes the cup away.

"Slowly, my friend. You must drink gradually throughout the day."

That afternoon she spoon-feeds me a watery soup with turnip. "I thought we would lose you. Today is the first day you're aware of your surroundings."

"I don't remember anything, only that I collapsed," I say. "How did I get here?"

"Eva let me take you in, and since then your body was fighting for life. The fact that you made it that far is a miracle. I had no medication to help you with, you fought it on your own. Now you just need to rest."

I touch her arm. "Thank you."

She sighs. "There isn't much of my doing. God has different plans for you."

"How long have I been here?"

"For almost a week."

"Have you seen Janina? How's she?"

Her face grows serious, overtaken by sudden sadness. "She was among the ones—"

She doesn't finish because a shouting in German makes her leap to her feet and charge away without another glance.

Minutes later, I see her walking among the beds and saying something in German to a man in Nazi uniform, a cap with scull on his head.

The man talks loudly but I can't understand a word. He points at some patients and leaves them alone while others are taken away by prisoners in striped clothing.

When they approach me, Krystyna says something to the man while he listens, his cold eyes on me. There are few more exchanges between them and the man's wrinkled face transforms into a curious one. Soon, he walks away, and no one comes to take me out.

The hope of surviving and seeing my son one day, renews within me.

That evening, I catch Krystyna's hand while she passes through. "You never told me what's with Janina." At this point, I'm convinced that she was executed, but there is also the spark of hope that I'm wrong. I want to be wrong so desperately.

She crouches before me. "Krystyna was taken out of the camp on one of those transports who knows where."

Her words make me swallow the painful lump that formed in my throat. "So, she's alive."

"I'm sure she is because she's a fighter like you."

The following days, I stay in the camp hospital gaining a little strength with each day but the news that comes to us isn't good at all. The transports are continuing, just like constant executions. We hear more of Germans dismantling barracks after the people who left or burning the camp's paper records. Crematoria work on full speed burning bodies of the dead. It's clear they want to cover up their atrocities before the Soviets come here.

I think of Władek, and if he is still alive. I wish I had that little dried violet flower he gave me, but I left it in my bed, and according to Krystyna, our barrack has already been dismantled.

We don't say it aloud, but we all expect the Germans to charge into this building too and shoot everyone in another attempt to eliminate proof of their crimes. This has already happened to many other hospitals, but Krystyna keeps reasoning that we are one of the last barracks and that we must have hope and that miracles do happen as I'm the solid proof of it.

On 22nd July, German guards force many people to march

in columns outside the camp. We spend that day awaiting the worse, jumping at every loud noise. I try not to hear the commotion outside, though today it's louder than any other day. There are still executions taking place while the Germans are fleeing.

It turns out, no one comes for us and two days later we hear Russian voices outside. The camp gets liberated.

We learn that Majdanek is the first German camp in this war being freed. I pray that soon other camps will be liberated as well and the lives that can still be saved will be saved.

The Soviets advanced so fast that the Germans had to run away so quickly they failed to destroy all the proves of their evil deeds. Now the world will learn of the hell they prepared here for us...

Before Krystyna leaves the next morning for home, we hug for a long time, while promising to write to each other. I thank her again for saving my life, for being there for me and my mother. Because of the good and strong women like her it was possible to survive the worst in this place.

I walk around the camp trying to find any familiar faces. Maybe Krystyna was wrong, and Janina is still here, but I can't find her or any other women who would know something.

"Bronka," Władek's voice makes me stop and turn. He's running toward me in the crowds of other prisoners. "You're alive," he says and brings me into his embrace. "I looked for you everywhere, but you weren't in your barrack. I thought..." He intensifies his hold on me.

"How good to see you, Władek. I was praying for you."

"When I realized that they were going to take our barrack for execution on the last day, I hid in the back of the latrines and waited." He sobs as he says it.

We stay hugging for a long time because there are no right words for all of this. Then, he takes my hand. "Come, I want to show you something."

He leads me to a crowd of other miserable looking men and

women like us in striped clothes who throw curses and spit at one of the SS guards that is tied up.

Władek pulls me closer and says, "He deserves your spit too, Bronka. For your father and brother."

The SS man's face is marked by pain, his eyes closed, every muscle tense.

I turn away from him. "I don't want this," I say through my tears." If not for Władek's support, I would collapse to the ground. "I want to be far from this place, please."

He doesn't say anything else but scoops me into his arms and walks out of the crowd. "I'm sorry. I will take you home." I detect a hint of sorrow in his quiet voice.

# FORTY-THREE
## ANETA

July 1944—Aneta's village

There is unusual commotion this morning among the German soldiers next door. It's like they're packing up instead of going for one of their excursions searching for Johann and the other partisans in the forest. This brings so much peace to me. It's been hard avoiding Erich for the last couple of days, since his sickly advances. I wasn't sure when he would make another move.

Honorata's brother told us yesterday that columns of Germans are fleeing west from Zamość. They are running away from the Soviets who keep advancing our way. I stopped by their barn yesterday to check on Ronia when her brother popped in for a short time. They still can't believe that their farm helper turned out to be a traitor.

According to her brother, the Resistance actively fights Germans, ready to back the Russians once they arrive here. Soon Hitler's forces will be out. That means that the Majdanek camp will be liberated too, and my friend will be free.

When I was there, I couldn't stop smiling at seven-month-old Ronia who was sitting with Adaś, Honorata's son, on the barn's floor covered with hay. These two are inseparable like twins.

On the way home as I navigate the dirt road through the village, a loud throat clearing makes me jerk my head to the side where Claus nods at me.

He looks around, then leaps my way. "We're leaving tonight. The word is that Soviets will be here any day now."

Heat radiates through my chest. Finally, we'll be free from them. This soldier is the only one that showed a sliver of humanity toward us. "Have a safe return home," I say and can't suppress a small smile.

"I would give everything to be back in my Bavaria, but who knows where fate will bring us next?" He beams. "But when I'm back at last, my family will not recognize me. The cream you gifted to me has done wonders."

I nod. "How old are you?"

"I will be nineteen in November."

"Well, you have your whole life before you."

As I continue walking, I think of our boys murdered by the Germans. They were stripped of their lives, like the boy that Johann signaled to execute in Zwierzyniec. A shard of pain pierces my heart while I remind myself that his hand was forced.

As I'm done with my evening chores, the soldiers stubbornly remain next door. It doesn't look like they are in a rush to leave. Not knowing when they are going to depart, I decide to take a risk and sneak out to visit the Steins with some food around eight o'clock. I haven't been there since yesterday morning, so I worry about them.

When I'm sure that the children are comfortably settled for the night on the hay, I exit via the barn's back door and waddle through the orchard and meadow, then forests until I reach the swamp area. The whole time I look in all directions making sure that no one can see me.

I navigate the wooded area around the swamp populated with slender and soaring black alder and downy birch, while listening to the lovely sounds of birds singing, insects chirping and frogs croaking. I feel so good here, far away from the danger of war, from malicious people. But my children are there right under the noses of the Germans, so I must go back immediately.

When I near the shack, I'm startled by a whistling sound from between Norway spruce and Scots pine trees. It must be one of the birds, surely, no human would be brave enough to come into this marshy area, unless someone knows it well.

I remain still, listening for more, but what I hear next has me almost tumbling.

"Aneta, it's me," his whisper echoes.

Delighted to see him, I run into his embrace, feeling at peace again. His touch electrifies not only my mind but every fiber in my body. I don't want him to let go of me. "It's you," I whisper into his ear, giving in to his closeness. The warmth of his skin and the so familiar woodsy scent mingle, having a tantalizing effect on my senses.

Just being in his arms brings such happiness to me but when our mouths entangle in a raw kiss, our hearts beat in the same rhythm. Suddenly, it strikes me that it's never been about only physicality with him. He is rooted deeply in my soul and the physical attraction between us is like cream on the cake. Our love reaches beyond our bodies.

"Erich's unit is stationed next door. I left the children in the barn, so I must go back soon."

"I know," he says through clenched teeth. "I've been checking on you though you couldn't see me. Leave the food for the Steins and I will walk you back," he says. "At least to the creek."

"You know they're here?"

"I've visited them a few times. They told me that you should be coming tonight. I wanted to see you before tomorrow."

"What's tomorrow?" The feeling of dread rolls through me.

"We're planning an ambush on retreating Nazi troops near Zwierzyniec. We're nearing the final days of war here in the Zamość area. Soon this land will be free from occupation. I'm ashamed that once I was one of the Nazis."

I caress his cheek. "You never truly were."

"Look at those love birds," a malicious voice says disturbing our moment together.

Erich snarls, while he aims his pistol at us. "When I saw you heading for the forests, I was curious enough to follow." He motions to Johann, "And that's when I saw you, brother. You both make a clumsy couple." He releases a derisive laugh. "I have to admit that I enjoy cooking two bunnies in one bonfire though."

"Stop, Erich. Put your pistol down and let's leave in peace. We're family." Johann's voice is quiet as if filled with hope.

Erich spits on the ground. "No way, brother. I dreamed of this moment for so long and you aren't going to ruin it."

"We're brothers."

"I don't care, damn it! To me you're just a traitor, nothing more. You betrayed me and the Führer."

"No, I refused to murder innocent people." Johann still holds my hand in his, bringing strength to me in this dreadful moment.

"You're just a coward. But you know why I couldn't wait to finally send a bullet through your rotten brain?"

Johann only sighs. I sense that he's sad, not angry at his brother but sad.

"You turned a blind eye when that monster used me and stole my sanity. Do you want to hear what exactly he did to me?"

Johann's chin trembles. "I didn't know because you never said anything, until you told Mutti about it. I swear I had no idea," he says in a tearful, breaking voice.

"I don't believe you. You only cared for yourself and to stay innocent, perfect Johann with the highest school grades while I was the outcast."

"You know I was always there for you. It was your decision to reject me, Erich. You hurt and kill innocent people. There is no excuse for that, no trauma from childhood can excuse it. It's sick!"

"I don't regret anything I've done," Erich says, turning his scowl to me. "After I burn this village and kill those damn Poles, I'm heading for Warsaw to continue the fight. The Soviets will not take it away from me."

"What?" I gasp.

A hard little laugh escapes him. "You don't need to worry about it, mistress. I already ordered my soldiers to do it at midnight, right before we depart. Your lover will be dead long before that."

Fear wraps around my heart, making me dizzy. I'm overwhelmed by the need to go back to my children and take them away from danger.

"Enough, Erich, she has done you no harm. Let her go and spare the village people."

In response he cocks his pistol. "Say goodbye to her. I can offer you that much as our farewell, but I can assure you I will keep her alive if she pleases me enough. Though you, my so-called brother, maybe soon will be running through green meadows with our parents." He smirks. "Though, I doubt there is anything more beyond this pothole."

I can feel Johann's body straightening as if he's about to lash out at him. My mind is whirling and the reality that my children will be burned alive in that barn breaks me.

"For the memory of our parents, don't do it, brother. I love you," Johann says through his clenched teeth. I can see that it costs him everything not to explode and jump forward but he's still trying to stop him without any of us being hurt.

"You can shove that love of yours up your arse. It's worth nothing, it's just a meaningless word. You think our parents loved us? No, brother, they never did. We were just an addition to a perfect-looking German family."

"Please, it's not too late. Put the pistol away and let's part in peace."

"Too late for that." He lifts his gun and squints while his lips curl into a snake snarl.

Johann lets go of my hand and charges at his brother, yelling at me to get down, but I feel frozen in place. Everything is hazy, my entire insides are on fire.

The distance between them is not so close, so only seconds later, before he's only halfway toward Erich, a shotgun splits the air.

# FORTY-FOUR
## ANETA

July 1944—Aneta's village

Johann isn't the one crumpling down. It's Erich who drops to the ground.

Dr. Stein stands with a small revolver in his shaking hand having sent a bullet through the back of Erich's head.

Johann kneels beside him and whispers in broken voice, "Brother."

There is no answer and when I near them, Erich's empty eyes stare into nothingness. His gaze was always dark and empty when he was alive and now, it remains the same, as if his soul was already dead when he lived. Maybe it happened that day when his uncle hurt him. So sad.

I gently pat Johann's back. "I'm sorry, darling. He was your brother, despite all."

Dr. Stein checks Erich's pulse and shakes his head. "He was going to kill you both."

"You don't need to explain, Doctor. You saved our lives," Johann says, then he pulls me into a hug. The way he holds me and the way he touches me, say all. He needs my comfort. My heart goes out to him.

A moment later he says, "I must put on Erich's uniform and pretend to be him."

This idea repulses me. "You can't."

"I must. He already gave the order to burn the village at midnight."

My legs are weak. "The children."

"I will go back as Erich and change his order. Then I will lead his unit out of your village to Zwierzyniec. It's where I run away from them and go back to the partisans."

"What if someone realizes you aren't him? You don't have the scar he has."

"We must take the risk. It's the only way. If Erich doesn't return now, they will start looking for him, and most of all, they will fulfill his order before their departure. Have you heard any names of his soldiers?"

"The one with the crusty chin that stands on guard is Claus and another one, tall and skinny and with hooked nose, is Bruno. That's all I know."

He rubs my chin. "I will be fine, darling. I love you."

I look up into his eyes, feeling like we both are swimming into an ocean of raw emotions. "I love you, too." I press my face to his chest and sob.

When Johann begins to pull the uniform from Erich's corpse, I turn around and realize that Mrs. Stein is outside too. They look at us with kindness, like loving grandparents would, and soon Dr. Stein helps Johann with the uniform.

Before parting at the creek, I say to my beloved, "Please, promise you will come back to me." I don't care to suppress my tears or sound like a schoolgirl. This is my heart and soul talking.

He takes my face between his hands. "I promise, my love, I will do everything to come back to you."

"I will be waiting."

His eyes glisten with unshed tears. "I will come back, even if it takes an eternity, but I will come back to you, my love." Our foreheads touch and his lips find mine, for the last time as if sealing the promise, before walking away.

# FORTY-FIVE
## ANETA

August 1944—Aneta's village

On 24th July, the Zamość region was officially liberated from the German occupation. The arriving troops of the Soviets were backed by the local partisans. It's hard to believe we are free, especially considering most of Poland is still under the German occupation. On the first day of August, the Polish Resistance started the Warsaw Uprising.

In the meantime, I've heard nothing from Johann. Was he able to fulfill his plan and leave the German squad when they went to Zwierzyniec? Thanks to him we're still alive and our village was spared from burning. I watched him leading the unit out, looking exactly like his brother. But I knew it was my Johann, the man with a good heart and sensitive soul.

There is more and more news of drunk Soviet soldiers looting and hurting women. Thankfully, they haven't come to us so far, maybe because it's out of their way and within forests.

I can't help but think that if Johann didn't remember the name of my village from when my sister told him, he would've never come here, and neither would his brother. They would be probably stationed in some of the other villages with better access to main roads and the town, from where Erich would be organizing his searches for partisans in the forests.

I don't want to even think of not meeting Johann again and learning the truth about him. His love is like the tinkling of a chime on a windy day. Its harmonious sound defines every fiber of my being while the wind of our lives continues. I pray he's back to us soon.

The morning after the Germans left our village, we moved back to the cottage. My mother-in-law is slowly returning to her normal self and criticizing my every decision. Well, at least I know she is fine, and her detachment from the world was only temporary and caused by fear. I always knew that once the war ended, I would move out, but with almost the entire country still under German occupation, I must stay here for now.

I shake off my thoughts and resume my task of throwing sheaves of rye onto the horse-driven wagon trying to fit them tightly, so I can fit as many as possible before bringing it to the barn. I've just started with this round, but earlier today I brought in three wagons.

I turn to pick up another bundle of dry rye when I notice two human figures on the road heading toward the village. They look like skeletons. When they near us and their striped clothes choke my attention away, my knees feel weak.

I drop the sheaf of rye and dart toward them, stopping only when I have them right before me. And after catching my breath, I'm unable to suppress my tears when focusing on the gaunt woman in the camp dress with white headscarf, soiled with dirt. Her skin is dry and flaky and if I was to describe her with only one word, I would use the word "frail". Not sickly or poorly but frail.

Only her eyes, now so sad, have the same shades of grayish blue. "Bronka," I whisper, suddenly forgetting the world around us, "you're back."

She sobs and we leap into each other's embrace, both crying.

In this very moment, it feels as if I'm holding the entire world in my arms. Still, I'm afraid that it's just one of my dreams and I'll wake up realizing she is not here.

"You're back, my beautiful friend," I whisper again unable to control emotion poring on me like a waterfall.

I realize that the man accompanying Bronka is Zygmunt's brother. He's also skin-and-bones, his head shaved, his skin ill-looking.

I put my arms around him. "Good to see you, Władek. Mother has been waiting for you." My throat is so constricted that I can't utter another word.

He clears his throat. "Good to see you too, sister." His mouth folds into the shy smile, one that defined him so well in the past. He always called me sister, since the day I arrived from Gdańsk. He strokes my hair, his tears more powerful than any words. I think of the past and realize with emotion that he never failed to treat me with kindness, and now, in this raw moment, I feel it so strongly. It's incredible that after what he had gone through, his heart is still filled with compassion and softness.

I wipe my tears for the hundredth time today and say, "Please, settle on the wagon as I only managed to put a few sheaves of rye on it. You will be comfortable."

Władek helps Bronka by supporting her with his hand while she scrambles up the wagon. He seems still so strong despite his gauntness and the exhaustion in his face. The tender and protective way he looks at her is not missed on me.

I'm so glad to have my friend back with me. I only hope I can have Johann back too. When we're all on, I turn to her and say, "Janina?"

Her eyes tell me all even before the words sound out. "She was sent away before the Soviets came." Her voice breaks, just like my heart.

# FORTY-SIX
## BRONKA

August 1944—Aneta's village

There were so many moments in the camp when I doubted seeing Aneta ever again. So now when she's so close to me on this wagon, I can't stop crying.

Władek takes my hand in his. I don't move it away but gently squeeze his. We went through so much together, so having him now beside me in this bittersweet moment feels peaceful.

When we arrive at their courtyard, a small black dog runs to us and cheerfully barks while his tail is wiggling. What a huge difference from the trained dogs in the camp.

"It's okay, Szarik, "Aneta says and laughs. "You know that someone special is here."

As we climb down the wagon, the door to the hut opens and Władek's mother runs out wearing a grayish apron. She brings her hands to her face as if not believing her own eyes, then she cries out and kisses her son. She hugs him for a long time. A wide pallet of emotions lingers in the air, and for a moment I feel like I'm intruding on their special moment.

But when two boys and a girl come outside, everything stops. I know that the taller one is Janek, Aneta's son, but the little scrab who's holding his hand is mine. His eyes betray it. Roman's eyes look at me from the precious face of our son. My heart melts and I try to swallow the lump that is stuck in my throat.

Aneta takes his hand and says pointing at me, "This is your mama."

"Jordanek," I whisper and spread my hands to him, but he only buries his face into my friend's skirt.

The realization that for him I'm just a strange woman hits me with the force of thunder. He was only four weeks when I had to give him away to save his life. He can't remember me.

Aneta puts her arm around me. "Don't get discouraged," she whispers. "He only knows you from that wedding picture that I have of you. Give him some time."

"That's right," I say, tears clouding my vision. "I looked quite different back then." I chuckle like it's a pathetic joke. In truth, I shouldn't be surprised about his reaction toward me. Everything went so fast since we were liberated that the only thing I thought of or yearned for was to come here and hold my baby in my arms. But Aneta is right, and I don't want to scare him away. After all, I'm just a poorly-looking woman, while in that wedding picture I appear happy and vibrant, with long hair and healthy skin. I will never be that woman ever again. She's dead, replaced by the broken version of me.

"Janek got so much bigger," I say trying to sound light-hearted while changing the painful subject. Soon we're introduced to the little girl whose name is Hania and who smiles adorably at us.

"Let's get in and have a bite," Aneta says, still holding me like she's afraid that I could faint.

"If you don't mind, I would rather clean myself first and get rid of my clothes," I say and avoid her gaze, ashamed of my condition. "I don't want to bring lice and fleas to your home."

"Bronka is right," Władek says and walks over to us. "We should bathe outside and burn those rags she calls clothes."

Aneta nods. "Of course, I will fill the metal tub, and you can wash yourself in private, behind the shed." Both women get busy warming the water and Władek helps them.

I want to help too but I lack the strength right now. The children return to the cottage, so I sit alone on the bench against the hut's front wall. It's incredible that she managed to keep them all safe through the war.

When the bath is ready, Władek encourages me to go first.

The space between the sheds is secluded, and no one can see me, so I undress and step into the tub with warm water. It feels so calming but at the same time surreal to be taking a wash like this instead of the cold showers when we'd always fret that they would release killing gas instead of water.

I shiver but chase away the thoughts of the camp, not wanting to ruin this moment. I pick up a pine tart soap bar that Aneta left on the side and scrub my skin and my entire body not caring for self-inflicted pain. It's been more than a year since I was able to truly wash myself.

When I'm done, I put on clean undergarments and a brown dress that my friend left for me. It fits me like a hanger but it's clean, and that's what matters right now. I call her over, afraid she wouldn't hear me as my mouth is still so dry, even after having a glass of water I still have trouble making loud sounds.

She appears and takes me in. "Beautiful," she says and hugs me.

"I'm like a skeleton," I say. "Even your tiny dress is too big for me."

She takes my face between her hands. "You're wrong. You're beautiful in and out and it shines through you. You managed to survive impossible because of your incredible strength." She touches my cheek. "Your hair will grow and skin shine, you will slowly gain weight. It will all return to you."

"Thank you," I say. "You know, it's what gave us the biggest strength in the camp: knowing that someone kind was near. We gave that to each other and it's why they couldn't break us so easily. And now I have you here in this fragile moment of gaining back my life."

"I'm here whenever you need me, my friend."

Her words remind me that we've felt that special bond between us from the moment we first met. We've become soul sisters, and that hasn't changed despite the harshness of war.

"I feel awkward without the head covering," I say. I guess the only good thing about it is that I don't have to worry about lice which would be impossible to eliminate if I still had my long hair.

She doesn't look at me with astonishment or question my words, but only says before walking away, "Let me grab you one and I will be back."

She soon returns with a beige scarf, and I feel so much better when coming out. I didn't lose my hair due to sickness; it was shaved by the orders of my oppressors. It was inflicted upon me just like the number I received in place of my name. So, I don't want people to see it, I don't want my son to see his mother like this. That little scarf brings me a sliver of security for now when comes to my vulnerability.

An hour later, we all gather at a long dining table. Wladek's mother serves beet soup, and a rye brea. Its savory flavor of sweetness mixed with sourness is delicious, so unlike the slop in the camp that was not edible.

We all keep quiet, only the sounds of our spoons hitting dishes and Wladek's occasional coughs breaking the silence. I'm relieved that they don't ask about the camp. While I keep forgetting myself and comparing how things are here and there, I don't want to talk about it.

"We must not eat too much right away," I say to Władek who sits beside me. "Our stomachs must get used to normalcy."

He nods but his mother is the one that speaks. "Yes, you must be careful." She eyes her son whose hand is shaking as he brings a spoon to his mouth. Mine is as well.

"I will go to Zwierzyniec to get Dr. Stein tomorrow," Aneta says. "He will do a medical check on all of you to see what you would benefit from the most, especially Władek's cough."

"No need," Władek says slowly. "It's just a cough. It will go away with rest and good food." The moment he utters the last word, a round of coughing comes.

His mom shakes her head and strains her deep wrinkles even more. "No, Władziu, Aneta is right. The doctor should listen to your lungs and check, just to make sure. He owes us that much for saving his life." She smirks.

"Stop, Mother," Aneta says treating the lady to a warning look. Some things still haven't changed...

I can't take my eyes off my little son who sits on Aneta's lap while she feeds him the soup. All I yearn for right now is to hold him in my arms, but I must be patient, not scare him away.

"Janek, I heard that you helped take care of Hania and Jordanek," I say and smile.

He returns my smile. "I only play with them and teach them talking. You know, Jordanek likes to play wooden soldiers the most and Hania brings her doll everywhere."

It turns out that I get to sleep in the guest room with my son, though my sunshine falls asleep on a separate bed. I can see that he gets more used to my presence and is curious about me.

The next morning, I notice Aneta anxiously glancing at the door every few minutes, as if she's hoping for someone to turn up. Who's she waiting for?

She wraps a block of white cheese between linen cloth and says, "I'm heading to visit Janina's daughter before going back to the fields. Would you like to join me?"

"I would love to see that little girl," I say quietly.

We walk through the village in silence. Dogs bark, people go about their chores, children play... The world goes on despite the tragedy of Majdanek where so many lost their lives, despite all the burned villages with their dead. The sun is shining as if nothing bad has happened in this world. I'm walking the village road, just like I had many times before the war, but back then my heart was young, before it got broken into a million pieces by losses.

When we turn into a small courtyard, a sturdy woman with a round face perches on a bench and smiles at two children playing with wood blocks on a grass. I recognize Honorata right away. She was always jealous of Aneta, so it's hard to believe that she's the one caring for Ronia.

"Good day, Honorata," my friend says and takes out the white cheese, "I brought some *twaróg*. Our cow gave birth to a healthy calf and now we have plenty of colostrum, and plenty of white cheese." She winks at the woman.

"You're so kind to share." She smiles and takes the small bundle but glances at me. "Good day, Bronka. Long time no see."

I detect no pity in her eyes, only careful softness. She has changed too. "Good day, Honorata."

"You came to see Ronia but without her mother." She says it more like a statement than a question.

"Janina was sent out the camp before its liberation," I say mechanically, like the words don't intensify my pain every time I utter them.

She nods, sadness runs over her face, then she turns to the children and picks up a little girl in a yellow outfit. "This is our precious Ronia." The boy cries, so Aneta swoops him into her embrace and he releases contagious laughter.

Janina's daughter is acting shy, hiding her face in Honorata's arm. Emotion constricts my throat as I admire this gorgeous baby. When I saw her last, she was slowly dying in that camp and now she's perfectly healthy and thriving.

I swallow a lump in my throat and say, "She's beautiful, just like her mama."

"I wish I had a picture of her mother to show her," Honorata says.

"I pray she will be back soon, so they can reunite."

"It's all God's will. I didn't want people to talk, so I baptized her with my son. But now it doesn't matter because *Szkopy* are finally out of here."

"You did good. Thank you for saving her life."

For a moment longer she says nothing, then hands the baby to me.

Ronia doesn't protest but giggles and touches my face. I hug her so close to my heart, unable to stop my tears from coming, tears of happiness that Janina's daughter is doing so well. She smells of milk and potato flour, at the same time sweet and subtle. Holding her brings so much calmness to me.

"She can stay here until her mother is back," Honorata says, her voice quiet. "I still nurse both of them and I treat her like my own."

"Yes, that would be best, at least until I gain my strength and move back to my parents' home and get settled with everything."

"Of course." The tension in the air that has been there since our arrival has disappeared.

"Thank you, Honorata, you're a good woman."

On the way back Aneta takes my arm as we navigate the road and says, "I hope that she will not cause trouble when the time comes to give Ronia back to her mother."

"It's like you would speak my own worries." I sigh. "She saved her life, and that's what matters right now."

"True, if not for her, I don't want to even think what would've happened."

I stop walking and look into my friend's green eyes. "I worry that she will not come back. She was already so weak when I saw her last, before I got sick." I wipe my tears away. "I hope she finds strength in her to fight for that little girl."

Her eyebrows draw together, and her steady eye contact is comforting. "We will pray for her. One must have hope in this world of wolves."

"She had this habit of reminding me every morning that I need not overthink but leave room for hope. I think it's what made me stronger."

"I can see that she's a remarkable woman."

"She truly is. We supported each other and that kept us going through a nightmare." We resume walking and I get this sudden need to tell her more. To tell someone how it was in there, only once, and never again. "It was a death camp."

She squeezes my arm. "You don't have to talk about it, I know it's painful."

"I want to one time because I want you to understand me and why I could never be that Bronka from before the war."

"I think I already understand," she says, sadness lingering on her words.

"You would have to be there to truly understand. One day, they ordered us to stay in barracks, they didn't even do the morning roll call to count all of us. We were told that anyone daring to look through the window would be shot. All day they played this cheerful music through loudspeakers, because they wanted to drown out the sound of shooting. But we heard it anyway. It went on through the whole day: the constant shooting accompanied by loud music."

"This is so terrible," she whispers.

"You know that they ironically called it as the *Harvest Festival*? Janina would have been dragged out and shot with the others if the night earlier we hadn't switched her camp number with that of the woman who shared my bunk bed and died of a broken heart."

She's blinking rapidly as if trying to process what I just told her, then she covers her mouth with her palm. "I don't know what to say."

We stand in the middle of the road, and by now I'm having trouble breathing. "Saying this aloud is draining. I don't know if I can continue."

"You must rest and be kind to yourself," she says. "I'm here for you."

"The irony is that when I saw one of the worst henchmen a day after the liberation of the camp, I found no strength in me to show him any cruelty. He was among the SS men who couldn't flee before Soviets arrived. People threw insults and spat at him. He just sat hunched over, his face showed only fear, nothing else but this haunting fear for his life. Was there any remorse in him, I don't know but I couldn't bring myself to spit on him. I just wanted to leave and never see him again. Nothing can bring my brother and my parents back."

"I'm proud of you for not stooping to the level of this troubled man with his lost soul. I'm sure he will get his punishment, and if not here, it's all in God's hands." She puts her hand on my back and brings me to a hug.

For a moment longer we stay in an embrace, then I say, "People say that time brings healing, but I don't believe it. It only gives us room to learn to live with that pain and emptiness. I would give everything to bring my loving husband back, to share another tea with my parents, to roll my eyes at my brother's silly joke. I would give my own life for them to be back here, but that's not possible. There is nothing I could give up for them to return. The wounds will never heal; they will bleed again and again, but that's okay because I would not want any different. It's the price of loving someone who left. That pain can only be mourned alone."

"You're right but as time will go on, those wounds don't have to define you. You must go on with your life and appreciate every moment with your son. Don't close yourself completely to connections with others."

Over the following days, I take Aneta's advice to heart and focus on resting. Not only does my body need it, but also my mind. We don't talk about my past anymore. I resolve not to ever speak of it to anyone. It causes unbearable pain in my heart and bleeds the unhealed wounds even more.

Then one evening I find her crying at the creek. She tells me all about her Johann and that he tried to get me out of the camp. I hope with my whole heart that her beloved will return to her. She deserves to be happy, this remarkable woman. If not for her, our children wouldn't have survived, the Steins wouldn't have survived...

On the fourth day, at nighttime, Jordanek falls asleep in my arms. This is so unexpected and sudden that I find it impossible to believe it. Having him in my arms while listening to his rhythmic breathing and healthy heartbeat, is the ultimate happiness for me. He's the reason why I'm still alive, the source of my strength. My everything.

# FORTY-SEVEN
## ANETA

September 1944—Aneta's village

As weeks go by, Bronka takes her time to rest, slowly regaining her strength, but she also cherishes every moment with her son. Władek started helping on the farm despite us telling him that he should take an easy for some time. He just doesn't know how to rest, finding solitude in farm chores.

Dr. Stein visited us and left medication for him and prescribed plenty of rest and good nourishment. But my mother-in-law is focusing her entire energy and effort on taking care of him. Dr. Stein and his wife are back to their old home in Zwierzyniec that during the war was occupied by a German officer.

There isn't a minute in the day when I don't think of my Johann. I haven't heard from him since that day when Erich died, and he took his place. I keep waiting for his return, believing that he's alive and just can't come to me now. Kostek has been trying to help me find out something about his whereabouts as he thinks that Johann was imprisoned by the Soviets.

He came back last week from the forests, and it's when I told him what Johann had to do to save our village.

"Warsaw is still fighting," Władek says one day at the dinner table. "Though I heard that the Soviets are just waiting on the other side of Vistula, not helping with the Uprising."

"Why would they be so deceitful if they helped to free our region from German occupation?" I ask. Our area is one of the first parts of Poland to be liberated from Germans. I believe it's only a matter of time before the rest of the country will be free as well, so Władek's words make no sense.

"We shouldn't be surprised," Kostek says between another spoon of *krupnik*, barley soup. "Look what's happening here. Communists, who're Stalin's puppets, are already spreading their propaganda and fighting for power. They've announced through the radio from Moscow about their establishment of the new government, denying our government in-exile in London the right to act on behalf of us, Poles. They go on with their activities in the liberated territories, of course under the protective wings of the NKVD. They even organized the entry into Lublin for the General Berling's army, just to turn our hearts toward their Stalin driven government." His nostrils flare now, but I can sense that he isn't done yet.

"They are organizing their Security Offices structures and along with the Soviet formations, they begin to destroy us, the fighters of the Home Army and the Polish Resistance," he continues. "There are already arrests, internments and deportations, and it's only going to get worse, to the point when they'll murder us."

Władek sighs. "The fact that they abolished the Zamość Ordinance under their so-called decree on land reform is disgusting. They parceled out the entire property leaving Count Zamoyski and his family with nothing. Basically, they confiscated everything from them. They even ordered their immediate leave not allowing them to stay here."

My heart breaks at this terrible news. Countess Róża is the sweetest lady, and she doesn't deserve this. She helped so many people, especially children, during the war.

"This is not right," Bronka says, her face even sadder now. "If not for Countess Róża, my son wouldn't be alive now, and so many other children."

"I never trusted communists," Władek says. "Our fatherland will never be fully free under their power. Like Kostek said, now we will be at the mercy of Stalin."

"It's why they don't want to help with the Uprising in Warsaw," Kostek says, his lips pursed, then he adds, "They're waiting for the Germans to kill all of ours and then they will triumphantly enter the city declaring their power. It's why so many of our boys stayed in the forests and are set on fighting for the free Poland, free from not only Germans but also Soviets."

No one responds and we all seem to drift into our own thoughts.

"I would like to thank you for the hospitality here." Bronka's quiet voice breaks the silence. "I realize that I've been taking advantage of you by staying here so long, so it's time I move with Jordanek to my parent's cottage."

"You can't," I say, surprised by her declaration. We went there the other day, and the house and other outbuildings are in decent condition but it's so empty there. "It's too dangerous to be there on your own now."

"She will be fine," my mother-in-law says. "Our hut is too small to fit everyone like this and it takes a lot of work to feed that many mouths."

Władek bangs his fist into the table causing dishes to clutter. "Enough, Mother. There will always be room here for Bronka and her son. Besides, Aneta is right that it's too dangerous in today's times for a woman to live on her own." This is a new side to him as before the war he never contradicted his mother or father and always stayed away from confrontations, kind of in Zygmunt's shadow. I'm so proud of him for speaking his mind and standing up for Bronka.

His mother gasps at him, the piece of bread in her hand forgotten.

He moves his gaze to Bronka. "It's not safe with the Soviet soldiers around, and after a year of no one living there, there is no cattle and no crops on the fields. It's not a good place for you right now. You must stay here with us until it's safer."

The way he speaks to her is gentle and respectful. I've noticed for the last couple of weeks the tender way he looks at her, but at the same time, he keeps the right distance. He understands that they both need time to get back into normalcy, though it's obvious that he feels something more for her than just friendship.

"Thank you, but it's not fair for me to overextend your kindness," she says and glances at my mother-in-law.

"We want you here." I purposely use the word "we" to give the opportunity for my mother-in-law to smooth things out. I know her so well after all these years spent under the same roof.

She takes the chance because she says, "Please forgive me, daughter, I was blinded to the fact how dangerous is still up there. Yes, you should stay."

"Thank you. In this situation I will make sure to help in the kitchen and fields, whatever you need me to. It's the least I can do," Bronka says and treats Władek to a warm smile.

His eyes shine with adoration as he returns her smile.

After dinner, I help cleaning while letting my thoughts take over. It happens a lot when I get distracted thinking of Johann. When will he finally come back to me? What's stopping him now when the Nazis are gone? Maybe he's hiding from the Soviets, just like so many partisans in the forests. Still, it's not like him not to let me know he's fine.

"Aneta, I need to talk to you," Kostek says pulling me away

from my thoughts. "I met with my friend today and learned something you need to know."

I wipe my hands with a kitchen towel. "Of course, let's step outside."

"When the Soviets attacked a German squad near Zwierzyniec, they took into custody their captain, and I think it was Johann."

I gasp. "So he's been under the arrest of Soviets, and we knew nothing of it." Conflicting emotions run through my heart. I'm relieved that he's alive but I worry so much about him. How are they treating him there? Soviets have no mercy for Germans, not after what happened in Stalingrad when so many died.

"You told me that he took Erich's place, so things line up here. The fact that he's gone without a word, now makes sense."

Panic sends adrenaline through my system. "What do we do?" I ask, feeling like I'm going to choke.

"We need to go to their post in Zwierzyniec and try to find out something. Maybe even try speaking to someone in charge to explain that Johann isn't Erich. It doesn't matter what he told them; there is no chance they would believe him. We need to pray that they would believe us though. I don't know if there is anything else we could do at this point."

"If he's even still there." The whole time I was hoping that he was with the partisans in the forests. How naïve of me.

"But if he is, and Soviets wouldn't believe us, I will see if our boys can organize an action to free him."

"Anything could have happened since the end of July," I say and put my hands over my face. "It's best that I go there by myself tomorrow. You don't need to bring their attention on you since you fought with the partisans for so long."

# FORTY-EIGHT
## ANETA

September 1944—Zwierzyniec

The next day I ride a bike to the town and after I explain that I'm there to report something extremely important, I'm soon being seen by a man in Soviet uniform, red bags under his eyes.

I sit in front of his desk while he scribbles something down and says, "How can we help you?" He smiles, revealing a gold tooth.

I summon all my courage and say, "I'm here because the wrong German soldier was arrested."

The pen freezes in his hand as he scrutinizes me. "That's interesting." His face features tighten. "And you were romantically involved with one of those criminals?"

I feel heat storming into my cheeks, but I embrace myself for calmness and say, "I would rather die," I look him straight in the eye, "than have anything to do with one of them."

His bushy eyebrows lift. "So according to you, we've arrested the wrong man?"

I bite on my bottom lip. His demeanor makes me uncomfortable, which intensifies when a tall officer with stern face walks in and pauses in front of the man who interviews me, his hands folded at his back.

The man with the gold tooth charges to his feet and salutes in Russian.

"I need the report from yesterday's interrogations," the tall officer says.

"Yes, Mayor Sokolov, it's right here." His servile tone of voice disgusts me.

"Very well then." The other man glances my way, "Please continue."

My interviewer drops to his chair and motions for me to go on.

I rub my hands down my skirt legs. "Yes, the man that you look for is dead, so the one that you have in custody is his identical twin and he's innocent."

The man rolls his eyes and sighs. "Well, let's start from the beginning." After grabbing the pen, he scribbles down something, then says. "Family name."

"Cietliwska," I say my maiden name, hoping it's safer this way. Nothing is going the way I hoped, and I have this feeling that he has already decided not to treat me seriously. He's probably deciding now if to arrest me.

"Given name," he prompts without looking from his paper.

When I was coming here, I was glad that I understand and speak Russian but now I'm not so sure it's to my advantage. By putting down my name, he probably adds me to their list of victims.

"Aneta," I say.

"I will take it from now," Sokolov's firm voice rings out from the back. "Please escort the lady to my office in five minutes."

The man's mouth falls open, but he quickly nods, and when the officer is gone, he looks at me sympathetically and says, "Now you have it coming." He orders another soldier to bring me to the mayor's office.

I know the man put on an act in front of me as I don't trust him a bit, but why would the other officer want to talk to me so suddenly? He seems harsh, still I have this inner feeling that I'm somehow safer with him than with the gold-tooth man, though those feelings make no sense. I often listen to my gut but this time I truly don't know what to think of all of this.

When I enter, Sokolov sits straight at his desk and studies me, his pointed nose and deep wrinkles under his eyes make him look serious.

"Please, take a sit." He points to chair in front of his desk. "You said your name is Aneta Cietliwska?"

"Yes, sir."

"And what's your father's name?"

Why would he be interested in my father who's been dead for over twenty years now? Is there something I don't know that Papa was involved with? "Szymon Cietliwski. But he was just an honest and hardworking fisherman. Gone way too soon."

He cocks his head to the side and smiles slightly. "You have his eyes."

"Excuse me?"

"You have your father's eyes." His face grows animated as if he's recalling something from the past.

'You knew my father?" I find it hard to believe this Soviet would have anything to do with my father, the Polish patriot and man with values.

He gives a slight headshake. "I knew him very well. We both worked on the same boat back then. That night when he perished in the storm, I wasn't there because I stayed home battling illness. It's the only reason I'm still alive."

"Well, this comes as a surprise to me," I say, trying not to betray my displeasure at this revelation.

"Every time at the end of the work shift, he couldn't wait to go back home to his beautiful wife and precious daughter. He adored you both." His steady eye contact is somehow comforting, the last thing I'd have expected when coming here. "I, on the other hand, valued his friendship."

"Thank you for telling me this. I only know him from pictures and my mother's memories." I blink away tears that stubbornly form. The truth is that I'm having a hard time processing his words, as if unable to believe him. Yet, it touches me that this man shared friendship with my father.

"My pleasure meeting the daughter of my dear friend. I see him when I look in your eyes."

"It's what my mother always told me." Something switches permanently between us and for a moment we aren't two people on opposite sides. "It surprises me that you decided to talk about this so openly, even though you know I'm here to ask for a favor." I give him a knowing look.

"I want to help you, only if it's in my power." His strong eye contact seems to back his words.

He might have sentiments for my father's memory, but his duties are his duties, and this might be just an attempt to collect information from me. I must be careful what I tell him.

"I overheard you declaring that we have the wrong man?" Just like that, the softness in his face is gone now and he's back to business.

Adrenaline kicks in because I know that he will evaluate my every word. This is life or death for Johann and for me. I tell him our story, only leaving out the fact that Johann joined the Polish Resistance because that would doom him even more. I stated that he hid until he had to save the village and take his brother's place.

When I'm done, he says, "I remember the German you're talking about. He did claim not to be that Nazi criminal we were looking for, but his brother. Of course, we had no reason to believe him."

"Is he still here?" I ask holding my breath.

He shakes his head. "He was sent to Stalingrad where he's to receive a sentence for war crimes."

Strong pain in my chest sets in while I try keeping my face composed. "What can we do to save him? He's innocent."

"I believe you but unfortunately, I don't have good news. If your German was still in Poland, then we could get him out." He sighs and lights a cigarette, and after exhaling bouts of smoke, he continues while my heart feels like it has shattered into pieces. "I'm afraid my powerful comrades won't let him go. They will simply not believe yours or his words, neither will mine. And if a miracle happens and they decide to believe you, they will have other reasons not to release him."

I can't keep myself at bay any longer. I put my face between my hands and weep at the realization that my Johann is in the clutches of Stalin's system. There is nothing I can do.

He gets up and walks toward me. The next thing I feel is his hand on my shoulder. "When you talk about him, your eyes are filled with love. I will try helping you by writing letters to the right people and hopefully someone will listen."

"Thank you, this means the world to me."

"I'm scheduled to go back to Stalingrad in a week, so I will make sure to find his whereabout and I will update you through my letter." His voice is quiet now. "This is the least I can do for my friend's daughter. Please, trust my honest intentions."

~

A month goes by while I don't hear from Sokolov. He promised to write once he learns anything important. Since then, my every day revolves around the hope of getting his letter. The knowledge that Johann is all the way in Russia treated as a Nazi criminal sucks the life out of me.

I hate feeling powerless and it's not like there is anything I can do at this point to help him. Even if I traveled to Stalingrad right away, it wouldn't change anything. Maybe by now he has already been sentenced...

The war is still roaring across Poland, and we've just heard that the Warsaw Uprising ended with Poles being defeated by the Germans. So many died fighting, so many civilians were killed, so many people taken into captivity by Germans. All for nothing because as Kostek has predicted, the Soviets will take over and Stalin will send his representatives to create government taking over our country on his terms.

"What are you thinking about?" Władek asks. "You've been so quiet lately."

Today we've busied ourselves digging potatoes in the field with the help of Bronka and Kostek. They drove home with a full wagon of potatoes to unload into the cellar.

We're chewing on bread and dill pickles.

"Not much. I can't get past the reality that Johann is in Soviet hands." I put the food down on a linen cloth due to lack of appetite and continue, "It paralyzes me that I'm not able to do anything." I already told Władek about Johann, which he took with an open-minded manner, stating that not all Germans were Nazis and there are the ones who opposed the regime or were against it.

"You know, sister, when I was in that camp my biggest weapon was to keep hopeful. Without it, I would not be here now with you," he says and stares into a clear sky. "You must do the same and never lose hope. Though you can't do anything to help him now, when the war is over things will change and so the ability to do more."

I sigh. "You always know how to make me feel better, brother. I'm sure Zygmunt is proud of the man you became." I feel more connection with him than I ever have with my half-sisters. "There is something I meant to talk to you but there is never good time," I add and smile.

"What's that? You know you can tell me anything," he says and takes a sip of water from a tin cup.

I look him straight in the eye and say, "I hate being a burden to all of you and it was never my intention, but since Zygmunt passed, I felt safer by staying here instead of going back to Gdańsk. It was better for Janek, and I believe it was easier for your mother to survive those horrible years."

"If not for you, I can't even imagine what would have happened. You kept all together and saved so many people." He takes both my hands in his. "Besides as my brother's widow, you inherit all. This farm is rightfully yours. According to old documents drafted by a lawyer that Zygmunt hired when they transferred the ownership to him, my mother is only guaranteed one chamber in the hut for the rest of her life. When the war ends, I will leave and look for a job in the town or city."

I shake my head. "We all know the circumstances Zygmunt married me, and Janek isn't his. It's not my place to stay here. I already went to Zamość last week and started the process of transferring the ownership to you. It's the right thing to do and I know deep in my heart it's what Zygmunt would want me to do."

"I'm speechless," he says quietly.

"This is your family farm, and I would never stand in the way. Though you will have to deal with me for a little longer." I nudge his arm playfully.

Emotion settles in his face and for a moment he looks like the old Władek, the kind boy before the harshness of war and the camp. "Thank you, I don't deserve this. It will always be your home and to me you will always be my favorite sister-in-law." His genuine smile reaches his eyes as he pulls me in for a hug.

"You're a good one, Władek and I know that when the right time comes, Bronka will see it too."

Minutes after we resume potato digging, Bronka and Kostek arrive with an empty wagon.

"You got a letter," Bronka says the moment she jumps down, white envelope in her hand. "The return address has the name of Sokolov, the man you spoke to in Zwierzyniec."

My trembling hand takes the letter and presses to my chest. Fear squeezes my stomach while hope spins my brain. What if it's a bearer of bad news? What will I do then?

I don't know how long I stand like this feeling numb, but Bronka touches my arm and says, "You should open the letter and stop tormenting yourself. I'm sure there is good news in there."

I swallow hard and snatch it open with my shaking hands, my fingers feel so fragile that for a moment I worry that I will drop the piece of paper and the wind will take it away from me.

*Dear Aneta,*

*I trust you're doing well. I apologize for not contacting you earlier, but it took time for me find out the fate of your friend.*

*Unfortunately, I don't have good news. Johann was sent from the prison here to Siberia. He's gotten ten years of hard labor. I couldn't save him, but I was able to prove his identity and thanks to that he was spared a death sentence. If they still believed he was Erich, he would be dead by now.*

*You must find strength in you to overcome all the pain in your heart and go on living your life, for the sake of your son, and Szymon's grandson. Your duty is to stay strong.*

*Do not wait for him because only few come back from Siberia. Even if he survives, which is unlikely, he will spend long years over there.*

*I'm sorry but you deserve the truth, so you can move on.*

*Please, don't hesitate to write back to this address should you need my help.*

*Your family's faithful friend*

I collapse to my knees and whimper. Everything around is just a blur... I want to die, to stop existing.

Bronka puts her arms around me and gently rocks me back and forth.

"No, God, please don't do this to me," I wail into her chest. "Not my Johann." Being sent to Siberia is worse than receiving a death sentence. He doesn't deserve this.

"Cry, my friend, I'm here for you," she says, continuing to rock me.

I gasp for air and succumb to crying because only tears can fill my broken soul. All strength abandons my mind and body. And then, there's just this silence that speaks more of the unbearable pain and sorrow than any words ever could. In this very moment, I understand that my life will be filled with this unspoken silence until my beloved comes back to me. Even if it takes the next ten years, or eternity.

# FORTY-NINE
## BRONKA

June 1945—Władek's village

With the war ending in May, villagers decided to gather in our barn to celebrate the final victory. The side with colorful ribbons hanging from wooden beams is designated for dancing while the larger part has tables filled with food, and patrons perching on chairs and stools. But no one dances. Too many losses in our hearts....

I smile at my Jordanek who now sleeps in my arms, after hours of running around the barn. I kiss his hair and inhale a fresh and slightly sweet scent of branches cut from birch trees brought here for decoration purposes. Its woodsy and earthly fragrance mingles with the one of wildflowers and herbs: mint, honey, rosemary, and many others. Like in heaven....

I wish Aneta could be here with me, but she already left for Gdańsk to look for her mother. I feel so lonely without her.

Janina died in Auschwitz... I think of her every day... Honorata plans to adopt our little Ronia.

Soon I let Piotrek take Jordan home for a nap. Faustyna's

son survived the massacre by hiding in the panel-covered ditch in the orchard, unlike his parents and sisters who were ruthlessly murdered. Two months ago, I spotted him begging for food near the church in Zwierzyniec. He's been living with us since and I love him like my own son.

Even after all the passing years, it's still hard for him to talk about his family, so we treat the subject gently. But I'm here for him and I plan to adopt him once I'm back in my childhood home. I hope Faustyna can see that her son is doing well and is surrounded by love. Of all the people, I deeply understand and feel Piotrek's pain. It's how I feel about Roman, my parents and my brother.

I feel so nostalgic by listening to the old song performed by a folk band.

*Oh my rosmarinus, grow*
*I'll go to the girl, I'll go to the only one*
*I'll ask her.*
*And if she tells me: I don't love you,*
*Uhlans are recruiting, riflemen are marching*
*I'll enlist.*

"Do you care to take a walk?" Władek asks when he approaches me, a soft smile at his mouth.

"Sure, it would be nice to get some fresh air." We walk out side by side, and I think of my fondness for him. He's been supporting me day after day in gentle ways, but most of all he's there for me, and even promised to help me moving into my parents' cottage once I'm ready.

We settle on a wooden log in the far corner of the orchard behind the barn. I pick a daisy from the grass thinking of the violet he gifted to me in the camp and how much hope it brought to my heart.

"What's your favorite flower?" he asks watching me in a tender way, which I've gotten used to.

"Violet," I whisper and smile.

His cheeks go lightly pink with pleasure. "You just made me so happy."

I put my hand on his arm. "No, Władek, you brought happiness to me when you handed me that precious violet. You brought hope to my heart and made me feel a woman again despite my poorly appearance."

He takes my hand in his, electrifying my skin, and then kisses the knuckles. "In my eyes you were beautiful even in that camp."

"You're a gentle soul. I've been overextending your hospitality way too long. It's time I go back to my childhood hut before someone else takes it over." I swallow the lump of emotions that formed in my throat. "It's so hard to think that I'm the only one that survived out of my whole family."

Instead of answering, he asks, "Do you believe in love at first sight?"

I think for a moment, realizing that it's not how it happened with Roman. "I believe in infatuation at first sight. Love either comes later when you get to know someone, or it doesn't."

"It's not what happened to me. When I saw you for the first time during your visit with Aneta, I couldn't take my eyes off you. But I knew your heart belonged to another man, so I hid my feelings."

His words not only touch me but surprise me. "You acted like you didn't even care to spend time with us, always going to visit your friends when we arrived."

"I can be good at acting."

"Don't settle for only acting. You deserve to be genuinely happy. There are so many pretty women that have their eyes on you."

He stares ahead into an apple tree, so when he doesn't reply right away, I turn my head to him.

It's when he turns my way too and caresses my cheek with his fingers. "I don't want other women. It's why I'm looking at you right now, the only woman I'm in love with."

I find myself swimming into his intense gaze, feeling no trace of an act from him. "I'm so broken. I can't offer you much. You know that."

"You must know that I'm only truly happy when I'm with you."

"It's not fair that I'm not able to love you the way I loved Roman. You should not be settling for this because you deserve so much more, and you can have it with someone else."

He brushes away a strand of hair from my face and says, "I understand that no one can ever take Roman's special place in your heart and it's not my intention at all. I know that the pain and emptiness after losing him will never stop, and that you've simply learned to live with it. But I also believe that one day the other part of your heart can be mine. You just need to give us a chance."

"It's not that easy. Don't you understand that you can never be fully happy with me and all the burden I carry?"

"We can be happy." He tilts my chin. "Look me in the eyes and tell me that you don't love me. If you do that, I will accept that we can be only friends, and I will never bother you again." His brows draw together.

My eyes flush to meet his. "I can't say that."

He takes my face between his hands. "Why, my beauty, why can't you tell me that?"

"Because I do love you. I'm just afraid."

"We will let things progress on your terms. Will you trust me and give us a chance?"

I feel like I'm going to choke on my emotions. "I will." The moment I say it, he closes his eyes and whispers thanks to God.

"I will love and adore you and Jordan and Piotrek for the rest of our lives," he says and engages us in a heart-stealing kiss that takes my breath away and makes me feel like there are butterflies inside my stomach.

It's not until this very moment that I fully realize how much I wanted him to be mine. "I'm yours," I whisper and kiss away the smile from his lips.

# EPILOGUE
## ANETA

Five years later, September 1950—Gdańsk

I tuck away Bronka's letter into my desk's drawer. It's admirable that she found enough strength all those years back to move on and give Władek a chance. They've created a beautiful family with their daughter Matylda, Jordanek and Piotrek.

I, on the other hand, will never stop waiting for Johann. I sent hundreds of letters to different parts in Siberia but never heard back from him. I've been in contact with Sokolov through the years, but he claims he's unable to find out Johann's whereabouts and the exact location he was sent. I even took a trip to visit him, but it was all in vain.

Still, there is this stubborn hope in my heart and soul that my beloved will return to me when his sentence is done. Five more years.

After I found out about Johann's imprisonment in Siberia, my life went on hold. If not for Bronka's support, I don't know where I would be now. With patience and love, she helped me drift away from darkness toward caring again for my son and Hania. She understood my struggles so well because she went through much worse when Roman was killed. She had no time to succumb to her pain or grief, instead she had to face the horror of that camp where Germans murdered so many innocent people. I don't think that I could ever be as strong as her...

With the end of the war, I decided to come to Gdańsk and find my mother. When I arrived in my childhood home in the Wrzeszcz district, she was there with my sister Weronika. I learned that my stepfather was killed in the air raid during the Soviet siege in 1945. At the beginning of the war, my other sister, Anna, ran away and followed a Nazi soldier to Paris. She was only eighteen at the time, so it caused a lot of distress for my mother. She's well now, as last year we received a letter from her stating that she's married to a Frenchman and they have two children.

I was so relieved to see my beloved mother alive and stunned to realize that Weronika was no longer a child but transformed into a young woman. She is so lovely without the damaging influence of her father and bossy attitude of Anna who always treated me with dislike.

Mama tried to make a living by sewing and my sister found a position to clean in the hospital. The clothing boutique on the ground floor of our villa still had the needed equipment and hidden stacks of fabrics, so we decided to re-open it, once we prepared a new collection. We all sewed under Mama's directions and created dresses that we thought would be perfect for the current times. We changed the boutique's German name to the Polish *Stroje Bałtyckie*, Baltic Gowns, and haven't looked back since then.

"I'm going to get Hania and Janek from school," Mama says, poking her gray-haired head into the doorframe of my office.

"Thank you, Mama," I say and smile. Janek is already eleven and Hania is nine, but my mother enjoys walking up to their school building and joining them on the way home.

They've become close through the years, which was a blessing as for a long time they missed the village.

We learned that no one from Hania's family survived the war. There were people coming to take her away from us saying that she should be growing up in the Jewish family. But since we moved to Gdańsk no one has bothered us. I could not bear to give her away.

When my mother is gone, Weronika pops in. "There is a man in the store stating that he must see you." We take turns assisting our patrons in boutique and when it's her turn, I usually tackle paperwork in my office, just like today. My sister got married two months ago to Wojtek, who works in a shipyard.

"Did he say what does he want?"

"No, he only said your name. He's a good looking fellow though skin and bones." She winks at me. She never stopped trying to convince me that I should start dating.

I roll my eyes but say, "Would you let him in?" It must be one of those sudden searches by Stalin's people, so the quicker I get over with it the better. They have been bothering us for a while now, but it seems they can't find anything because they never arrested me like so many others who worked for the Polish Resistance during the war. Rejecting their "checking" would mean putting us into trouble.

I make sure to get busy analyzing bills, so when the knock comes, I respond firmly without taking my eyes off my papers. I must appear relaxed and act like I have nothing to hide from them, but when the man says no word and seems to just be standing at the door, I lift my gaze and freeze.

Speechless, I blink rapidly to make sure that my eyes aren't fooling me. It must be only an illusion that he's standing here, my mind's cruel tricks... Is this hollow-cheeked man with beard and deep wrinkles under the eyes truly my Johann?

When he says, "Netuś," the loving sound of his voice and the yearning look in his bluest eyes slow time...

I rush into his embrace. "I thought—"

I don't finish because his parched lips hungrily possess mine. His touch is tantalizing, his taste soul filling, to the point that I can't get enough of him, unable to quench my thirst for his presence. I brush his bruised cheeks with my fingers, still worrying that it's just a dream from which I will wake up at any moment.

He strokes my hair; his rough-skinned fingers build a yearning sensation in the deepest part of my being. Then he kisses away my tears from my face. "Oh, darling, how I've missed you. Every second of my life." His voice shakes with emotion, the same one I feel so strongly in every particle of my body and soul.

I take his hand and press it to my chest. "I can't believe you're here," I say, enjoying the way he holds me so close. I've never felt safer than right now in his arms. For a moment longer I listen to his heartbeat.

"I came to you as soon I could, because I knew you would wait for me," he says, the painful softness of his eyes reflects the years of hardship, but also loneliness and longing. "I was finally given amnesty and released, though many other prisoners who were lucky to survive were freed much earlier."

I cuddle into him. "I'm so sorry I could do nothing to help you."

"If not for Sokolov's intervention, they would have sentenced me to death for Erich's crimes. He came to see me in the prison before I was transferred to Siberia. It's when he told me that you made him promise you that he would do all in his power to help me."

"I thought he lied to me and did nothing for you. But now I understand he did what he could. Maybe Papa haunted him in his dreams." I smile through my tears.

"I don't doubt that, especially if you got your strength of character from him." His beautiful and contagious laughter echoes through my spirit, but soon his face grows earnest again. "The thought of seeing you made me survive the unthinkable in that frozen hell. Having you and Janek in my heart kept me alive."

I brush my lips over his and whisper, "I love you forever."

# A LETTER FROM GOSIA

Dear reader,

I want to say a huge thank you for choosing to read *The German Next Door*. If you did enjoy it and want to keep up to date with all my latest releases, just sign up at the following link. Your email address will never be shared, and you can unsubscribe at any time.

*www.bookouture.com/gosia-nealon*

At the end of November 1942, the Germans officially began their operation of displacing Poles of the Zamość region from their homes and farms. It was part of the German General Plan for the East created in June 1942, which assumed the creation of the "Lebensraum", the German living space in the east.

The action was carried out brutally because after the German forces surrounded a certain village, they only gave the villagers one hour to grab immediate belongings that would fit in a hand luggage, while everything else had to stay.

The elderly and sick, or anyone unsuitable for work, were often killed on the spot or during segregation. Everyone else was sent to temporary camps in Zamość and Zwierzyniec for selections. Many got deported to forced labor in Germany or to concentration camps in KL Auschwitz or KL Lublin, known as

Majdanek, while some were subjected to the process of Germanization, mostly children.

But the largest and most brutal and bloody stage of displacements began in June 1943. The German forces focused on killing the villagers, like in the village of Sochy where they murdered around 183 people, mostly women and children, burned everything and bombed by aircraft.

Among the displaced, there were about 30,000 children who got deported, while around 10,000 died or went missing, and nearly 4,000–5,000 were chosen for Germanization.

It's estimated that over 110,000 inhabitants of the Zamość region and 300 villages were displaced from November 1942 to August 1943.

While doing research, I learned that thanks to the Countess Róża Zamoyska and her husband, the Count Jan Zamoyski, hundreds of children were saved. They opened an orphanage where the children were taken care of, but they also helped so many other people. The Countess Róża was known for her kindness and bravery, and people in the Zamość region called her the *Angel of Goodness*. She was a remarkable woman.

KL Lublin, known as Majdanek, was the German concentration and extermination camp located on the outskirts of the city of Lublin in the southeastern part of German-occupied Poland. It was the most primitive camp where the prisoners suffered diseases, hunger, murderous labor, fear and threats, executions and gas chambers, and their bodies were burned in crematoria. There are no words to describe the terrible atrocities.

While researching, I focused on the stories of women who survived Majdanek. There was one thing that stood out to me as many women talked about it: the way women supported each other in that camp. They often shared food and confided in each other about their problems; they were united by a great bond of friendship, cordiality and loyalty. What mattered was who was inside when the lights went out in the barracks. It was easier to survive when a friendly person was nearby. It was important to not be blind to those who were weaker and tired, to establish contact, to understand and support, to try surviving together the worst hell on earth...

My dad told me about his uncle who survived that camp and that thanks to his bravery he found a way to escape.

Majdanek was the first major concentration camp to be liberated by Allies at the end of July 1944. With Soviet forces approaching Lublin, the Germans quickly evacuated, failing to destroy the proofs of their crimes. It's why Majdanek is the best-preserved camp of the Holocaust.

I hope you enjoyed *The German Next Door*, and if you did, I would be very grateful if you could write a review. I'd like to hear what you think, and it makes such a difference helping new readers to discover one of my books for the first time.

I love hearing from my readers – you can get in touch on social media or my website.

Thanks,

Gosia

www.gosianealon.com

facebook.com/GosiaNealonHistoricalFiction
x.com/GosiaNealon

# ACKNOWLEDGMENTS

I'm thankful to God for the love, perseverance and strength. Tears come to my eyes when I think that this is my sixth novel.

I think of my sister and her children; my husband and our children; my parents; my brothers; my niece; my nephews. My heart is full for having you in my life.

I'm thankful to my exceptional editor, Natalie Edwards. Working with you on my books has been a dream come true.

I'm thankful to the entire team at Bookouture for their brilliance and professionalism.

As a mother of three boys, I'm thankful to my children's teachers, especially Mrs. Faith Baker for her excellence in teaching, hard work and compassion.

I'm thankful to my readers. I love bringing new stories to you.

# PUBLISHING TEAM

**Turning a manuscript into a book requires the efforts of many people. The publishing team at Bookouture would like to acknowledge everyone who contributed to this publication.**

### Commercial
Lauren Morrissette
Hannah Richmond
Imogen Allport

### Cover design
Eileen Carey

### Data and analysis
Mark Alder
Mohamed Bussuri

### Editorial
Natalie Edwards
Lizzie Brien

### Proofreader
Claire Rushbrook

**Marketing**
Alex Crow
Melanie Price
Occy Carr
Cíara Rosney
Martyna Młynarska

**Operations and distribution**
Marina Valles
Stephanie Straub
Joe Morris

**Production**
Hannah Snetsinger
Mandy Kullar
Ria Clare
Nadia Michael

**Publicity**
Kim Nash
Noelle Holten
Jess Readett
Sarah Hardy

**Rights and contracts**
Peta Nightingale
Richard King
Saidah Graham

Printed in Dunstable, United Kingdom